AF207402

Shadows Gray

Book I of the Lost Trilogy

By Melyssa Williams

Melyssa Williams

Red Team Ink
DBA of Zealot Solutions, Idaho LLC
5447 Kendall St.
Boise, ID 83706
Copyright© 2016 by Red Team Ink

All rights reserved. Without limiting the rights under the copyright reserved above, no part of this publication may be reproduced, stored in, or introduced into a retrieval system, or transmitted in any form or by any means (electronic, mechanical, photocopying, recording, or otherwise) without prior written permission.

This is a work of fiction. Names, characters, businesses, places, events and incidents are either the products of the author's imagination or used in a fictitious manner. Any resemblance to actual persons, living or dead, or actual events is purely coincidental.

For permission requests or information about discounts for special bulk purchases please contact: redteamink@gmail.com. Substantial discounts on bulk orders are available to corporations, professional associations, and small businesses.

Printed in The United States of America

Library of Congress Control Number: 2017930050
ISBN: 978-0-9982349-5-3

Title: Shadows Gray
Description: First Edition

Prologue

My name is Sonnet Gray and I was born in 1737. My mother was born in 1880, and my father in 1174. If that math doesn't trip you up, then perhaps the fact that I'm currently doling out lattes in the 21st century will.

By the accounts of those who know me best, I'm 18 years old, but could just as easily be 20, or even 16. Sleeping and waking in more than a dozen different eras, makes it a little difficult to keep track of such things. There's an old saying that applies I think. I'm as old as my gums and a little bit older than my teeth. That seems to sum it up well enough I believe. Anyway, my family and I are Lost, like our ancestors were before, and will be after us.

I remember almost nothing of the eighteenth century, from the time of my birth through the first four years of my life. I do recall visiting it briefly again during one of my journeys, but it never felt like home to me. Moreover, my time there reminded me of my sister whom we had left behind, and as such I couldn't wait to leave. Each time I saw a babe in white lace, I thought of Rose. Every time I saw a beautiful young woman with light blue eyes, I thought to myself...*could it be her?* I wondered if she had lived her whole life in that century, while her mother, father, and sister had been forced to move back to the 1500s.

I was left with little time to fret and ponder however. Before I marked another birthday in that century, we traveled again, though this time it was just my father and I.

My mother, shaken with sorrow and drunk with sadness, had not made it even a month after we left baby Rose. Desperate to find her child, and sick with guilt, she neither ate nor slept. Slowly she wasted away until she became little more than a hollowed out wraith of a woman. Given my age, it doesn't seem as though I should remember her at all, and yet I do. A least a bit anyway. She was a vague, shadowy woman with yellow hair and a listless voice. My father tells me I have her eyes, which were a disconcerting light blue color.

As for my little sister Rose, I have only Dad's tales in lieu of my own recollections. I do know that she had flaxen hair that was golden like our mother's, and that her eyes were blue like mine. Where I'm taller than average with rather gangly arms and legs, Dad said that Rose was just a tiny thing, and that she was almost bird-like in a way.

She was three and I was four years old the night we disappeared and she was left behind. It was the first Leaving we had been subjected to since her birth, and no one could have predicted that she wouldn't possess the same ability as the rest of us. Of course, she wasn't the first child born to a Lost family who wasn't Lost herself, but none of us ever want to think that it could happen to one of our own. There are always whispers though as to why some cannot wake in different centuries with the rest of their family. For instance, there are those that are half-Lost, born to one Lost and one non-Lost parent. Rarely do they ever have enough magic in their blood (for lack of a better word) to accomplish the journey. The sickly don't always make it either. There have been plenty of cases where the ill or the very old and frail have been left behind.

It's likely that we'll probably never know what happened that night. We only know that three of us woke up in Italy in the 1500s, when there should have been four. Little Rose had not passed through time with us. Mother, in her grief, starved herself for two weeks. She would often sit motionless, staring off into the nothingness for frightening amounts of time. When she wasn't doing that, she was out in the sun, pacing back and forth restlessly. When she finally grew tired of all the sadness and the grieving, she combed her hair, put on the cornflower blue dress that my father had stolen for her, and then calmly walked off a cliff. My father took her death hard. He started drinking heavily that night, and hasn't stopped since.

The first few months were frustrating for me. I arrived in this century for the first time and found it incredibly fast-paced, noisy, confusing, and generally overwhelming. Everyone had gadgets pressed to their ears, and they drove cars from place to place instead of walking. I had never seen automobiles before, but of course I had heard of them through people who had traveled much farther in time than I had.

I found out quickly enough in this new time that I'd need papers to identify myself if I wanted to get a job, a house, or anything else that one would need in order to exist in this time period.

A mutual friend of a mutual friend, who was shady to say the least, stole an identity for me that came with a number. They told me it was a Social Security number, but that didn't sit well with me. I didn't like being assigned a number, because to me it seemed like some sort of a trap. Unfortunately, we needed to find ourselves a place to live, so it was a necessary evil that would just have to be tolerated. It was winter now. Dad and Prue were both sick again, so for several months I became Emily Winn. I told people that I preferred to go by my middle name, Sonnet, so I could at least hold onto some small semblance of myself. Finding a job was not easy, but then it never was. It was always the same whenever and wherever we ended up. The Lost cannot take much of anything with them when they travel through time. They can only take their family, and whatever they happen to be holding in their hands when they pass on, so I have learned to rely solely on music to provide me with an income. I have a low, throaty voice that serves me well, and I find singing to be a pleasure that the people of each and every century will stop and listen to.

This decade proved to be the hardest as far as finding employment, but I finally managed to secure a job at a coffee shop that had live music and poetry on the weekends. The wages and the tips are enough to feed me and Dad, and to keep him in cigars and alcohol. There is no need for other things, and no need to save our pennies, because the expression *you can't take it with you* is never truer than when you are Lost. I sew extra money into my nightgown hems so that I am not destitute when we pass on again, but it rarely helps. If you are suddenly living in ninth century Germany, no one is going to recognize your $50 American bill.

The Lost stick together, and as everyone knows, misery loves company. No one wants to be lonely. It's a comfort when we have others there to go through our trials with us. Those who aren't Lost could never really understand the problems we have to deal with, so we tend to stay lost in groups of our own kind. If we stay in too large of a group, we end up becoming far too conspicuous, so most of us keep our groups at fewer than ten. As it stands right now, our group consists of eight, though we may take on others as time goes by. Even at our current number we've become rather noticeable, so we have to do our best to keep a low profile.

Our group was varied, to say the least. We had my father, who had sort of found his place as a drunken storyteller, and then we had a married couple who claimed to be my second cousins, though personally I have my doubts about that. If I'm being honest, my opinion is that they were kicked out of their last family group due to the fact that they were both ridiculously annoying, and irritated everyone with their bickering to the point of distraction. In addition to them, we've got Old Prue, who has to be at least a hundred years old, and a pair of brothers named Matthias and Harry, who are both elderly themselves and lifelong bachelors. Then there's Israel Rhode, a man who stands several inches over six feet tall, with strikingly black skin, a gleam in his eye, and a warm smile that makes him completely unforgettable. For the past several years, these people have been my family. Together we speak almost every language you could possibly think of. I myself speak five different languages, because when you live in as many places as we do, you tend to pick them up rather quickly. This little family of ours is all we've got. We are not immortal, though certain legends may say we are. No one knows whether the Lost age differently than the rest of mankind. There are different thoughts on the matter, and no one seems to agree. One man might say he fell asleep clean shaven, and then awoke the next morning in a different time and space sporting a full formed beard.

Chapter 1

I've been wondering about a man I've seen at the coffee shop. He gives me the feeling that he has been keeping an eye on me. Since there is nothing remarkable about me (my boss tells me if it weren't for my voice and the way I froth milk, he never would have hired me), I can only assume he is Lost and looking for others to be with. It's common for our type to land in similar places, in similar decades. Sometimes we narrowly miss each other, while other times we seemingly come together as though it were fated. It's as though whatever it is that seems to tug at our marionette strings has a specific goal in mind, but does not share it with us.

The man in question is young, tall, and aimless in appearance. He always looks as though he went out to fetch the morning paper and the door slammed shut behind him, locking him out of his house. His hair is a bit too long and his face is on the scruffy side of smooth. He wears glasses when he reads the paper but takes them off to pinch the bridge of his nose when he drinks his coffee. He also sits at the bar and pretends not to stare at me. This isn't an attractive description, but he's an attractive man in an unkempt, confused sort of a way. I know he isn't staring to start something romantic. If it was love at first sight he was looking for, he'd be much more apt to turn his owlish eyes towards my co-worker Penny, who is far more beautiful and alluring than I am. Of course, she does have her faults. She's terrible at frothing milk, and her poetry is a thing of horrible legend, but men rarely find either to be much of a turn off. This particular man keeps his eyes on me however, though I must admit that his reasons for doing so simply escape me. Tonight, I caught him staring at me again, and I accused him of doing so.

"It's your coffee," he replied wistfully. "You make it so strong that I can't even blink, or get my eyes to focus. It's all your fault."

"I make it the way I was trained to make it," I answered, primly. "If you aren't manly enough to handle it, I could make you some warm milk instead."

He looked wounded by my words and without another word he took a big chug of his coffee, swallowing it both slowly and pointedly.

"Well...anyway," I continue, wiping an imaginary spot on the counter with my dishtowel, "It's rude to stare, and you're always staring at me. You should stare at Penny instead. She's up on the stage right now about to read her latest poem."

"I'd rather drink warm milk," he said, shuddering almost comically. "Will it be about goats and chocolate again?"

"I think it was supposed to be a metaphor."

"I don't even want to think what it was for," he said as he glanced over at the stage, and then back to me. "Anyway, I didn't mean to stare at you. I just sort of get lost in my thoughts I suppose."

"Constantly? You're constantly lost in thought? That's a lot of thinking. You should really try to give it a rest. Maybe try switching to decaf," I said as I turned and jerked my thumb at the pot behind me. I know my conversational skills can border on the inane at times, but I've never been all that smooth when it comes to conversations with handsome men.

"Pointless, boring, and sleep inducing...just like warm milk, or Penny's poetry," he said flatly.

I smile in spite of myself. Penny is sweet, but it's a pleasant change to be ranked higher than her in the estimation of a handsome man. Now don't get me wrong. I certainly have no delusions about myself. I am tall and lanky, with dark, nondescript hair that neither curls nor straightens properly. My light, ice blue eyes might be fascinating in their own way, but more than likely they just creep people out. I've been told by 21st century girls that I have a horrific sense of fashion (evidently t-shirts with kitty cats are not haute couture in this era), and it seems that I lack the conversational skills to come up with witty responses at the appropriate time, especially when I'm talking to someone of the opposite sex.

6

Someone once dryly commented that I was a keeper, but I have the distinct feeling that their comment was more sarcastic than sincere.

"Actually, I'm only scoping you out because of your grandma," he said as he raised his cup to take another sip.

"Prue?" I asked. I wasn't sure whether I should be disappointed or wary about the sudden change of subject.

"Elderly woman? Accent? Dispenses cryptic advice with her food? Ring any bells?" he asks.

"Her name's Prue. How do you know about her, and why are you scoping out my grandma anyway?" I asked. I wonder if he knows my father as well, since they've been selling Cajun, Irish, Southern, and Italian food from a cart several blocks away. Prue is an excellent cook, but thanks to her heavy accent, her fiery, take-no-prisoners personality, and her tendency to swear at the customers, she and Dad don't pull in much in the line of income. Truth be told, Dad's a bit useless since he's almost always drunk, so he doesn't exactly pull in the customers either. Although Prue's cooking is amazing, they certainly won't be featured in any upcoming restaurant reviews, at least not favorable ones anyway.

"She made me this really spicy gumbo and pasta thing," he explained. "It may or may not have been alligator."

"So what? Don't go back then if you didn't like it. And it's not illegal to cook with alligator, if that's what you're getting at," I said tersely. To be honest, I was more worried about the fact that my Dad may have picked his pocket than I was about any indignities he may have suffered from eating alligator.

"What are you talking about? I loved it, and I love her. I asked her to marry me and she hit me with her rice spoon. If it's illegal to cook with alligator, I'll cheerfully hide your grandma in my house to keep her away from the authorities. I was hoping to get her to talk to me. See, I'm a photographer, and I'd love to get a picture of her."

"Oh, really? Well I suppose you can ask, but she'll probably turn you down," I said in a much more relaxed tone. Prue doesn't like photos. In fact, most of the Lost don't like having their picture taken. We're timeless enough as it is.

"I did ask her, but she started waving her spoon at me again and I got scared. I guess I was hoping that you might be willing to butter her up for me. I'm a pretty decent photographer. You can even see my work if you like. These are all recent and from the area," he said as he pulled out a folder with several sheets of photos.

In spite of myself, and the fact that I should be refilling coffee right now, I leaf through them politely. They actually are quite good, at least to my untrained eye. I see a young boy that I recognize from the street where I live. The photo captured his mischievous grin and his missing front teeth perfectly.

There was another photo with a couple of teenagers holding up a large fish, both grinning and looking deliciously sunburned. After that was a woman who was nuzzling a tiny baby. I think I've seen her around as well, only she was still pregnant the last time she was in the coffee shop. Another photo had a girl around my age, or maybe just a bit younger. She was leaning against a tree with her skirt billowing back against her knees. Her arms are crossed, and the way she's staring off into the distance makes it appear she doesn't even know she's being photographed. Her feet are bare, and her hair is long and straight. She seems to be small and delicate, like a fairytale princess.

I think it is my sister.

Chapter 2

"Where did you take this?" I ask hoarsely. I feel as though my world has tipped sideways and I am dizzy and nauseated.

He peers over his coffee cup at the photograph of the girl I feel certain is my sister, Rose. "At the river," he says. "It was during the fair last weekend. Know her?"

Suddenly I feel ridiculous. Of course, I don't know her. Of course, it isn't Rose. How many times have I thought I've seen her, been certain I've spotted her? I do the same with my mother. Any woman with yellow hair and light eyes really. That quickening of my heart and breath, that butterfly feeling in my stomach, and then they turn and I see they are nothing like my family at all. I feel foolish and desperate. And yet, she is so very much the way I imagine Rose to look. I imagine her all the time, but it's pathetic. My little sister has been dead for hundreds of years.

I clear my throat. "No, no I don't know her. She looked familiar though for a minute, that's all."

"Well, I didn't catch her name, but she's a beauty and the camera loves her. Got a couple shots of her in the crowd as well. Do you have any muffins left?"

"Hmm?" I say distractedly. "Oh, sure. They're day old though, still want one? I'll charge you half price."

The photographer eats his muffin, drinks his coffee. We listen to Penny's poetry – he's right, there was mention of a goat. I stifle a giggle. When he leaves, I clear his plate and find his business card, *Luke Dawes, Photography*. I pocket it in my apron to show Prue and since he leaves a nice tip, I decide to vouch for his character so that maybe she'll let him photograph her. She is so old. I wouldn't mind having a snapshot to sew into my hem to remind me of her when she is gone.

I'm home late that night as I always am on weekend nights. The shop stays open late and I'm the only one who can close it because I'm the only one trusted enough to do the changing out of the cash register and balance the books. Israel comes to collect me, as he always does, and we walk home together through the night, since his car is low on fuel and the night is warm.

Israel is a good man to walk with; he's not talkative and we fall into an easy rhythm. He has been with our group since we came here – no, since just before I suppose. We met him in our time before this one, which was Portugal in the 1850s. I have traveled thirteen times in my life, and lived in four different centuries. There is no rhyme or reason to how long we stay, no pattern, no way of anticipating how long our times will be before we move on unwittingly. Portugal was short. My time here now has been two years, longer than most. I do not get attached. I have all that I need, or fiercely say that I do. My father is irritating and difficult, but he's mine. Prue is as well. The others have been with me long enough to love them dearly but they will most likely not be with the three of us forever. At some point someone will distance themselves and we won't make a jump through time together, but we will meet up with others. Sometimes you are lucky enough to find someone from your past again, but it's rare. Once we met my uncle, my dad's brother, who has always been a wanderer and a loner. I hadn't seen him – well, no one had – since he had wandered away from us when I was ten, but we somehow made a passing together anyway and ended up in Portugal together. He seemed happy enough to see us and we all made plans to stay together this time, but no one was completely surprised when he wasn't around the night we all traveled again and woke without him. Every so often the loneliness is more than you can bear; but it's easier for some to be the one to force it upon themselves than to be the one who is left behind. I wonder if Luke is like that, and then I remember no, he is not Lost, he merely wants a photograph of my grandmother. He probably has a wonderful family, people who are never further away from him than a phone call or a letter or a boat ride. I kick rocks all the way home and my fists are curled in my jacket pocket in muffled, stifled anger. Israel is silent and in the darkness, his African skin blends into the surrounding so that he looks like a walking set of clothes with no body. I feel as though I am strangely alone.

There is no familiar sense of comfortable camaraderie in our silence tonight.

* * *

I wake the next afternoon to the smell of strong tea and bread. Amelia and Will are at it again, arguing in the living room. They're the only married couple in our little family, and the way they go at it, I'm not sure how long they'll hold that union. I can hear their tone of voice, if not their words, although I can guess at the conversation since it rarely differs. I can also hear the sound of the television with the ever running game shows. It sounds like Family Feud. Matthias and Harry, our bachelor brothers, are huge game show fanatics. They were so excited to be back in an era with television, they almost wept with joy. I baby them, seeing as how they are both so old. Matthias, I think is elder, but neither recognize birthdays anymore. After seventy, they cheerfully say, we stopped counting.

I stumble out in my favorite old shirt, a soft gray one with faded pictures of horses, and a pair of plaid pajama pants. I have changed from the white, old fashioned nightgown I wear every night. The risks of waking in an unknown era are vast enough without calling attention to myself by an odd set of clothes. The nightgown, while a little eccentric in this day and age for a young woman, is the best I can do. I yawn and give Harry his customary high five as I walk by the couch. He loves this century. He loves smacking people's hands instead of shaking them.

"Sonnet," Amelia or Meli for short, calls out as I reach the kitchen and open the refrigerator. "Sonnet, tell this bum we need to go out! We need to go out, Will." She turns her attention to her husband and props her cute, heart shaped face on her hands. She stares pointedly at him.

Will is short and small and wears glasses. He reads a book and sips orange juice and doesn't pay her the slightest attention. Will and Meli have been married for several years and they haven't agreed on anything since. Meli frets and mopes and stomps around the house when she isn't working as a nanny, and Will indulgently pats her head occasionally, but mostly ignores her. Their devotion to each other and to their respective pursuit's border somewhere between ridiculous and inspirational. Last week their daily arguments were focused on whether or not to have children. Now it seems Meli just wants a date night.

"Mm hm, you should take her out," I agree while I put bread in the toaster. "Where's Prue? Did she and Dad leave already?" I peer at the clock. It's nearly 10:30.

"They were doing corned beef and cabbage today so they had to leave a little earlier than normal," Will replied.

"That's going to stink in this humidity." Meli wrinkles her nose. "They should stick to the Cajun stuff, it sells better. Are you going down there, Sonnet? Please change your clothes, honey."

I butter my toast and glance down at my shirt. "What's wrong with it? You don't like horses?"

"At least put on jeans. Come on, Sonnet! You could be so pretty if you'd put in a little effort, you know. Comb your hair, put on some make up. Let me take you shopping. Don't you think I should take Sonnet shopping, Will?"

"I like Sonnet the way she is."

Point one for Will. "I promise to comb my hair," I say as I leave the kitchen.

"And put on jeans! And some lip gloss!" she hollers after me.

"No lip gloss," Matthias says disapprovingly as I pass the couch. "That stuff is not for nice girls. Only street girls wear color on their faces." Matthias doesn't get out much. Plus, the last time he dated anyone was 1912, so I can't fault him his logic.

I do comb my hair and change my pajama pants for jeans, although I doubt either one improves my outfit much. It looks sunny and hot outside today, so I grab my favorite hat with a Budweiser logo on it. I've never actually had a Budweiser but they make excellent caps.

It is unseasonably hot once I step outside our little house. The heat hits me in the face like hot steam from one of Prue's soups. It makes the peeling paint more obvious and makes the whole house seems dried out and shriveled in size like a giant raisin left in the sun. The wooden planks of the porch are warped and our mailbox leans to one side. I flick a bug off my favorite spot to sit, our porch swing, and fluff the indoor/outdoor paisley fabric of the cushions before I leave.

It's not a long walk to where Prue and Dad have their vender's cart set up, but I swing by the coffee shop on my way and get an iced tea from Micki, the manager. By the time I reach the food cart, I am ravenous and could eat whatever Prue slaps on a paper plate for me. It's melt in your mouth meat with salted potatoes and cabbage. I do so love the Irish.

Prue is tall and very tan and leathered looking in complexion. She does have the sort of face that a camera would love to capture, simply because she is unusual and seems out of place wherever she is. Of course, like the rest of the Lost, she is. Her long salt and pepper colored hair is done up in braids that are then twisted around her head several times making her look large and rather intimidating. Her skin is the color of mocha and her ethnicity is always a debatable question. Prue isn't my grandmother by blood, but it doesn't matter. She has traveled with my dad and me for as long as I've been alive. She's been with Dad since he was a teenager, after he lost his own parents. She speaks several languages naturally, but mostly lapses into a mixture of French and Native American. She makes sure to swear in English so that everyone can understand it though. She's accommodating like that.

My father is tall and dark haired like me, but his eyes are brown. He looks like he should be a college professor of something literary, and he is in fact a bit of a history buff. I suppose we all are experts in history since we experience more of it than the normal person, but he especially loves dates, times, and facts. He has that air of musty books, reading glasses, and bow ties about him. No one would be surprised if you found him perched right on a library shelf. He is aimless and sad much of the time, and our whole group has a tendency to mother him. Everyone wants to see him smile, laugh, and forget, but he rarely does. He is not a man of rainbows and sunbeams, my father.

I sit on the concrete wall behind the food cart and swing my legs as I eat my lunch. I praise Prue as much as possible, telling her how wonderful her cooking is and how nice she looks today. Judging by the scowl and the way she smacks my knee with a fork, I'm guessing she isn't buying what I'm selling. I decide to abandon the compliments, take the fork away from her, and tell her about Luke Dawes, the photographer.

"And he didn't say, but I bet you he probably pays for his models," I finish by taking a sip of tea through my straw, and trying to sound casual. Prue is extremely fond of spending money.

She grunts and stirs her pot of cabbage. She removes a bay leaf and flicks it in my direction. Getting Prue out of customer service would probably be an excellent idea. I remove the leaf from my jeans.

"He takes nice pictures. Just think about it. I saw some of his photos and he's talented. There was a girl who looked like Rose." I shouldn't say it, but I do. We don't speak of my sister much. If it's possible my dad looks even more sad and lost, and I immediately regret my impulsive carelessness.

Prue on the other hand, softens her gaze and puts the lid back on her pot.

"Baby Rose. God bless her. I hope she had a long, happy life. Wish we could have gone back and seen what happened to her. I 'spect she had a real good life, that little one. *I'm sure old Babba found her real quick.*"

I'm sure Old Babba found her real quick. One of us says that each and every time we remember Rose out loud. It's like the words are our mantra, our chant, to ward off thinking about it any longer. Old Babba was our neighbor there, an old woman who came by the house we were living in nearly every day. We talk ourselves into believing that Old Babba would have found Rose the next morning after we had traveled on without her. The worry of what may have happened, what could have happened, is too much to bear. So we comfort each other with the same words and talk ourselves into accepting it as truth.

I'm sure Old Babba found her real quick.

Saying it doesn't make it so.

"Well, in any case, whether you want him to take your picture or not, Prue, he also wants to marry you for your alligator gumbo recipe. So there you go, you heartbreaker." I wink at her as I jump off the wall and dodge her large tan hand as it reaches out to slap my head. Prue doesn't tolerate cheekiness.

"You're the one who needs to get married, little missy!" She huffs. "You isn't getting any younger." She eyes me up and down. "You isn't getting any purtier either."

"Hey! Why is everyone always trying to change me? And I'm way too young to get married in this day and age. Besides, who would I marry?" I twirl my cap around backwards.

"You might be a tad young in this day, but wouldn't you rather travel with a husband in case you wake up in another time where they pick out the husband for you?" She puts her hands on her ample hips and purses her lips.

I roll my eyes. "All right already, I see your point. Tell you what, I'll get married, if you will."

She continues to glare at me.

I take my life in my hands, and give her a hug squeezing hard. She squeezes back and then shoos me away impatiently.

"Go away, child! You are scarin' away all my good customers."

"I'm going. Dad, do you want to walk with me? Dad?"

"What's that, dear? Oh no. I'm going to stay with Prue and help her with her customers. I'll see you later tonight." He smiles wistfully at me, and picks at his fingernails. It's one of his many nervous habits. His others include, pulling on his eyebrows, twisting his tie, and rolling his short beard whiskers between his fingers.

I give him a kiss and walk back the way I came. I won't go to work until later this evening, so I have time to visit with Emme, my closest friend here. Her home is a small apartment not far from the coffee shop and I know she'll be there. I'll probably find her eating a very late breakfast and reading one of her trashy romance novels, with her pretty manicured feet propped up on a table. Emme is Lost, but she didn't travel here with me, she's one of another group. I want her to come with me, and she may inadvertently since her apartment is close by.

When we travel to another place and time, we do so when we are sleeping and anyone who is Lost and is nearby generally goes as well. That's why families can stay together for long periods of time. We sleep together at all costs. When I work late at the coffee shop, everyone in my house stays up for me. There are no slumber parties when you're a little Lost girl. The daddies don't travel for overnight work, the mommies don't go out of town for Girl's Night Out, and the teens don't go away to school. The risk is too great. So, with Emme being not far away from my own home, she may get pulled in with our group. Time will tell. Time always tells. I know that if she doesn't, I will miss her forever, almost as much as I miss my mother and Rose.

Her apartment is one in a large building. Each has a little balcony with a screen door, and Emme's balcony is full of flowers and potted plants, hot pink geraniums, purple pansies, and orange tiger lilies. She has cute little stone bunnies peeking out from beneath one, and a ceramic cat is nestled in the daisies. We each have a weakness for furry animals, but Emme has the good sense to indulge hers in lawn ornaments instead of wearing them on a shirt like I do. She has a doorbell that plays music, but I don't press it. Instead I let myself in and call a greeting as I walk through the door.

There is Norah Jones music playing when I arrive, and Emme is exactly how I imagined. She is lying on the couch with a book in her hand and a plate of cookies on her belly.

"Hullo, doll!" she says merrily. "Come have some dessert for breakfast. Whipped these up myself last night!"

I take one gingerly. "You baked?"

Emme laughs. "Yes, I baked. Had a client last night and that's what he wanted to do, so that's what we did. Takes the cake doesn't it?" She winked.

I pause. "Were you both fully clothed when you were umm, baking?"

"Mmm, well, I'll leave that part up to your imagination, but believe me when I say there was no hanky panky. He just wanted to bake, the love. He was a cutie too. Hey, maybe I could set you two up?" She wiggles her perfectly shaped red eyebrows suggestively.

When I first found out what Emme did for a living, I couldn't help but be a little shocked. She isn't much older than I, but has been doing what she does for...a time. It's the profession that never goes out of date, she says. I suppose she has a point. Nudity is always in style, at least in some circles. I try not to think about it.

"Everyone and their brother are trying to set me up," I grumble, biting savagely into the cookie. It's a gingersnap.

"That's because you're hopeless on your own, Sonnet. Look at what you're wearing. Good God, are those horses?" She looks aghast at my favorite shirt. I wipe off the cookie crumbs, and puff out my chest proudly in defiance. "You should really let Meli take you shopping. I'd give you some of my stuff if you weren't so dang skinny. Have another cookie."

I oblige and settle into the chair opposite her couch. Her book's cover is of a half-naked man holding onto a gorgeous woman. It's a tough call who has the better hair.

* * *

It's Friday night, and the coffee shop is packed with customers. Our busiest night is always Friday because of the lineup of singers, and specialty prices on drinks and snack food. I spy Luke in the back, in one of our comfortable leather armchairs, but it's too busy to go say hello or socialize with anyone. Matthias and Harry wander in at about half past seven for coffee and to hear me sing. That's a compliment coming from them, as they don't like to leave the house very often. I make them a whole pot of French press coffee, and serve it to them with a pitcher of cream and lots of sugar packets. They never have any money because they never leave the house to make any, so I'll have to pay for the coffee out of my wages. I get a small discount, but Micki is notoriously tightfisted.

When it's my turn to sing, I don't bother taking my apron off since I'm still on the clock. For atmosphere's sake, the lights are low tonight, giving the shop an air of an old time piano bar or an old fashioned elegant club. I imagine myself wearing a sparkling floor length gown, blue maybe, or red. I'm sitting on a piano, my hair in loose waves, and the audience is sophisticated, sipping champagne instead of cappuccino.

The song I've chosen is from World War II and I've picked it for Matthias and Harry. They were both there, in that very war. They recognize the first few chords from the guitar I'm playing, and salute me from their chairs. Harry's chin wobbles bravely, and I have to look away so my voice doesn't do the same.

I'll be seeing you
In all the old familiar places

That this heart of mine embraces
All day through.

In that small cafe;
The park across the way;
The children's carousel;

The chestnut trees;
The wishin' well.

I always sing with my eyes shut. It isn't my intention, but they tend to just drift closed and I lose myself in the music. I'm not a very good guitar player. I've only been playing for a few months, but some strumming is better than no accompaniment at all. I sing mostly for Matthias and Harry, but also for the love of singing. If I'm honest, I also like to see if I can impact the man in the back with the camera.

I'll find you
In the morning sun
And when the night is new.
I'll be looking at the moon,
But I'll be seeing you.

When I finish the last note, I open my eyes and smile at the applause. Of course, this little group of locals would clap politely for anyone, but I know I sounded decent, maybe better than decent. I blow Matthias and Harry a kiss and put my guitar back down by the tiny stage. I can't help glancing back at Luke and I see him fiddling with his camera. Did he take a picture of me? I feel flattered and then instantly feel ridiculous for feeling flattered. I really must get out more if a mere acquaintance can dictate my emotions. I planned to walk casually off the stage, but instead I nearly trip on a speaker cord. A hand helps me up from my stumble. As I rise, my eyes flicker once again to the back. I no longer see Luke, but what I do see frightens me and steals my breath.

Sitting where Luke had been, in the oversized leather armchair, is a small woman. Her red calico dress is old fashioned, but it doesn't look out of place on her timeless, otherworldly beauty. She is willowy but small in stature, with a frame like a little bird. Her blonde hair is almost yellow and hangs all the way to her tiny waist. It is parted on the side and half of it hides her face, but it is a face I know. A familiar face from my memories and from my dreams. This time I cannot talk myself back into reality. I cannot convince myself it is a coincidence, a fluke. A moment of déjà vu. She is too entirely like my mother and I know my mother is dead.

I suppose I should say that *our* mother is dead, because I am certain that beautiful girl is Rose Gray.

Chapter 3

I land right back where I had stumbled a split second before. The woman helping me is so surprised that she almost lands on top of me since her hand is still in mine. I feel as though I've been hit with something, a blow that knocked me off my feet. I am stuck in a frustrating state of things being in slow motion, and yet it's all happening too fast for me to control. I can see the vibrant colors of the woman's shoes that are directly in front of me. I can smell the vanilla from the latte on the breath of the man who leans down and helps me up. I can still hear the last strum of my guitar hanging in the air by my ears. I am terrified that when I stand again Rose will be gone. I half leap, half claw my way to standing again. When I gaze desperately into the back of the crowd, my fears are realized and my heart feels as though it has stopped. She is gone. The leather chair is empty.

I know I am almost sobbing and making a spectacle of myself as I push my way through the crowd to the chair. I think I see Luke out of the corner of my eyes, but I am uncertain and unconcerned. There are two different exits to the coffee shop and I don't know which way to turn. Right would be the main entrance that leads to the street, and left is the back entrance which has more parking spaces. I choose the right.

When I swing open the big door and step into the night air, the silence is a black hole that makes my air expel out of my lungs in a whoosh. I can see far down the street in both directions and there is no one. There is no one here and I have chosen wrong. Pushing back through the crowd and going out the back is hopeless now. Rose is gone. I sink to the sidewalk.

I must have sat there for a few minutes, staring blankly into space as calm, silent tears cascade down my face. I notice when someone sits down beside me, but I don't respond. I hug my knees to my chest. The only way I acknowledge him at all is to sniff every few seconds to prevent the snot from running down my face. It's the only polite thing I can accomplish right now. Despite what I think is a heroic attempt, Luke abruptly stands and leaves back through the coffee shop door. I can't help the pitiful broken laugh that escapes me, but in less than a minute he is back. He sinks down to the sidewalk with me and hands me a rough paper napkin.

"Best I can do," he says. "Men's stall is out of toilet paper."

"Sorry," I croak and accept the napkin. "I always forget to check in there when I'm stocking for the next day." I blow my nose politely at first, but then with more gusto. I take longer than I need to and wipe my eyes, putting off what I think could be a weird conversation and explanation.

"If this is how you always end your act on stage, I think you're a little hard on yourself," Luke finally begins. "You weren't that bad. Kind of good actually. Although your guitar picking needs work."

I can't help but smile, lopsided though it is. "I know. You're a big guitar expert, huh?"

"The world's leading air guitar expert," he corrects me. His tone changes from silly to gentle. "Want to talk? Or do you need more sandpaper to blow your nose with?"

"I just thought I saw someone I used to know." My response is very lame and I know it. But how do I explain that this someone I used to know I last saw over two hundred years ago? I look down, embarrassed, and see my horses on my shirt galloping across my chest. They would look so mighty and strong if they weren't soaked with my tears and upside down.

"And that someone owes you a million dollars? That's why you're so upset, because you lost them again?" Although his words are light and teasing, his eyes are piercing and I am uncomfortable under their scrutiny. I make a show of wiping my eyes with the soggy napkin again, if only to collect myself.

I smile widely and hopefully with an air of sanity. I fear it comes across as desperate and crazy though. I am surprised when he doesn't develop a sudden recollection of what he should be doing, where he should be going, and leave never to see this tear stained wreck of a girl again. Instead he stands and offers me his hand.

"Well, let's get some caffeine and strategize, shall we? This isn't a big city and we can find your special someone. It's not the end of the world kid.

Chin up." I stand awkwardly at his side, and he uses his knuckle to rub my chin and lift my head.

I feel very conspicuous when I walk back into the shop. I am hesitant and worry that every head will turn and stare at me. The deranged, clumsy girl who made a spectacle of herself now has the job of refilling their mugs and bringing them their peanut butter scones. They're probably terrified I'll spill a pot of hot coffee on them, or drop a butter knife on their toes. But aside from a couple of sympathetic looks, I seem to be mostly ignored. I'll take it. Ignored is home to me. Ignored is where I dwell quite comfortably, thank you very much.

At the bar, I take off my black apron and tell Micki I'm taking a break. I pour Luke and myself two coffees in matching white cups that are ridiculously large. We sit at the only table available, a cozy spot for three people in the back corner of the shop. I watch him sip his coffee for a moment as I squeeze honey into mine from a bear shaped plastic jar. The concentration gives me something to do. The honey is cold. It seems to take forever before it plops into my coffee. Finally, if only to break the quiet, I speak.

"That girl that you photographed, the pretty one with the blonde hair? She's my sister. I saw her here tonight. It," I stumble over the inadequacy of my words. "It surprised me." *No, it rocked me. It paralyzed me. It undid me.* But I can't say those things.

"How long has it been since you've seen your sister?" His question is so innocent, so appropriate, yet I want to laugh like a loon. How can I tell him I last saw her was in 1741? He'd pat me on my crazy head, pay for his coffee, and disappear into the night. And I wouldn't blame him a bit. Not a bit.

"I haven't seen her since we were children. I thought she was dead, actually." How to explain this? "It's only been my dad and me since I was four." Let him think we are a broken family. Let him think my mother was there for Rose and we have simply been separated since a divorce.

"Must have been quite a shock. I'm sorry." His words are kind, but his eyes remain unconvinced and skeptical. He knows I'm not saying everything.

I wrap my hands around my hot mug of coffee.

"I asked Prue to let you photograph her," I blurt out suddenly, hungry for a change of topic. Something safe and ordinary. Something away from this mess of emotions that is eating me up inside. "I don't think I convinced her though. You might have to take one when she's not looking or something."

"And risk death and maiming?" His wooly eyebrows shoot up into his too-long hair. I fight an urge to smooth them back down. "That's okay, I don't need to die for my art. I did take some of you singing though, I hope you don't mind. You can see them if you like. I'll develop them tonight most likely."

"You don't use digital?"

Luke shrugs. "I'm an old fashioned guy. I like the process of developing the photos almost as much as I love taking them. But anyway, maybe we can use the pictures I got of your sister to help you find her. Something that would give us a clue to where she lives or who might know her or something. I'll be Cagney, you be Lacey. No? Fred and Daphne?"

My blank stare must be a giveaway. I don't have any idea what he is referring to. Who are those people? He laughs.

"Sherlock and Watson then?" He continues. "No? Just what is your name anyway?"

"Sonnet Gray. But I get to be Sherlock. I'd better get back to work." I stand up and wonder if I should shake his hand, hug him, something. What do social people with friends do?

"Goodnight, Gray," he says. "Stay out of trouble. I'll bring in those photos tomorrow night."

I'm so tired when I get off my shift. Matthias and Harry wait patiently for me, sometimes sitting at their table, sometimes helping me by taking out the trash and wiping down tables. They don't seem to have noticed my antics from earlier and they don't seem as though anything is amiss. They didn't travel with us until about ten years ago, and they never knew Rose. They know the story though. All the Lost have stories. It's after midnight by the time I finish getting the shop ready for opening tomorrow morning. I feel bad on nights like this because no one at home can fall asleep without me for fear of traveling on by themselves. No one can sleep until we are all together. Meli will be irritated because I know she has to watch the kids tomorrow early. We walk home in silence and enter our little brown house quietly. I was right about Meli, she shoots me a glare and a tight-lipped goodnight before she shuts her and Will's bedroom door a little more forcefully than necessary. Prue gets her nightly glass of water and reminds me to run the dishwasher if I'm going to dirty a plate tonight. Dad pecks me on the cheek with his dry lips, and absentmindedly settles into the couch with the reading lamp still on. He sleeps there more often than he does in his bed, so I pull an afghan over his legs and switch off the lamp. Matthias and Harry tell me I sang beautifully and they retire for the night to the room they share, whistling *I'll Be Seeing You*. Israel is eating soup from a blue pottery bowl in the kitchen and I join him.

"What's wrong?" He asks. Israel sometimes seems as though he knows me the best. His brown eyes look concerned.

"Do I look that bad?" I joke lightly. I wipe some coffee grounds off the horses on my shirt.

"You look like something bad happened," he responds, leaning back against the counter.

I look like I've seen a ghost, I think. *Because I did.* Instead I choose my words carefully and speak softly so that my dad, curled up on the couch, can't overhear.

"I saw Rose today. I know it was her. I know I'm not mistaken. Do you think I'm crazy? Or imagining things? Is it possible that she didn't stay in that century, and that she can travel too? That she's Lost?" Now that it's out, I can't seem to stop blurting things.

Israel is silent so long I fear what he will say when he finally does speak.

"I've seen my family in the strangest places," he says. "Sometimes I'll turn a corner, and I'll see someone and I'm so sure it's my mother. Other times I stare so long and so hard at someone that their features will start to resemble more and more my father. I see my brothers in every little boy their ages. I always hope that we'll meet up again one day. It's good to hope, Sonnet. Hope doesn't make you crazy. The absence of hope does."

"You don't believe me then?" I feel like crying, but I also feel angry.

"Will that make it better? Do you want me to believe?" (*In your delusions?* is the unspoken ending to his question.)

"Do what you want," I shoot back. I turn my back on him and rummage through the cupboard until I find what I'm looking for, Nightfall pills. Sleep being so important and vital to coordinate with your group, a Lost man long ago developed Nightfall pills. Although I am exhausted and weary to the bone, I know I will need their assistance in turning my brain off and falling asleep tonight. I swallow two of the lavender pills and go to bed, leaving Israel in the kitchen still silent.

Despite the pills, which usually knock me into a dreamless comatose kind of slumber, I am fitful and restless all night. I feel stuck in that not quite asleep, not quite awake state, the kind you feel at the very ending of a nightmare. I'm too groggy and disoriented to wake up fully, but never reaching that refreshing, rejuvenating energy you get after a good night's sleep. I feel as though my insides are shutting down, and everything is heavy. I am being pulled under by a suffocating fog and strange dreams. My room is so dark and my dreams are dark too.

At first, I am young again, eating bread in our stone home in the seventeen hundreds. I can see my mother sewing something by the fire. I am lying on a pallet next to her, and I can see her bare feet. The fire burns hot, I can feel it on my face, legs, and arms, like gentle sunburns. I hear my dad humming, but I can't see him. I hear a little scuttling sound and then little three-year- old Rose, lies down beside me. I can see her light blue eyes, mirror images of my own. She wears a white gown and holds a small wooden toy in the shape of a bear.

As I watch her, she begins to grow. Her features grow up, her baby fat melts away. I look down at my own legs and they are growing too. Rose reaches out and strokes my cheek, then my hair. I still feel the fire burning brightly beside us. I still hear my dad's hums, see my mother's feet. Rose stops touching my face and her hand reaches down to hold mine. She holds it softly for a moment, then tighter, then tighter still until I want to say *stop, that hurts!* Her hand squeezes and it feels larger now, not like that of a small three-year-old. It squeezes violently then and pulls out of my grasp with such force that the nails scratch me. I cry out both in my dream and in reality, waking myself up as I gasp for air.

I throw off the blankets and fumble for the light on the stand by my bed. I turn it on half sobbing. The place on the bed next to me is warm as though a body had been there only seconds before, and I cradle my bleeding hand feeling frightened and very small.

Chapter 4

I bring my blanket from my bed and wrap myself in the recliner. I spend the rest of the night next to the couch where Dad sleeps, snoring blissfully away like he always does. I am freezing cold, shivering and trembling, chilled almost to the bone. My teeth chattering, my fingers and toes alternating between a state of numbness and bone-chilling pain. It's not the temperature of the room, it's the way my body reacts to fear. It was the same when I was a little girl scared by a dream or a thunder storm. I'd cocoon myself in quilts and shake like a leaf until the fear subsided.

To be frank, I am not one of those girls you read about in mystery novels. If something goes bump in the night, you can be sure I won't be the type to head down into a dark basement to investigate. I'm not going to traipse off into the spooky attic looking for mysterious answers or calmly take a shower when a serial killer is on the loose in my neighborhood. I'm more of the "yell for help and hide under the covers" type. So, what happened in my bedroom frightened me. I want nothing more than to reach out to someone, anyone, but knowing Prue would probably beat me with the bat she keeps by her bed just for such purposes. I curl my legs up in the chair and try to fall back asleep.

Whatever happened had to have been a strange nightmare to cause such anxiety that I scratched my own palm and wrist. The dried scrapes looked like the leftovers of a cat fight, dark red and jagged. They followed the lines of my hands where a palm reader would foretell my happiness or the length of my days, and then continued all the way past my wrist almost to the crook of my elbow. Four parallel lines. They ache even now.

I am so grateful for morning because it means a chance to do something, anything, to make me less jumpy and paranoid. I go into the kitchen and noisily begin breakfast at the first hint of dawn. The sun has barely risen and shines as brightly as it can through our old dirty window and faded lace curtains. I take out pots and pans, crack eggs, and dip bread into vanilla and cinnamon-scented milk. I let the slices sizzle on the griddle with bacon and make coffee. I am being loud in the hopes that my household will wake up. I am being a chef in the hopes that they won't kill me.

Israel is the first to enter my little sanctuary and I want to throw my arms around him. I am shaking off last night like the bad dream it must have been and am determined to dismiss it from my mind.

"Why are you cooking?" Israel yawns, taking out plates from the cupboard. He looks tired. No, worse than tired. He looks like he was up all night. Perhaps we all ate something a bit off, perhaps we all had terrifying dreams.

"Because I'm hungry," I say happily. At least I am trying to sound happy. The truth is I sound squeaky which is an uncomfortable sound for a deep-voiced girl like me. I clear my throat and turn the kettle on for tea. Israel has spent most of his years in Europe and he prefers his caffeine in the form of tea leaves rather than coffee beans.

We don't speak again as I flip the toast slices and add eggs to a pan to fry. My bacon is burnt and all my eggs end up breaking, so I scramble them hurriedly. I sip hot coffee from my favorite mug, one shaped like Elvis Presley's head. Elvis is my very favorite artist and silence with Israel is one of my comforts and familiarities. *He is my rock*, I think to myself.

Soon Meli and Will come in, and then Matthias and Harry. I serve them all, handing out little feasts on our best cracked dinner plates and making witless conversation about anything I can think of. I seem to be talking now just to keep myself from thinking too much, and it sounds like chatter to my ears. I even out-talk Meli which is remarkable in and of itself.

"Here is your English Breakfast, Iz." I hand Israel his tea in my other favorite cup, the one with a fat orange colored cat pictured. I also have the same cat on a t-shirt, though Emme once tried to burn it after she claimed she only wanted to borrow it. I know better now than to believe her when she compliments my fashion. I had to cut off the burnt bottom just to salvage it, and now it's so short I have to wear it under overalls. Which is a sort of revenge on Emme, so it worked out well. It's a double whammy fashion disaster now, she says. It's my favorite outfit.

Israel takes the cup, but his dark eyes look concerned when the sleeve of my white nightgown falls back towards my elbow. He has seen my scratches. He reaches out and rubs them lightly with his thumb. *What happened?* He mouths. He knows already somehow that I don't want to speak of it with the others.

I shrug as though I either don't recall or it isn't important enough to mention. I suddenly don't want to talk anymore and I definitely don't want to talk about my arm. It begins to throb again.

I eat, but the breakfast tastes wooden in my mouth. I wash my bites down with coffee but it tastes of nothing. I feel as though I want to jump out of my skin, especially the skin on my arm and wrist.

I hear Meli and Will debating something, and Harry interjecting gentle admonishments to them. I see Prue come out from her bedroom and push my father's leg off the coffee table as he snores on. I am aware of Israel watching me, looking perplexed. I see Dad finally pick himself up off the couch and fold his blanket neatly, fluffing the pillow he leaves behind. I see and hear all this, and yet feel far away, distant like I am on the outside of our kitchen window, peering in. I'm hearing snippets of conversations and softly spoken words. If it was just a dream, why is it affecting me so? I need to get a handle on myself. I need to get out of this house. First however, I need a bath.

Our bathroom is old, like the rest of our house, but it has a wonderful, deep tub. After years in other centuries, where you'd never find something like that, much less instant hot water, I avail myself of baths frequently. It is a luxury that I dread missing when we leave, and inevitably we will.

An embarrassing amount of my tip money is squandered on bubble bath and oils. I may not have good clothes or fancy hair, but I guarantee I smell good. This morning I pour in a ginger and pear concoction that I paid far too much for, and only use for special occasions. It's a ridiculous limit I've sternly set for myself. If I wake tomorrow in dusty Egypt four hundred years in the past, I am really going to be angry with myself for wasting what I had left in the bottle. So, I pour in a few more drops before sliding in up to my nose in fragrant bubbles. I can't help the sigh that escapes me when I hear knocking on the door only a scant few seconds later.

Without even moving the rest of my body, I can reach the doorknob and I open it obediently. It swings by my head and I don't even open my eyes to see who it is because I know it's Meli. She probably was left at the breakfast table still talking, as everyone wandered off, and now she'll be looking for a captive audience.

Sure enough, when I open my eyes just a slit, Meli is sitting on the counter beginning a long narrative about Will, work, babies, marriage, the house, and any other topic that comes to her mind. I do love Meli dearly, but she is not helping the pounding in my head from my nightmare and it is building to a rousing crescendo. I "mmm" and "uh huh" while I shave my legs (not a requirement of womanhood I shall miss if I do wake up in Egypt centuries past).

I wash my hair, then scrub my face with a pink washcloth I bought used at a garage sale. It has a white ribbon around the edges that is silky when dry, but rough when it gets wet. The initials T.S. have been embroidered in one corner. I like to wonder who T.S. is or was and how her handiwork ended up in someone's garage sale and finally in my hand. Was T.S. someone's grandmother? No one these days would do such an old fashioned thing as to hand-embroider a washcloth. But I am an old fashioned girl, literally, as old fashioned as one can get. I would have been alive many years before T.S. and I will be alive many years after she is only a memory. Unlike, her I will have nothing to leave behind for my descendants to sell, and the thought is vaguely sad to me. I decide to embroider myself my own initials on my own set of towels. Take that, Fate or Destiny or God or whoever pulls my marionette strings. I may be a puppet, but I can be a rebellious one.

Meli's conversation seems to wane and I sink lower into the ginger and pear bubbles. She finally accuses me of not listening, but it's good natured since Meli is all bark with no bite. When she leaves, I towel myself dry and ponytail my wet hair. Quickly, I put on my denim coveralls with a striped tank top, and pull out my old battered sneakers from their spot under my bed. An eerie feeling comes over me as I look around my dimly lit room. The bulb in my lamp is low wattage, and the only window is hazy and hard to see in or out of. The memories of last night still haunt me, and I can't be here any longer.

My imagination seems to be running a mile a minute, as I grab my bag and slam the door shut behind me. I swear I can still smell the smoke from my dream. The smoke that curled around my mother's bare feet as they swung back and forth in her rocker, the smoke that felt hot on my little girl face. That same smoke from the fire that lit up Rose in bright, yellow light right before she reached for my hand, and held it softly. All this before her gentle child's grip became, something sinister and painful.

The scratches begin to hurt again as I hurriedly left my house, hastening for anywhere but here. I can't go to Emme's this early in the morning or she'll do worse than attempted arson on my clothes. She isn't a morning person. I wonder where I can find Luke Dawes. In the bright, cheerful light of day, outside in the city, I am feeling much less nervous. I realize that now more than ever I want to do whatever I can to find my sister. If I could look at those photos Luke said he had taken of her...would they give me anything to go on? Any clue to her whereabouts or existence? I can think of no other route to Rose other than these photos, so I pull out his business card looking for the phone number or address of his shop. There is a number, but I will have to use a payphone to dial it. I must be the only teenager in all of America who doesn't own a cell phone. I don't see the point in learning how to use one if it will only be ripped away from me soon enough. Besides, who would I call?

There is a payphone, dirty and old, in the front of a service station on my right, and I jaywalk across the street quickly to get to it and feed it my coins. It rings and rings and no one picks up. Impatiently I wait for the voicemail and when it finally begins speaking to me I am informed that his photography shop is located at the corner of Poplar and Monterey Streets, beneath a yoga studio. It isn't far, which explains his proximity to both my coffee shop and Prue's food cart.

Prue parks in that area most times as it's close to a schoolyard and a business complex both, although the thought of her feeding small children alligator stew makes me roll my eyes. Not to mention with her people skills, she'd probably stew the children along with the gators. The business men and women in their expensive tailored suits and spiked heels will pay twice as much for her strange cooking as other customers, but their tips are terrible. They think she's avant garde and ahead of her time, and call her 'a risk taker in the kitchen,' and 'the city's best kept secret!' Actually, she's far behind their time but she definitely has the best kept secret.

It doesn't take me long to reach Poplar and Monterey. Luke's section of the complex is the only rundown little square of the shiny business complex. Even the yoga studio is sparkling and clean, and the tiny perfect office spaces that surround Dawes Photography are symmetrically square shaped with gleaming windows and perfectly hung signs. Luke's space looks like the room that time forgot. The windows haven't been washed in what looks like a very long time, the sign is crooked and it's so dim inside it's impossible to tell if he is even open for business. The windows, besides being filthy, are covered with fliers for musicals, concerts, dog sitting services, apartments for rent, and estate sale notices. On quick glance, they all seemed to have expired several months ago. The whole building complex reminds me of a beautiful smiling head with one brown, crooked tooth in its gaping mouth. I reach out my hand, turn the handle of the door and enter the brown decaying tooth, leaving the rest of the shiny head outside sparkling in the sun.

A set of bells right above my head jingles as I step inside and close the door behind me. Even the bells sound a bit tired and worn out. When no one greets me, I reach up and shake the bells more vigorously.

"Hello?" Luke's head pokes out from behind a door in the back. His voice sounds extremely surprised at the realization that something resembling a customer has actually arrived. When he sees it's me, he looks even more surprised. "Gray? Come in. I was just eating breakfast in the back here. Do you want to join me or is there something I can do for you? How are you?" He seems to have a lot of questions and his sentences run together as though he is speaking exactly what is going through his mind. He looks as disheveled as ever and needs both a shave and a haircut. He has a plate of food balanced in one hand as he holds open the door with the other.

"Um, sure, I can stay for a bit," I answer. Well, of course I can, isn't that what I'm here for? "And I'm all right, thanks. You?"

He takes a bite as the door swings shut behind us and waits a moment to finish chewing before answering me. "Good. Hungry?"

I think of my breakfast feast, sitting in my stomach like a brick and shake my head. I do peer at his plate of food though. "Wait, that smells familiar. Is that Prue leftovers?"

He nods happily. "She said it's an old family recipe - shepherd's pie."

I snort. "It's an old recipe, all right, all of Prue's recipes are old. And it isn't shepherd's pie, it's squirrel pie." I watch his bushy eyebrows for a reaction. They shoot up and take residence in the sandy-colored hair that falls over his forehead and stay there for a minute, before settling back down over his hazel eyes. He takes another bite.

"I can support squirrel control. Little buggers got into my film last year."

"I can't imagine why," I say dryly. "You keep such a clean, organized storeroom." I look around at my surroundings and gingerly sit down at a small bistro style table. Other than the table, there is a tiny refrigerator, one chair – which I am perched on - a cot with a rumpled quilt and pillow, and lots of both books and boxes stacked everywhere. There is also a tiny counter alongside an even tinier sink and an open door that leads to the world's smallest bathroom. Does he employ elves?

"Hey," he chewed, narrowing those hazel eyes, "Did you come here to make fun of my squalor or to see those photos of Rose?" He remembers. Well, of course he remembers. Who could forget the girl who tripped over her own feet, made a scene in public, and then cried buckets as he tried to sop up the salty tears with restroom paper towels?

"To see the photos, please," I say meekly. As meekly as possible. I've never been very good at meek, but in my defense I haven't had much practice.

"Okay then, I'll get them. Stay away from my squirrel potpie." He leaves back through the door we had just come through, the one that leads to his shop. I hear drawers opening and closing and then he returns with a folder, a similar one to the one I looked though before. It feels like lifetimes ago, before I knew that Rose was perhaps alive. Will I categorize everything that way now? Before Rose's Appearance, and After? Everything before seems so fuzzy and distant and so unimportant now. He pulls out three photos and sets them before me. I feel as though there are butterflies in my stomach causing me to break out in a sweat. I push the hair back from my forehead and neck where tendrils have escaped my ponytail. My hands shake as I lay them back down in my lap as my eyes focus on the photographs.

It is the girl I saw in the coffee shop. There's no mistaking the red calico dress, and the long sheet of white blonde hair cascading down her tiny frame. As was the case in the original photo of Rose I had seen, she doesn't seem to be aware that her picture is being taken, and is looking off to the side. Her feet are bare, something I hadn't noticed before. Was that the case when she sat in the leather armchair in the coffee shop? Has she no shoes? Is my sister suffering? I wonder as a lump forms in my throat and threatens to make me cry. The same dress, no shoes. What if she's only just arrived here, in modern day America? Is she used to traveling, to being Lost? What if the magic or power that we have has only just begun to materialize in her? Is she scared, confused? The tears building up behind my eyes and threaten to spill over. Frustrated with myself for my weakness, I savagely stab a bite of squirrel pie with the fork I grab out of

Luke's hand. The chewing gives me something to do while I get hold of myself and blink the tears away.

Luke gets up from the overturned plastic crate he had been sitting on, and opens his tiny refrigerator. He puts down a bottle of water in front of me, twisting off the top first.

"Thanks," I mumble and drink deeply. "I don't usually cry this much." I am trying to sound apologetic, but it comes out sounding defensive.

"No problem, it's hardly the first time I've made a pretty girl cry." He speaks lightly.

Pretty? I straighten my overalls that have bunched up in front. I look again at the photos in front of me. I don't see anything else that could give me a clue to finding Rose. The tree she leans against could be any tree. Luke had said she was at the fair, but that only means she was there that particular night. It's not like she lives there. No one lives in a fairground. I don't know what I thought I'd find. Maybe I just wanted to look at her again, feel some connection.

"Can I have them?" I ask. "I can pay you for them if they're for sale."

He waves away my offer. "I can't sell them anyway. I didn't have her permission to photograph her. Really, I was just trying out a new camera that night and wasn't paying too much attention to what I was capturing. I'll end up throwing the other ones from that night away. You can keep them if I can keep the ones of you singing last night."

Was it only last night?

"Why?" I laugh. "I'm not going to be a star someday if that's what you're hoping." I won't be around long enough to be a star, I thought.

"You photograph well," he answers, reaching behind him to the counter and handing me more prints. They are of me on stage at the coffee shop, singing with my eyes closed. My guitar partially covers the horses on my

36

shirt and my legs are crossed Indian-style the way I always sit when I am singing. It must have been mere seconds before I opened my eyes and saw Rose sitting in the chair that Luke had been in when I began my song. Had he gotten up and moved closer to photograph me, while she sank down in his vacated chair? I look peaceful even with my mouth open singing. I'm surprised how pretty the girl in the photo looks. I don't think I look like much in real life, but the camera seemed to bring something out in me. Perhaps the shadows shaded my face in the right way, or the light reflected making my skin look luminescent.

"The camera loves you, Gray. If your barista talents and singing career don't take off, you can come model for me. Hey, all this could be yours!" He gestures grandly at his sad little shop. I can't help laughing. I like the way he makes me forget to finish crying.

Chapter 5

By the time I leave the little dingy photography shop, I think it may be late enough in the morning to stop and see Emme. I let myself in the way I always do, and find her in her favorite spot on her couch reading yet another novel. I see her pretty pink toenails as they swing over the end of the couch. Her strawberry red hair is piled haphazardly atop her head in a messy bun that looks ravishing on her, but would make me look like a homeless lady.

"Hang on, luv, just let me finish this chapter."

Instead I pull her romance novel out of her slim fingers and replace it with the photos Luke took of Rose. She scowls at me, but then glances over them.

"All right, I'll bite; what am I supposed to be looking at?" She sighs dramatically. Everything about Emme is dramatic, but in a good way. She is British for the most part, though she's traveled as much as I have. She plays up her British accent, it especially helps in her line of work adding to her charm and overall cuteness.

She is petite and curvy, a few years older than myself, with lots of wavy strawberry curls, twinkling brown eyes, and a self-deprecating sense of humor. She is the type of woman who is by nature a leader and a force of nature. If she were to trip and fall flat on her face you'd wonder, why you hadn't done it first. Emme's Lost family consists of only herself, her mother and her little brother Joe. They live in the apartment next door. They have been here a while, longer than my group, and they are beginning to wonder if they are stuck in time. Five years, Emme says. That's a long time for the Lost.

"It's Rose, my sister, Rose. I'm positive of it," I answer, flopping down on the floor by the couch since she hasn't made room for me and is sprawled from end to end.

"The missing one?" She cocks a pretty eyebrow that has been penciled in red. "Blimey, Sonnet, are you sure? How old is the picture?"

"A week or so and it was taken here." I can feel the excitement bubbling up again. "I met the man who took the picture, and I saw her myself at work last night. Now I just have to find her again."

"She doesn't know you then, is that it? Did you tell her who she is? I mean, who she was?"

"She ran off before I could talk to her. The only thing I can think of is that she is Lost too, but either she moves on less frequently than her family does, or maybe this is her first travel."

"Well, she does look a little confused," Emme agrees, staring at the photos once more. "She's very beautiful."

"I have to find her and bring her home before one of us travels on again, Emme. If you had just arrived here, where would you hide?"

"Mum and Joe and I stayed at the homeless shelter for a bit when we got here. Or since it's still summer, she might be sleeping in one of the parks. Otherwise, I don't know, Sonnet. Your guess is as good as mine. The Lost know how to blend in, you know that. Where'd you guys stay when you got here?"

I think back to two years ago when we first woke up here. We were all laid out on the riverbank at the edge of town, like beached fish. Prue had woken first and already had a fire going and was looking as nonplussed as usual to have woken up in an entirely different spot than where she had laid down to sleep. It was hardly her first travel, of course, and nothing much affects Prue. If Israel is my rock, Prue is my mountain. I had gone over to her, my heart in my mouth the way it always was when we traveled, and she had wrapped her big arms around me and rubbed some warmth into them and the goose bumps right off.

Amelia and Will had gotten up soon after, and Will spent the next several hours calming down his hysterical wife. Dad looked a bit sadder than normal, which is sorrowful to the point of death. Israel went off to find food and to find out what he could about where, and more importantly, when, we were. Matthias and Harry traded stories and attempted to fish with tree branches.

Israel came back with stolen clothes and reports of a modern American town. I traded glum for forced excitement and couldn't wait to see the cars he talked of. One drove by on the road above the riverbank and it was the only thing that made Meli stop bawling (after screaming first, of course). We stayed at that riverbank for a few nights, scoping out and learning as much as we could. We spent the next several days in an abandoned farmhouse a few miles away, an old trick of the trade for the Lost. Every town has a house or two that is empty and forgotten.

"She seems like a loner," I say doubtfully, thinking of the crowded homeless shelter and having a hard time imagining Rose there. "Parks aren't a bad idea though...there's the big one that edges up to the campground. No one would notice an extra camper." I am lost in thought and my thoughts lead me back to my nightmare from last night. My scratches start to ache again, dull and throbbing, starting in my palm and traveling up my arm. I am so focused inward I don't see Joe pop up from behind the couch until he lands on my lap and I jump out of my skin.

Joe is five and was only an infant when Emme and her mother arrived. He is an imp, with red hair and freckles and a mischievous personality that makes Emme look like a saint.

"Gotcha, Auntie Sonnet!" He crows, triumphantly, pumping his fist in the air.

I wait for my heart to resume its normal beat and resist the urge to thump his cute little red head. "You scared me half to death, brat!" I tickle him, which is of course what he is waiting for and the whole reason he is on my lap to begin with. When he has had enough and is properly winded, I roll him off my lap and onto the floor. He scampers off in search of snacks in the kitchen.

"Mum is out today so I've got him all day," Emme explains. Emme's mother, Bea, does all sorts of needlework and sells them, or attempts to, at craft shows and flea markets. Sometimes she even lays them out alongside Prue's food cart, but since Bea is terrified of Prue she only does it when she is really anxious for customers. Bea is sweet and shy and easily embarrassed, but Prue is – well, Prue is Prue.

"We should take him to the park," I suggest casually, examining my fingernails. As usual they are chewed short. Emme's are long and shaped and the contrast makes me sigh. I resolve to stop biting them first thing tomorrow.

"So you can look for Rose?" Emme's nose is tucked in her book again. "Have you thought maybe she isn't Rose, but just someone who looks like...well, like the way you imagine she would look today?"

"Of course I've thought of it, but I'm telling you, she's exactly how Dad describes with plenty of Mother thrown in, and even a little of me. Our eyes aren't exactly common," I remind her, pointedly.

"Your eyes are creepy. Oops, I meant to say creepy in a beeooteeful way." Emme laughs.

"You're no help at all," I answer, crossly. "Tell me what to do!"

"Simmer down, luv, don't get your knickers in a twist. Let's piece this puzzle together, shall we? Rose was left behind when you, your mum, and your dad disappeared back in what, the seventeen hundreds?"

"1741, I think."

"What do you remember? Anything about that time? If she was left behind, what would it have been like for her?"

"Well, it was France. It was cold or at least my only memories are of being cold. I think I remember," I falter, "I think I remember the night we left. There was a fire in the hearth and Mother was in her rocking chair."

Of course, it's my dream I'm really thinking of, but it describes what Dad has told me of our home there. It felt so real, as if it could be more of a memory and less of a dream.

"We lived in the countryside and there was a neighbor woman named Old Babba, kind of an old crone lady. She hobbled around with a walking stick and muttered a lot. I never understood much of what she said. I think I might have been a little scared of her. She used to come by almost every day, share her hen eggs and goats milk with us. We always hoped she found Rose the next day, and we always assumed she would have raised her or at least found a family to raise her."

"Didn't it occur to you that she would be Lost, too?"

"But she didn't come with us that night."

"What if she's only a half-sister?" Emme asks, lightly.

"Why?" Then it dawns on me. "If she wasn't full blooded Lost she could be traveling less frequently? I suppose only my mother would know and she isn't exactly here to ask, is she?"

It's not the first time I've been bitter about that. More often than not, I simply miss my mother. I miss the long talks we should have had, the lessons, and the companionship. But occasionally, like now, I am simply angry with her. Angry that she left me to fend for myself, and to never know her the way a daughter should.

"I've never doubted Dad is Rose's dad too. I mean, I guess I haven't thought about it, but he has never alluded to any," I pause, feeling awkward, "unfaithfulness on my mother's part."

"She doesn't look like your dad at all, but I suppose that's hardly proof. I don't look like my dad, the bloomin' sod, thank my lucky stars." She winks at me.

Emme's dad was some sort of con man from what I can gather. He wandered off after Joe was born and apparently no one looked very hard to find him. "Anyway, anything else you remember?"

"Not really." I frown. "Everything is fuzzy, I was only four. The next thing I knew I was in Italy two hundred years earlier. Mother killed herself and Dad started drinking. Not exactly the best part of my life."

"Well, it's probably good you don't remember," Emme says, kindly. "I bet your dad remembers enough for both of you. No wonder he stays smashed."

"I suppose."

"Talk to him? If it is Rose, he should be told. Might sober him up."

Trust Emme to find the bright side of things.

* * *

Dad lounges at his usual spot, a lawn chair he brings to set up next to Prue's food cart. By the time I arrive, it's lunch hour for the business executives from down the street, and I warily keep an eye on Prue's behavior as she dishes out buttery rolls stuffed with savory meat and onions.

"You know what this needs?" Asks a portly gentleman in a suit that looks entirely too hot for the weather.

Prue narrows her eyes. *Dear man, please shut up*, I think to myself.

"A side of potatoes!" He looks around as if the entire world would be pleased with his insightfulness, and then looks to Prue for her approval.

Instead, he gets a sharp whack with the silver tongs she has in her hands and a glare that could melt a glacier.

"Potatoes?" she barks. "You ever hear of a little sumpin' called The Potato Famine, you ignorant child? Why would I want to even look at a potato again, never mind cook 'em up for the likes of you? You get out o' here, you windbag! And give me back that roll, you don't deserve it." She snatches the roll out of his chubby hands and in spite of it having a large bite taken out of it, plops it unceremoniously into the next customer's fingers. The portly man turns purple and stalks away. The young woman who has suddenly gotten custody of a meat and onion lunch opens her mouth, closes it, and orders a soda with a squeaky voice. Prue smacks a can of cola on the cart and demands five dollars. She has raised her prices by two dollars just in the three minutes I've been standing here. Also, she makes potato dishes all the time, but I'm certainly not going to point that out to her.

"Dad? Come for a walk with me?" I whisper, conspiratorially.

He smiles as much as I've ever seen him, which is to say, briefly and with only the smallest bit of mirth, and nods. He unfolds his long, gangly legs out of his chair and together we leave Prue's little lunch area, heading for the small sidewalk that follows along the river. Dad hunches when he walks, the way he always does, and our long strides match each other's perfectly. We eat up the sidewalk.

"What is it, dear?" He asks, but I know it's only a formal request, not a burning desire to know what is actually going on with me. I don't believe it's that he doesn't want to know, he simply hasn't thought enough about it to develop any curiosity about me or my life. I wonder if I ever cross his mind in more than a vague, forgetful way.

There is no way to gently break what I'm going to say to him and so I dive right in to the heart of the matter.

"I think Rose may be Lost. I think she is traveling and she's here. Now." Here means nothing to the Lost; now means everything. It's the place in time we pay attention to, not the location.

I am surprised when he doesn't break stride and when his face shows no emotion. I suspected shock, disbelief, a roll of his eyes, or an unbelieving laugh, but not this. No reaction at all.

"Did you hear me, Dad? I've seen Rose."

"Where?" He asks, and it sounds as though he is choosing his words carefully. His voice remains neutral.

"At the coffee shop. And she was at the fair last week. I have pictures of her to prove it." I pull them out of my cover-all pocket where I had folded them and placed them. There's a crease through her pretty red dress where I've folded it. I hand the photos to my dad.

He finally stops walking and looks, but he doesn't move to take them out of my hands. He swallows hard and I watch as his eyes well up.

"Yes, yes, that certainly does look how I imagine your sister would look at your age. She looks like your mother, looks like Carolina." He begins walking again, his hands in his jacket pocket, his back hunched over.

I stand there for a second, put the photos back in my pocket, and then run to catch up to him.

"Dad?" I am torn between impatience at his reaction and empathy for his response. I love my dad, but he is a mystery to me and at the moment I have other mysteries that are more pressing. "Sit down and talk to me, Dad!" I pull on his sleeve and pull him down with me on the giant root of a tree. We both unfold our legs and lean against the tree, him pensively and me gingerly. I am on pins and needles.

"Tell me about Rose. Did you know that she could be Lost? What are you thinking, Dad?" I am practically begging and I am beginning to be angry at him for forcing me to be.

He pinches the bridge of his nose as he does when he encounters something unpleasant, such as see the bottom of his whiskey bottle or have a heart-to heart with his daughter. Then he rubs the back of his neck and opens his mouth. Just like the poor accosted woman who suddenly had a meat roll in her hand, he closes it again. Then opens, and almost gets a word out then closes it again.

"Oh forget it!" I snap, standing again and brushing off the pine needles from my legs. "I'll get Prue to talk to me if I'm such a bother to you."

I feel his hand in mine as I start to stalk off, feeling righteously upset. He pulls me back down.

"You're not a bother, Sonny," he says. Only my father calls me that and I can't help that it softens up my hard heart considerably. "I'm just not prepared...not prepared for...Rose." He shakes his head. "Your mother loved her so."

More than me, the one she chose to leave? The one who wasn't enough for her after she lost Rose? I don't want to think about that.

"I'm sure Old Babba found her real quick," Dad whispers, his eyes filling up again. One fat tear rolls down his unshaven face and gets lost in his mustache. He pats my hand consolingly.

At that, I know the conversation is over. I sit for a moment, hoping I am wrong, but Dad just stares into space, rolling his short beard whiskers between his fingers. He doesn't even seem to notice that they are wet.

Chapter 6

I leave Dad where he sits, perched uncomfortably on the tree root. I leave quietly, but I feel like stomping off like a small child. I feel like screaming, running, beating my fists against a wall. Why is it so hard to get through to him? He must care. I know he does. Then the realization dawns on me, like sunlight breaking through thunder clouds, he cares more than I know. And that is precisely why it frustrates me.

What exactly don't I know?

Prue is packing up her cart when I return, hot and sweaty from my little river walk. It's a humid day and my feet are hot and sticky in my shoes. I plop down dramatically on the stone wall behind the food cart and sigh loudly. It gets no response. This childishness of mine needs to stop. I am eighteen years old. Well, I think I am.

Prue gives me no reaction other than to demand I move and count her tips, a large mason jar with a few meager handfuls of change. As cranky and ornery as I am feeling, I am certainly not in the mood to take my life in my hands, so I obey.

"Nearly eight dollars," I tell her, handing her the money. "Not bad for a couple hours work." I make more than that in a busy morning shift at the coffee shop in less than half an hour, but I certainly won't tell Prue that.

Prue shoves it in her apron pocket and scowls. "Lazy rich people," she snorts. "Can't leave more than a measly quarter each. Ought a smack some sense into 'em, since the good Lord knows their mamas never did. Where you been, girly? Where's Noah?"

Noah Gray. My father. My dear, sweet, unbearable father who I was cruel enough to leave sitting beneath a tree, half inebriated and full of sorrow. I feel like such a heel. It's as though I have two emotions when it comes to him, impatience or guilt. Neither is something to be proud of.

"He's back on the river path. Prue, can I ask you something?" I begin to pick at my nails in my effort to look casual and to give my hands something to do besides shake. Prying into Prunella O. Broin Boulander's business is like feeding sharks. It's best left to professionals and those with excellent life insurance policies.

"If you ask it while you're pushing my cart, go ahead," she agrees.

Obediently I begin to push, my hands clenched tight on the handle of the worn food cart while I form the words that will leave my dysfunctional brain and travel out of my mouth where I will, most likely, instantly regret them. I can still see the original owner's slogan *Vic's Organic Hotdogs!* printed but faded on the cart's handle.

"I was wondering how many times exactly you've traveled? And have you ever heard of a Lost who traveled only occasionally? Like, say a couple times their whole life? And what do you remember of when we left behind Rose? Do you think my mother could have had an affair? And if we meet up with other Lost at least once in a while, do you think there is a reason for it? I mean, what if we are all thrown together for some purpose and we're missing it? We're missing the whole point, Prue! Because there has just got to be some reason for why we exist! Some reason why we are chosen. Special. Some reason for the places we go, the times we visit," I stop realizing that in all my babbling I have left Prue behind. She is several paces behind me, frowning mightily. Hastily I retreat, with the cart.

She stares at me as though I have three heads. Her arms are crossed against her substantial chest and her feet are planted firmly and widely in the pavement of the sidewalk. Her dark brown eyes are narrowed, almost in suspicion.

"What you about, girly? Where's all these fool questions comin' from? Your daddy been putting ideas in your purty head?"

Since I've never heard Prue call me pretty – or purty – I almost get distracted in a petty way from my diatribe.

"No, Dad's been doing the opposite of talking to me. I just... I don't know. I want to know why we are the way we are. Don't you ever wonder?"

"No, not particularly," Prue snorts again, but the way she says it, it sounds like 'purticoolerly.' Her accent is completely untraceable: unique, bizarre and a melting pot of languages and dialects. All of the Lost speak like that to a certain extent, but the difference is that Prue doesn't mask hers. "What's the point of wonderin', child? We ain't ever gonna know why we are the way we are. Just accept it. Our kind's been travelin' 'cross time for centuries, we always will. Might as well enjoy the ride, my da' said. Enjoy it or let it kill you."

"How do we even know it's centuries?" I argue. "No one bothers to keep records, no one passes down their stories to the next generation beyond the good old 'when I was a boy...blah blah blah,' no one finds out anything, no one questions anything, Prue! Doesn't that make you crazy?"

"Honey child, you have done lost your mind. What do you want us to do, keep diaries? Save the world? Learn how to navigate or somethin'?" She chortles and begins walking again, her short legs making short work of the sidewalk as only Prue can, leaving me behind now. "Hey! Maybe we could go back and invent microwaves the next time we move! Or plastic wrap! That's stuff'd make us a fortune!" She slaps her knee in mirth in mid-stride.

"Well, why not?" I ask reasonably. "Why haven't we done that? Why haven't we bet on the World Series or killed Hitler as a kid or warned everyone on the Titanic?"

"Don't be a fool, Sonnet Gray." She is stern now, the laughing is over and she is irritated with me. Irritated and hot by the looks of it. She uses her apron to mop her forehead. "No one can change their fate. If those people were meant to drown on the Titanic I guess they went to their holy reward, sure 'nuff. And I don't reckon I ever heard of a Lost meetin' Hitler, otherwise I 'spect they woulda stabbed him through his dark heart. You can be sure I will if we meet sometime. Right through the heart with my best bread knife. That'll teach the little bugger. Or maybe the apple corin' one…it's duller." She sniffs and picking up stride, fairly sails by me, her head held high and visions of murder on her mind. Once again, I hurry to catch up.

"Okay then. We can't change history. You've been through a lot more of it than me so I'll let you be the judge of that one. Fine. But tell me what you remember from all the places you've been? Is there a pattern?"

"What you mean, like knowing where we're endin' up next? Don't you think if I'da figured that out by now I'da warned ya?" She has gone from irritated to incredulous.

"But what do you remember from all the places, Prue?" I press.

Sighing, she stops walking once again and looks me right in the eye. "If you're gonna do this to an old lady, Sonnet, at least buy her a Coca Cola and get her outta the sun." She nods her head towards a diner on our right. It's the Up All Night Diner and the only place that stays open later than the coffee shop. They are in direct competition with us, and even have a sign advertising the City's Best Coffee– the cheekiness! But I will buy Prue ten Coca Colas if she will only sit down and talk to me.

Prue insists on parking the food cart right in front of the picture window so we can keep an eye on it in case a mad, serial cart thief is on the loose in the neighborhood., She also has to make sure we bully the waitress to get the table that is directly in front of the same window. I order her the largest Coca Cola with a slice of lemon, just the way Prue likes it, and we settle into the red, vinyl booth.

"Now why you wantin' to know all this history that don't concern you?" Prue begins once she drinks half her soda through the straw and burps. "You got sumpin' you need to be telling me?"

My mind races frantically and I don't know whether to tell her of Rose. I can't decide if I'm hesitating because I don't want her to know, or I just don't want one more person disbelieving me. Finally, after I have torn a napkin to shreds with my fingers, I take the plunge. "I think Rose is here. I saw her. And I don't know whether it's by accident or design. I'm afraid this is our only chance to meet up with her if she's really Lost, and if it is, I'm afraid to travel on until we find her." There. I've said it.

Prue looks as though she has swallowed her lemon slice whole. Her eyes are narrowed and her forehead has more creases than a pleated skirt. I am even more surprised to see her large, brown hands trembling.

"You saw Rose? She's here?" I have never heard Prue whisper in my whole life, yet she is whispering now.

I nod. "I'm positive it was her, Prue. Do you believe me?"

Prue doesn't speak for a minute. She twirls the straw around in her glass absentmindedly. When she speaks again it is no longer in a hushed whisper, but in the regular voice I know, firm and not to be trifled with.

"I don't see how it could be, Sonnet. That doesn't make a lick of sense. If she had the same powers we do, she woulda never been left behind in the first place. Lots of girls have blonde hair and blue eyes. It's just wishful thinkin.' That's all." She stands and motions for me to do the same. "Come along home, girly. I gotta go shopping today and I gotta get my cart home first."

Not as vague as my father's, but a dismissal just the same. I pay for her drink, since she marches right past the waitress with the cash register without even pausing, and goes back outside.

"Do you want me to go back and get Dad?" I ask.

"Nah. He'll make his way eventually. Now if you do the pushin', I'll tell you 'bout some of those other things you was asking about, all right?"

Obviously throwing me a bone, I think. It's not what I want to find out most, but it's better than nothing. "All right. Tell me about your first travel, and when you get to here and now."

She chortles. "Land sakes, Sonnet, I can't remember my first travel! My da' said I was just a babe. I was born in Quebec in 1920, but I don't remember nothin' about that. I was only a year old when we traveled from there, I think it was to some God forsakin' part of Russia. We were there for 'bout three years. I don't think the time frame was too much different from 1920 though...my da used to say something 'bout being stuck at the turn of the century. Next we went to Ireland, 1845. I remember that all right; I was about five or so and we stayed for four years. Never did get outta that dang potato famine." She scowls. "Wonder I cook Irish food a'tall nowadays. Anyway, where was I?"

"After Ireland, 1849. You would have been nine years old your next travel."

"Right. Yup, I remember being nine and bein' right here. First time in America, it was, least for me. Da said he'd been before. Anyways, we came here in 1755, over in New York. Couldn't make up our minds which was worse, the Indians or the colonials or the British. They was all bossy if you ask me. But I came back later when I was twenty and that's where I met my first husband, he was a Huron. His mama was the one who taught me to cook that puddin' you like."

I nod. "But what happened between your first two visits to America? Where were you?"

"Oh criminy, child, I can't remember everything! We was in London for a while, that was in that Victorian time frame. Whole time and place was annoying. I hated it there!"

I can't picture Prue, her ample waist and bosom tucked into a corset and a bustle! The thought almost makes me laugh out loud. I'm surprised she lasted in that era for any length of time at all.

"Had to work as a maid for this uppity, whiney British gal who claimed to be a lady. It was enough to make me want to sleep all day, tryin' to travel on again. Hmm from there, thank God, we ended up in Chile, I think. I don't know."

"Well, after your husband here in America, where did you go? Were you sad to leave him?"

"Well, honey, bein' married ain't never sat too right with me. 'Course that didn't stop me from trying again three more times!" She guffawed. "But by the time I'd been with him a couple years, I wasn't too sad to move on. Bet he was as mad as a hornet when he woke up and I was gone though! I was always tellin' him I was gonna run off with a proper English gentleman so I imagine he was runnin' through the countryside looking for some dandy with his wife! Ha!" She slaps her knee in mirth.

"Then what?" I press. Is anything going to give me a clue to our crazy mixed-up existence?

"Well, where was I?" We have reached our little brown house now and Prue sits down heavily on the front stoop. She motions for me to sit as well. "If you want to hear all this we'll sit here. If I go in, I'll just start gettin myself pulled into one of them game shows that the boys will have on."

The boys, of course, are Matthias and Harry, who are in their seventies if they're a day, but to someone nearly twenty years their senior, they'll always just be boys.

"So's anyway, after that I spent some time in Central America. Stayed there a right long time, too. My longest stop. Probably the closest to feeling like home now I think about it. Stayed so long and got so comfortable, I got fat!" She chuckles, slapping her thighs.

"Was it hard to leave if it felt like home?" I've never had that feeling before, no place has felt like home yet. I hope no place ever does. Leaving is hard enough when you don't particularly like where you are anyway.

"Oh shore, I guess so." Prue shrugs. "The next stop was Belgium and that's where I met up with your daddy's parents. Been with Noah ever since. Closest thing to family I ever had, and that's probably counting my Da. Never saw him again after I married my Huron boy. Didn't approve."

I have trouble imagining Prue as a beautiful rebellious daughter who chose love with a Native American warrior over her stern father, but I like the imagery. Separating yourself from family when you're Lost is saying goodbye forever. They'll be no reaching out after a few years to your estranged parent asking forgiveness, or showing up on their doorstep with a suitcase trying to apologize. She must have been very angry or very in love. Knowing Prue, I'd put money on angry with a side of vindictive.

"Well," I say trying to make my voice sound steady and casual, "If Rose was Lost, and I'm only saying if, what would pull her towards this same century, this same town? Would a bond do that? Have you ever heard of that, the Lost following each other? Remember when Uncle Zed met up with us that time? Kind of like that?"

"Well, I ain't never met up with anyone from my past. I reckon I'd remember that, even if my memory is a little foggy sometimes. I never did meet my Da again, and we had a bond."

"A strong one?"

Prue wrinkles her nose. "Well, not that strong...he always drove me a little batty. And I think he was secretly happy to marry me off even if he put up a fight. I 'spect we was ready to say goodbye." She sighed. "It was just me and him, you know, but we'd had enough time together for one lifetime. Then I ended up in Belgium. After that I 'spect you know the rest, girly."

This whole conversation was interesting, but hardly enlightening. I don't know what I expected, a pattern, I suppose. Something to go on, some way of reaching out to Rose or to know it's possible for her to be reaching out to me. Something. Resigned, I reach out and help Prue to her feet.

"Tell me about your marriages, then?" I ask, not letting go of her hand.

Her eyes light up at the thought. "Ahhh, marriage! That was sumpin' I never could get right, although they were entertaining enough. Well, there was Roger – I met him while I was a maid for that hateful woman. I cain't recall her name now. Anyhow, he was a real nice bloke. Those were his words: 'Prue, I'm a real nice bloke, you oughta marry me!' And it wasn't a half bad marriage either. He was one of my husbands who was Lost, so we got a few years together in Chile before he died of the cholera.

Bad luck to travel anywhere that bloody disease was," (Was it my imagination, or did Prue actually look a little teary?) "But no matter, that was a long time ago.

"Also married your grandpa's brother, Jonah, in Belgium. 'Course he turned out to be shiftless and we parted ways purty early on. He was Lost too, but no matter, cuz we'd said all we needed to say to each other, including goodbye. So when I traveled on with your daddy and Zed and some others in their family, I didn't mind too much he didn't tag along. And after that, well, it was just Abe. You remember Abe?"

I do remember Abe because he's the closest thing to a grandfather I ever had. He had a handlebar mustache and always had candy in his pockets. I was between ten and twelve when he was around. He knew we were Lost and he even believed us, but he said he married Prue for whatever he could get out of her. Even if what he could get was a couple years of good cooking, he'd take it.

"Abe was a rock star," I say.

"If that means he could eat like a horse and never pick up after himself, I reckon he was. Come on girl, I'm tuckered and I'm missing Jeopardy!"

This may be the longest conversation I've ever had with Prue, and I enter our home feeling a little better about the whole world in general.

* * *

I am staring at her bony white knuckles, mesmerized. Her fingers are so long and pale and knobby, I can't look away. I must know I am being rude because I will myself to stop staring, but I cannot. My mother raps my knees under the table as a warning and when I pry my eyes off the knuckles to obediently look at her, she glares at me.

"Sonnet, eat your stew and stop that daydreaming," she says firmly.

She sets down another plate of stew in front of Old Babba and her white knuckles. Old Babba will suck it down like she did the first plate, noisily smacking her lips, making more noise than Dolly, her pet goat, when she eats.

Old Babba is skinny, rail thin, with milky white skin, and sunken black eyes. She doesn't have much hair and what she does have is baby fine thin. It's even thinner than my little sister Rose, whose own hair is very fine and so light in color it is practically clear.

Old Babba finishes her stew and the moment she swallows the last bite, she turns her small black eyes on me with such ferocity and speed, that I yelp and fall out of my chair.

"For goodness sake, Sonnet," my exasperated mother says, righting my chair. "Go lie down and rest your eyes. This fidgety nature of yours makes it impossible to enjoy a meal. Go on!" She shoos me towards the big fireplace and clears away my plate. I am sorry to see my half-eaten stew being carted away when I am still hungry, but I am not sorry to leave Old Babba. Her scary eyes and bony knuckles grasp her spoon greedily.

"She's not the one to watch, Carolina," Old Babba says to my mother. "She's nothing. But the little one...the little one is different."

"Rose is no different than the rest of us," snaps my mother, and I am surprised to see her treat the old woman so. She is always reprimanding me on my lack of respect and manners with our elderly neighbor and yet she is barking at her now. "I don't want to talk about this. You've said your peace and I'll thank you to say no more."

Old Babba cackles. She is just like the witch in my Hansel and Gretel story. She will put me in a giant bird cage and feed me chickens to plump me up before she eats me. After that her knuckles and fingers won't be so bony anymore. She will fatten up and her back will straighten and become strong. All her wrinkles will become smooth, and her hair will turn glossy and spill over her shoulders like a younger lady's. All this will happen because she will make me into stew. A stew so good she will smack her lips over and ask for seconds.

I awake in a panic in my own bed, eighteen years old and terrified of a witch in a gingerbread cottage. I am afraid it is more memory than dream.

Chapter 7

The next morning, I worked the a.m. shift at the coffee shop. I have a love/hate relationship with the morning shift. On the one hand, I earn better tips for some reason, but on the other there's no singing or guitar picking. In fact, Micki gets to pick the music selection that runs on our compact disc player and it is, in a word, boring. I want to add extra shots of espresso to everyone's drinks as an apology, and in the hopes that they won't fall asleep and drool on my counter.

Today Penny works with me because mornings are always busy, and sure enough there is a lovely selection of elevator music playing softly. Our customers approach the counter like zombies.

"May I recommend the triple shot Irish Cream mocha with whip and sprinkles?" I chirp to the man next in line, who appears as though he may slip into a coma at any time.

He takes a deep breath and to my great disappointment, orders a non-fat, decaf, sugar-free vanilla latte, not too hot.

"One cup of 'why-bother,'" I tell Penny, who is making the drinks that I place orders for.

The next lady wants a skinny mocha, the next a half dozen muffins and cappuccinos for her co-workers. Three hours go by like that, with nary an interesting customer, until finally someone familiar darkens my cash register.

"Coffee. Black," says Luke. He looks, as usual, like he just rolled out of bed, forgetting to shave. On him, it seems to work.

"Can't interest you in a toffee cream breve? My specialty?" I cajole.

"Are you kidding? This some sort of entrapment? You know darn well a troop of well-organized macho men would jump me and demand my Man Card if I ordered something like that. Coffee. Black."

"Well, you don't have to order it like you're 007," I retort, feeling proud of myself for knowing a pop culture reference from his own time. "Tall coffee," I tell Penny. She smiles at Luke and suddenly I wish I'd done something prettier with my hair, or worn something other than my tie-dye long sleeve t-shirt. Penny is so pretty and so ... perky. I should be perky, but frankly the energy it would take to keep up that kind of perkiness would take more than a toffee cream breve.

"Take a break?" Luke asks in a whisper as Penny hands him his coffee. He is whispering to me and I feel a delicious sense of importance. (Could it even be perkiness?)

I take off my apron and leave it behind the counter as Luke fixes his mug of coffee beside me.

"Umm, pretty sure the macho men you fear so will take just as much offense to you pouring on the white chocolate sprinkles and the twelve packs of raw sugar," I point out.

"No way. Even 007 drinks his black coffee with white chocolate sprinkles, nutmeg and a little sugar. You're out of 2% by the way."

"I wasn't before you dumped out half your coffee and used it all."

"I was topping it off." He feigned hurt. "Your customer service needs work."

"Fill out a comment card. Now what do you want? Or did you just come in to annoy me?"

"I mostly came in to annoy you. But also I wanted to talk to you."

"There's no way on God's green earth I can get Prue to pose for a picture."

"Pose?" He looks truly horrified. "I don't pose. Geez, it's not like I work for some kiddy photo shop, you know. I'm a professional. My specialty is candid shots, un-posed. Just like your frou-frou espresso drinks, I have specialties too, only mine cost slightly more." He frowns at his cup.

I remember his hole-in-the-wall studio. 'Slightly' was an overstatement. "All right. Shall we sit?"

He chuckles and it takes me a moment to realize he's chuckling at me. "Yes, we *shall*, madam. Did you major in old English or British Literature or just been watching too many Jane Austen movies lately?"

Major? Oh, college. Maybe I am closer to twenty years of age if he places me as a college graduate. I probably shouldn't tell him the last school I attended was in a Portuguese commune, founded by a Baptist missionary. My graduating class was myself, the missionary's daughter Molly, and a Portuguese boy named Henrique.

"Umm, too many Austen's. You got me. What do you want to talk about?" I purposely steer us away from the leather chair that I had seen my sister sitting in the other night, and instead lead us toward the same table that Luke and I had sat at the last time we spoke here.

Luke settles in his chair; he is too large for these tiny bistro style chairs. He leans his elbows on the table, cupping his face in his big hands. He holds my eyes with his for a moment before he speaks.

"How long have you been here?" It's the way he says it, not the question that throws me. Instinctively I know what he really means. There is no unspoken law against telling a normal person about living as a Lost, but it's hardly ever to anyone's benefit. The odds of anyone believing you are slim to none, and if they did believe it, they are probably some sort of wacky conspiracy theorist. Those types who spends their free time spotting aliens and building traps for Bigfoot, or wants help working on the time machine he's building in his mom's basement. Luke doesn't look like one of those types, but isn't that what everyone says about their serial killer neighbor? *He was so quiet, kept to himself mostly...I just can't believe he builds time machines in his mom's basement...*

"What do you mean?" I ask treading carefully.

"Here." He gestures widely. "But mostly, now. Where did you come from?"

I don't reply. I'll let him dig himself in a little deeper.

"I know what you are, Sonnet. At least I think I do. It won't hurt to tell me the truth. I know why your speech is old fashioned and why you try to adopt an American accent and why your family put the fun in dysfunctional. You came here from another era, didn't you?"

"What are you, some kind of intrepid rogue reporter?" I respond lightly. "Following up on leads and finding clues in dark alleys? A private eye, maybe? Is this your life's work, undercover for the Lost? That is what we're called by the way, if you want the technical Latin term."

"No dark alleys, I'm terrified of rats. And I don't work as a gumshoe or a reporter. I have been putting together clues for a few years now though. Also, I knew a guy who was Lost and he pretty much told me everything." Luke winks at me, breaking some of the tension I'm feeling. "He rented a room from me before I moved into the palatial palace you saw in my office. His name was Armando and when I met him he was wearing a ruffled shirt and awfully tight pants. I knew he was strange, but I didn't realize just how strange until later when he started talking to me. He was extremely good natured and polite. It turns out he was so afraid of what I'd think of him if he accidentally skipped out without paying his rent that he actually convinced me he was time traveler."

I roll my eyes. "I really hate that term."

"Sorry. Armando traveled alone, but he found a few others at the shelter and they kind of corroborated his story. Together with their testimonies I started realizing maybe my own mother wasn't as colorful a storyteller as

I had always thought." My stare must be blank because he continues on, explaining. "My dad was a no-show by the time I was two. Mom used to try to make excuses for him, at least I thought they were excuses. She would explain that he *had* to go, how it wasn't his fault, and that he had to move on even if he didn't want to. I pretty much ignored her excuses, and she married my stepdad when I was just a kid. After that we kind of quit talking about my biological dad.

My mom has always been a free spirit and believes in all sorts of things that others don't like unicorns, fairies, and peace on earth. So I didn't pay much attention to the things she said. But after meeting Armando and his buddies, I wasn't so sure. Course, with my luck, it could be that my father really is a deadbeat dad, and living with a second family somewhere in this century. Who knows? But when I started eating at Prue's cart and talking a little to your father– and then met you, well, I put two and two together. Especially after the Rose episode, it became pretty obvious."

"Rose was left behind when she was three years old," I explain, finally speaking. "No one knows why and we all just assumed that she lived her life in that one time frame. When I saw the photo, I knew, that it was her. And I was even more certain when I saw her here." I rub the spot on the back of my neck that starts to tense up whenever I feel stressed or tired. "So you can see how desperate it is that we find her before one of us travels again? If we don't travel together, we may never be in the same place at the same time again."

"Yes, I can see that." His playful demeanor is serious now. He looks worried on my behalf which strangely, makes that spot on the back of my neck feel better suddenly. "So, what's your theory? Why is she here, now?"

"I wish I knew. I don't know if she's been one step behind us all these years, or if she's only come into her abilities recently as an adult. She'd be about seventeen now, give or take."

"Ahh, seventeen. I remember it like it was only three years ago...which it was. And I thought my problems were huge at that age."

"You have no idea. Teenagers these days," I make a humph-ing sound that to my chagrin sounds exactly like Prue. I am the world's youngest old woman! I feel myself turn red.

Luke laughs. "You're okay, Gray. How long do you think you have?"

"Five minutes," I say, promptly, as I glance at the clock on the wall across the room.

"You're going to time travel – excuse me, I mean travel through time – in five minutes?" He looks slightly terrified.

"No, I thought you meant until my break was over. As to the other, your guess is as good as mine. The longest I've heard of any Lost staying put is about eight years, and that could have been a lie. We could be gone at any time. Every weekend I give Micki notice."

"Very considerate of you."

"Yes, but now he ignores me."

"So how does it work, this time travel stuff? Do you have to step some through a portal, fold a bend in time, open a secret door or wardrobe or something?"

"Nooo. We go to sleep and when we wake up we're some place different."

"That's not nearly as interesting as a portal. And I suppose it doesn't have to be in the light of the full moon either?"

"No. And no I can't go back and kill Hitler as a child either."

"That was not my next question, although it was on the list."

"There's a list? Because I'm down to three minutes. And no, I've never met myself in the past, and no, I've never been further ahead in the future than I am right now. And no, I didn't get to meet Elvis either."

"I bet you say that to all your intrepid gumshoe reporters. What I really want to know is, can I come with you?"

It turns out that I don't get to answer Luke's strange question because Penny spills a whole pitcher of boiling hot soy milk all over the place. I rush to help her clean it up, and then make an ice pack for her burned hand. I never should have left the frothing job to an amateur. By the time I convinced Penny I can handle the rest of the shift alone, I have a whole new line of customers. I can see Luke still sipping his coffee, but after a while he gets up and leaves, catching my eye long enough to wave. I spend the next three hours making drinks that would offend manly men everywhere. When Micki comes in to relieve me, I'm tired and the spot on the back of my neck feels as though it's been twisted into sailor's knots. I sink into the most comfortable chair available and wait for Israel to pick me up. I hope Prue cooked a big dinner, and I hope with equal fervor that it doesn't involve squirrels.

I wait and wait, my eyes as tired as my feet, but Israel never comes. Finally, at half past seven, I use the phone in Micki's office to make a call. Seeing as how we don't have a phone in our little brown house, I dial our neighbor lady, Gladys.

"Gladys? It's Sonnet from across the street!" I have to yell into the receiver because Gladys is rather deaf.

"Who?"

"Sonnet Gray! From across the street!"

"Oh, hello dear. How are you?"

"I'm fine, Gladys. Would you peek outside and see if Israel is home?"

"Who?"

"Israel Rhode!"

64

"You want to know if he's home?"

"Yes, please!"

"You say you live in the house across the street?"

"Yes!"

"And is Israel there?"

"I don't know! That's what I need you to find out!"

"Well, why don't you look around, dear? He's a large man, I'm sure you won't have to look very hard. Did you check under the beds?"

I sigh. My feet hurt, and Israel had promised me earlier that he would pick me up in his car. Israel is the only one with a car at our house and even though he is a terrible driver, it beats walking. "That's a good idea, Gladys. I'll check under the beds. Goodnight!"

"Goodnight, dear! It was lovely talking to you, please call again soon!"

"I will. Goodbye." I hang up the phone and leave the office. I can't help but look around the busy shop for a glimpse of someone with yellow blonde hair and a red dress, but my efforts are fruitless. I exit through the doors in the back and start my trek home. It's nearing autumn and the leaves are turning and falling to the ground. The weather is still a bit humid and warm, but with enough of a breeze to make a cold-blooded person would want a jacket. It's an overcast day, so even though the sun is up, it's darker than it should be. It feels like a late summer thunder storm is coming. A small pile of leaves swirl in a tiny funnel cloud by my feet as I walk by. I crunch them with my shoes like I used to do as a little girl when I would follow behind Prue walking to the market each day.

One of the reasons Israel comes to get me when I work evening or night shifts is the fact that we don't live in the best of neighborhoods. You don't bother picking out your dream home when you know you won't be there long. Anyway, we can't afford much rent between my coffee shop tips, Meli's babysitting, and Prue's food cart. Will works as a handy man, but he doesn't find much. What he does make he uses to constantly improve Israel's car, which he loves and covets. Israel works as a medical intern, which is a fancy name for saying he doesn't get paid period. But maybe by the next time we travel, he'll know enough to set up his own practice and then we can all live in a house that's on the right side of the tracks, so to speak.

For the time being though I almost love our dilapidated brown house with the sagging porch and peeling paint. Well, as much as I almost love anything. I am like most Lost, distancing myself from attachments to the point of coldness. I put up walls that nothing can scale because I fear the loss that inevitably comes. Even my love for Prue and Dad, while strong, fierce, and loyal, has realistic and practical elements to it. I wonder if I will ever love anything or anyone with complete abandon. If I will ever feel safe enough to do so.

The breeze whips itself up into real wind and more leaves are ripped from their branches where they spent the summer growing. I watch them rippling down to earth in lovely arcs and patterns. If the sun was shining more, they'd be glinting and I could see their bright colors. As it is, everything seems to be a distinctly different shade of gray like a black and white film

I make my legs move faster despite being tired. My hunger and my dislike for the dark compel me to get home quickly. I don't like the way everything is becoming gray and sinister and the way I seem to be only living person in the world right now. Usually this street has someone on it. Where is everyone tonight, I wonder uneasily? Most of the hair from my ponytail has come loose as the wind continues to blow whipping it around my face. The dilapidated street is still empty and void. There are no children out playing softball or kick the can. No cars pass me, and no one waves a friendly hello as they check their mailboxes. All I hear is the sound of my own breathing, and my footfalls on the pavement.

Chapter 8

Prue has not fixed squirrel pie for supper, but instead has pulled out
practically everything that is wrapped in foil or wax paper in the
refrigerator and announced that it is, 'help yerself to leftovers night.' Then
without so much as a goodnight to anyone, she stomps off to her room
and slams the door. I'm not sure Prue has ever simply closed a door, she
always slams. I think now of the father she mentioned earlier, and if he
ever tired of shouting at her not to slam the doors. I smile at the image
I've conjured in my head of a teenage Prue, stomping around and giving
bossy orders to all of humankind. I also think of her father's
longsuffering, and perhaps anxious desire to marry her off to an
unsuspecting boy. I load up my plate with rice, okra, jambalaya, sweet
potato pie, and one fat tamale. Then I make my way over to the couch
where Meli and Will are already eating. Will nods at me and waves his
fork in a strange bowing gesture, which is about as much conversation as
I've ever had from Will. Without warning, Meli then launches into a
soliloquy about her day. I try to listen, I really do, but with a start I realize
that Israel isn't home. I swallow my bite of tamale in a hurry and
interrupt Meli to ask his whereabouts.

"I don't know, I expect he had to go in to work. I haven't seen him. Dear,
have you seen Israel?" Meli turns to her husband. He shakes his head and
uses the remote control to turn up the volume on the episode of Cops that
is showing. "He hasn't been around too much lately. Did you see his car
out front?"

I shake my head, realizing I hadn't seen the Blue Beast, out front either.
"Oh well." I shrug, trying not feel hurt at Israel's neglect of me. "He'll turn
up. He always does. What were you saying?"

But we are interrupted this time by the front door opening and Matthias
and Harry stepping through with someone else. I am so surprised to see
Luke in my house that I choke on my jambalaya and almost spill my plate.
Will reaches over, his eyes still glued to Cops, and pats me hard on the
back.

"What in the world are you doing here?" I demand in between my coughs.

Luke eyes my plate with interest. "Harry and Matthias invited me. We ran into each other near the coffee shop. I came back by to see if you had time to finish our conversation, but you had already left. Is that okra?"

"Help yourself. It's all in the kitchen," I reply moving my plate away from his ravenous gaze and plopping back down on the couch. I don't know why, but his being here annoys me. Maybe it's because I look like I just worked a double shift and my house is embarrassing. Perhaps it's because Meli is looking at me with amusement in her eyes and a million questions on her lips.

"Hush up!" I anticipate as she opens her mouth to speak.

I stare at the television, feigning interest in the ridiculous show, until Luke brings his plate of food over and squeezes his tall body unceremoniously onto the couch between Meli and myself. He stretches his long legs out and balances his plate on his lap. I can't help staring at him. We've never had a guest in our house before, unless Emme counts, and here he is making himself at home eating far more than his fair share of leftovers. I fix my ponytail, trying to look casual. I give up when I realize there is a sticky, crunchy section of hair that is probably dried caramel syrup. I tuck the crunchy part behind my ear and wear the green hair band on my wrist instead.

"Which conversation did you want to finish? The one about wanting to come with us?" I ask. I have been curious all day about where that talk of ours had been heading anyway.

"I misspoke," Luke replies spearing more okra with his fork. "Or rather, I phrased it wrong. I wasn't looking for an invitation. I just meant to ask if you thought it was possible. If we go on the assumption that my father was Lost, of course. Is half-Lost enough to time travel?"

"I think so. But maybe not without your father. Prue and I were talking about how maybe there needs to be a bond strong enough to help you travel. If you were just half-Lost and no one else around you was Lost, it wouldn't be surprising that you never traveled."

"I was thinking the same thing. Either that, or I've never traveled because my dad is actually a used car salesman in Topeka with a dozen illegitimate kids running around the world."

"Also a distinct possibility." I can't help smiling. "There has to be a way to find out. Did you ask Google? Google knows everything." I don't care overly much for computers, but I find the fact that you can discover the answer to anything on Google pretty fascinating. Penny showed me once at the shop during a slow shift. Since then I've Googled everything from cucumbers to chameleons to Elvis Presley. Penny wanted to Google me, but I stopped her. I don't exist, well at least not in this computer age. I once wasted a whole weekend doing online searches for Rose, but came up with nothing. She was probably given the surname of whomever adopted her, and Dad never knew Old Babba's real name.

"No, never thought of that. I guess maybe I don't really want to know. Am I eating squirrel or alligator or anything I should know about?" He looks suspiciously at a forkful of food before eating it.

"Who knows? Most of Prue's recipes are top secret. Keep your cat locked up."

"I don't have a cat. Hey, pets! Can pets be Lost?" Luke looks more interested in the answer to this question than he did about the answers to his missing father.

I laugh. "Sorry, no. At least, not as far as I know."

He looks almost crestfallen. "I was hoping my dog that ran away when I was twelve didn't really run away."

"Who are you?" Meli suddenly bursts out. I'm so impolite I forgot to introduce Luke to the rest of my strange little family.

"Sorry, Meli! Luke, this is Amelia and her husband Will. This is Luke Dawes." Will does the same fork bow to Luke that he did to me as a greeting, but Meli shakes his hand warmly.

"You know who we are? What we are?" she marvels.

"I know," I smile grimly. "He doesn't look like someone who builds time machines in his mother's basement does he?"

"Is she always this strange?" Luke mock whispers to Meli, who giggles. "Half the time I don't know what she's talking about. So, are you saying you've never had a pet?"

I don't know when I ever said any such thing, but Luke is right, of course. I don't know anyone Lost who has a pet.

"Well, I don't really have what it takes to commit to an animal," I respond dryly. "In case you hadn't noticed, I'm not very reliable."

"That's terrible. Every kid should have a dog, or a kitten, or a tarantula or something. I had a fish."

"And a dog," I remind him.

"Yes, Munkles."

"Maybe he ran away because he was embarrassed of his name," I suggest, stifling a laugh. Luke glares at me, but his eyes are twinkling with good nature.

"I should go. I told my mother I would stop by and see her newest painting." Luke stands up and collects my empty plate with his. I follow him into the kitchen.

"Your mother is a painter?" I ask with interest.

"At the moment. Last month she was a sculptor. Luckily, my stepdad makes a lot of money so he can afford her artistic pursuits. We're all just happy she's off her violin phase, that was incredibly painful."

"I can imagine. When I started teaching myself the guitar it was a little painful as well. It belongs to Micki, so I can only practice at the shop."

"Will you miss it?" He asks. He has already jumped to the correct conclusion that the guitar, just like a pet, won't travel with me.

I shrug trying not to think about it. "It's only wood and strings. I've left more."

"That sounds cryptic. Boyfriends, lovers, husbands?"

I roll my eyes. "Yes, several husbands."

Luke winks at me. "I knew it. I'm watching you, Gray. See you around."

And with those parting words he is gone, leaving me alone in the kitchen with nothing but a sweet potato pie to keep me company.

* * *

Despite feeling tired and taking a Nightfall pill, I am unable to fall asleep. After putting on my white nightgown, I sit on the window seat in my bedroom, staring out the window. Penny gave me a portable compact disc player and several compact discs when she upgraded to an Ipod. I find the whole thing amazing and mind boggling, although Penny laughingly assured me it is nothing but a dinosaur. Besides the music selection Penny gave me, I have checked out a whole stack of discs at the library and right now I am listening to a band called Air Supply.

I cross my legs under my nightgown and turn up the volume as I watch the Blue Beast finally pull up to the curb below my window. I see Israel's tall dark figure get out of his car and walk slowly, as if he is tired, up our crooked steps to the front door. I glance at the glowing time on my alarm clock: 11:47. Someday we will lose Israel. Of all of us here in our house, he is the most disconnected at times. He stays out late and sometimes I don't think he comes home at all. I'm scared that it's only a matter of time before we leave without him. I wish he would only be as attached to us as we all are to him, but I think that a solitary life has hardened. It's as though he has already said his goodbyes ahead of time. But me, I can't be like that. He keeps me grounded and makes me feel secure and safe. He is a huge part of what I call home, the home that is a part of my soul not just a town or a house. When he is gone, it will be forever, and I will never get that part of my soul back.

I pull the little ear buds out of my ears and run out of my room, my bare feet barely skimming down the steps. I round the corner at the bottom of the stairs and throw myself headlong into Israel. Anyone else would pull me off them, and laugh at my impetuousness, or ask me what is the matter. But not Israel, he just holds me as tightly as I hold him, as if he knows exactly my reasons. He holds me firmly, his chin resting on the top of my head. I suddenly remember that I never washed out the caramel syrup, but he doesn't belittle me by pulling away first. I leave a wet spot on his button down shirt from my leaking eyes. He cups my face in his hands and looks at me with his deep chocolate brown eyes.

"Go to sleep. I'll see you in the morning."
Someday that innocent expression will be a lie, I think, as I trudge back up the stairs. Someday I will wake up and he won't be there, just like my guitar, just like Penny, or Micki or Air Supply or toffee cream breves or Luke Dawes. What will I have when I don't have the ones I have now? Prue will pass away eventually, along with Matthias and Harry, and even Dad will – sooner rather than later if he doesn't stop drinking so much. Meli and Will eventually will have children and go their own way. Then will I be middle aged and traveling alone?

I wish, not for the first time, that I had Rose. It is selfish, this obsessive need to be near her, and I can't lie to myself. Of course, I am worried for her, and scared of what she may have been through without us by her side. I don't want her to travel alone anymore, but ultimately I am terrified of being completely and utterly alone. I push open my cracked window to let in more of the night air. I feel stifling hot suddenly, and my nightgown feels more like a heavy velvet cape trapping me beneath its folds. The breeze through the window lifts the ends of my hair and I close my eyes. I can still hear the wind moving quickly through the trees below. *Shhh*, it tells me, *hush*.

* * *

When I wake the next morning, I have an idea, as if sleeping has brought me clarity of mind. I will not go on the assumption that Rose is traveling alone, but rather look for other Lost who may know her. She herself may be hard to locate, but perhaps her traveling partners, if they exist, will be easier to find. Also, I have laundry to do and the Laundromat that I frequent isn't far from the shelter and the soup kitchen. It is a good place to start if I hope to find people like me.

I skip a shower and instead wash out the sticky strands of hair in the sink, throw on my cleanest clothes, and grab Israel's car keys on my way out the door. I have only driven once and it was a bit of a disaster. Israel tried giving me a driving lesson once but I nearly hit Gladys' cat and Iz wasn't the most patient teacher, but I am not going to walk clear across town with three baskets full of laundry. Typically, Emme and I go together with her mother, Bea, driving. Bea spent quite a few years in her twenties in the 1960s and knows her cars. It doesn't look that difficult and since I'm the one who helped Israel study the driver's manual, I know most of the rules and laws. I see the same cat now as I slide all my laundry in the backseat.

"Shoo!" I clap my hands at it and slam the door extra hard hoping to frighten it away. It sits on the curb washing its paws, and eyeing me with its green eyes.

I have to figure out how to adjust the driver's seat which takes a minute. Finally, I slide it up quite a ways so that my feet can reach the pedals. *Gas on right, brake on left*, I take a deep breath. I can't seem to move the gear shift and then I locate the small button where my thumb should be and press. Still nothing. I press the brake lightly and the button simultaneously and the gear shift jumps several positions. I try it again, putting it back in Park so that I can do it more slowly and make sure I will end up in Drive and not in Reverse. What are 1 and 2, I wonder, and Neutral? I don't remember these from the driver's manual, and I hope with fervor they aren't necessary to get me to the Laundromat. I edge incredibly slowly away from the curb and even remember to signal, although there is no one behind me or in front of me to see it.

"Stop watching me, cat," I mutter, as I pull the Beast into the street. "You're making me nervous."

The whole city seems deserted and whenever I do pass someone I try to look as casual and confident as possible. I am sweating with nerves and driving at such a crawl I know I probably could have walked it quicker. With each turn or stop I make, I grow a little more confident. By the time I am halfway to my destination, I am calm enough to turn on the compact disc I brought with me. Since I am usually in charge of the music as a passenger in the Blue Beast, I find the controls without even looking at them. I turn up Fleetwood Mac good and loud. I also feel confident enough now to pry my left hand off the steering wheel and dangle my arm out the window as I drive. I am even feeling a bit smug, maybe even perky, until I get to the street my destinations are on and then I begin to panic a bit. The parking situation is less than ideal. The Laundromat is recessed in the middle of an old brick and mortar building that still has a huge wrap-around sign advertising Woolworths even though there is no Woolworths to be found. The Laundromat itself is being hugged, nearly squeezed to death, by a sub sandwich shop on one side and a beauty parlor on the other. Upstairs, two stories high, are what appear to be office buildings or maybe cheap apartments. I cruise by very slowly trying to determine, by craning my neck, if there is an alley or something behind the building that can be used as an alternative to parking on the street. No such luck for me, and I sigh turning the Blue Beast around the block trying to prepare myself for parallel parking.

I bite my lip and crawl to a stop in front of the spot that looks the most available. It's a space between a pickup truck and a van that looks large enough for a tank, yet still too small to wriggle the Beast into properly. I wipe my sweaty palms on my skirt and check the rear view mirror the way I've seen Israel do. Parallel parking *was* in the driver's manual and I *do* recall reading it, but the head knowledge doesn't seem to be helping. I put the Beast into reverse and crank the wheel, but it takes me a full minute to get up enough courage to release the brake and press the gas. Instantly I know I have turned the wheel in the wrong direction as I am edging away from the sidewalk and the parking space instead of into it. I creep back up to my original starting point and try again, this time turning the wheel the other direction and saying a little prayer. It feels like it takes a week, back and forth, back and forth, one inch at a time, but I finally get the car where it needs to go. I am feeling quite pleased with myself as I pull two of my laundry baskets out of the car and slam the door shut with my foot.

The bells above the doorway to the Laundromat give a rusty jingle as I enter and my eyes adjust to the dimly lit space. I am the only one here at the moment, although a dryer spins noisily nearby with a pink plastic bin bouncing on top. I pick my washers and deposit my coins from my tip jar at the coffee shop. Although the driving, money, and less than convenient locale for my wash day seems like a hassle to some, it is worlds better than ways I have previously laundered my clothing.

I spent the largest chunk of my teenage years in the eighteen hundreds, first in Europe as a 13 year old, and then in Portugal later at the little missionary school. Wash day was every Monday and without Prue's capable hands and knowledge, Dad and I would have worn dirty clothes every day. It was such a difficult and time consuming chore, just fetching the water took the whole morning. I remember trying to keep up with Prue and her thick, strong legs as we went back and forth from the river to the big copper cauldron that was the laundry's ultimate destination. By noon, my shoulders and back were aching and my fingers were cramping from grasping the buckets so tightly. Dad would chop wood almost all day long, stoking the fire between his chopping and taking swigs from an always present bottle of homemade whiskey. Why we gave him an ax I will never know, but desperate times call for desperate measures I suppose.

The next step in laundering was the scrubbing with lye soap. This hurt the calluses on my hands that had formed from all the wringing out of the clothes, and the carrying of the buckets. For some reason that wasn't even my least favorite part. The worst was the sewing on of all the buttons we had removed so they wouldn't be lost or broken during the scrubbing. I can't say why I hated that part the most. I think it was because we were almost done, the hard part over with supper in site, and still we had these blasted buttons. I always wanted to rush through it, sewing on buttons willy-nilly, not caring what it looked like or if they lined up properly on the clothing. After all, we'd rip them all off next Monday anyway, so what was the point? But Prue, despite her large overworked hands, had nimble fingers with a needle, and liked things done properly. If I slacked off, or if my stitches were too large and not pulled tightly enough, she'd pull it out and make me start anew. I would sit there daydreaming of being brave enough to not obey Prue's commands, and make my fingers pull that needle in and out, spurred on by the smell of biscuits, last night's ham, and fresh tea brewing. The sun would be gone by the time we finished, and supper never tasted as good any other day of the week as it did on Mondays.

I finger my blouse buttons now, remembering, as I watch my pile of clothes toss merrily in the washing machine in front of me, turning and spinning in the suds. If only someone had invented washing machines earlier, I think. No, as much as I hated Mondays back then, I love the memories of them just as fiercely now. I can still feel those calluses phantoms on my palms and fingers, leftovers from memories past.

Chapter 9

I leave my clothes spinning and tumbling around, and walk back out in the sunshine towards the shelter and soup kitchen a block away. I admire my parking job again as I walk by the Blue Beast. It's a warm day and my plaid woolen skirt itches my thighs, and I realize the last time I wore the skirt I had worn it with winter tights. A woolen skirt is not the smartest thing to be wearing in late summer, but I haven't washed my clothes in nearly two weeks and it's the only clean thing I had to put on this morning. Besides, I think it dresses up my plain white cotton blouse nicely, although I suspect Meli will find something wrong with it and purse her lips and sigh when she sees me.

The shelter and soup kitchen is a place I know quite well, though I haven't dropped by in quite a while. When we first arrived here we spent long hours here, eating a free meal, sometimes serving to help out, and playing Checkers with other people who were down on their luck as well. Prue spiced up the lunches, bullying her way into the kitchen, and Dad, Matthias, and Harry would make friends as they sat on the hard plastic chairs, sipping coffee and telling stories. Israel was the only one who never spent too much time in this place, instead he spent his time, looking for houses cheap enough to rent or merely squat in. He also went out trying to make connections with doctors who might give him a job or teach him the practice of medicine.

I swing open the large, doublewide glass doors and the familiar smell of hot steam, chicken, boiled vegetables, and cleaning supplies hits my nose. The long tables are clean and empty, the chairs all pushed in neatly. It is only late morning and the only people here will be Jim, the director, and all his volunteers getting ready to serve the lunch crowd. Jim is a heavy set jovial man, with a large nose, pink cheeks. His white hair is both frizzy, and wiry. He is upbeat and nothing ever gets him down. Once a long time ago, he was threatened with a knife by an angry homeless man high on drugs. Jim left that situation not only alive, but with a new friend. He still goes each weekend to visit him in prison, bringing him leftovers from the soup kitchen.

I spot Jim now, moving in the back of the kitchen at a speed that is surprising for a man of his bulk. He claps his workers on their backs and spurs them on as he makes his rounds, checking the food, and the dishwashing station. As he slings a white dishtowel over his shoulder, he spots me and shouts merrily.

"Sonnet Gray! Is that you? Are you on the schedule today? It must be our lucky day!" He beams and steps out of the kitchen towards me, where I am waiting and smiling by the salad bar.

"No, I'm not on the schedule, but I'll help out if you like." I embrace him fondly. "I'm doing my laundry and wanted to stop by and say hello. How are things?" I pop a carrot in my mouth from the salad bar and he shakes his finger at me playfully.

"Now, now, that carrot is going to cost you two hours of manual labor young lady! Suit up! You know where the aprons are." Jim shoos me towards the kitchen, and I obey grabbing a long white apron as I pass them on their hooks. I have worn my Budweiser cap this morning, so I can skip the hairnet, which is a plus.

"Any new regulars?" I ask busying myself by pulling out huge stacks of white plates and setting them on the counter. "Say, a girl about my age, blond hair, my eyes, red dress?"

Jim is counting plates for a moment and does not answer. "We need bowls too. Clam chowder today," he responds. "Umm, blond hair, blue eyes, huh? Well we've been busy lately, lots of newbies. It's been a good summer for camping, hiking, and hitchhiking, so we've had a run of those types. Been so busy actually, I haven't had time to meet everyone. But I guess if she's real regular I'd know her all right. If she's only been here once or twice, she'd have gotten lost in the shuffle. Might ask around."

"That's what I'll do, thanks Jim. Serving at noon straight up?"

He nods absentmindedly, going back to counting stacks of dishes. The kitchen moves with efficiency, bustling and moving along with its tasks like clockwork. All of Jim's volunteers are well trained and hustle quickly, baking the chicken, stirring the peas, mashing the instant potatoes, and whisking the gravy. This room, this teamwork, and these smells will be one of the things I remember most about my time in the twenty first century.

After the dishes are pulled and stacked in convenient rows where the customers can easily access them, I start slicing small squares of chocolate cake and plating them. The rows multiply fast and before I know it I have enough tiny white plates of dessert to feed an army. It's noon straight up and Jim is propping open the front doors. I lick the frosting off my fingertips and when I catch Jim narrowing his eyes at me for this health code offense, I wash my hands and take my place in line with the other volunteers prepared to dish food and offer small talk. Before I get too busy though, I remember my clothes in the washer across the street and I take a couple of minutes to rush across and switch them to the dryer.

In less than an hour we have served the line of people and although I have greeted several regulars by name, I haven't served so much as a pea or a pat of butter to my little sister. When everyone is seated and eating, that's our cue as volunteers to make ourselves a plate of food and join them. I pile mine up with salad and then ladle clam chowder into a bowl. I grab a roll and carry my tray over to an empty seat by two of my favorite people, Margery and Ed, both volunteers. Margery is the sweetest, nicest person you will ever meet, with a high pitched voice and a tendency to wear a lot of costume jewelry. Her husband, Ed, is bald up top but with a long, gray beard and mustache. He has several tattoos and is a good 75 pounds overweight, all of it centered in his belly. Margery looks like someone who attends PTA meetings for fun, and ED looks like he is in a biker gang. Together they are sweet as pie and if anyone has seen Rose, it'd be these two. They seem to know everyone, but I ask the same question I had asked Jim earlier and wait for their answers as I blow on my chowder.

"Oh yes, I've seen her!" Margery chirps, nodding vigorously. "Remember, Ed? She was in here last week, or maybe it was two weeks ago. And I saw her again down by the river when Jim and I took the leftovers to feed the homeless out there. She didn't want any though, little thing looked at me like I was crazy and like she'd never seen peanut butter and jelly sandwiches before. Strangest thing, I wondered if she was on some pills or something, she looked real confused or lost."

You don't know the half of it, I think. Aloud I say, "Do you think she was living out there by the river?"

"Well, I don't know, honey, could be. It's been a lovely summer so the city has had its fair share of homeless, especially down there where the camping's good. They're clearing out now though, the nights are getting colder already." As if her words were a premonition, Margery pulls her cardigan closer around her shoulders. Ed wraps his arm around her and rubs her arm, while continuing to eat his chicken.

"Was she alone? Did it seem like she had friends or anyone with her?" I prod.

"No, no, I don't think so. There were a lot of people there that day, and here in the soup kitchen that time I saw her here, too. But I got the impression she was alone."

"Did you see her, Ed?" I turn my attention to him. It appears I've gotten all the information I can out of Margery, and it's doubtful her husband will be any more help, but I have to try.

Ed gnaws on his chicken wing before responding. "Nah, darlin', I remember her real vaguely, but I didn't notice any more than Margery did. You say she's your sister?"

"Yes, and it's very important that I find her." I sigh. "Will you do me a favor? If you ever see her again, will you tell her that her sister, Sonnet, and her dad are looking for her? Tell her she can find us through Jim?"

"Sure thing, honey," Margery says standing and clearing all of our plates. "Come on now, let's get that dessert served. I am craving some chocolate!"

Rather than make everyone line up again and be served in order, Jim likes the volunteers to serve them their cake and coffee at their tables. It also makes for more chitchat, which is almost as important to some as the food. I can fit twelve small plates of cake on my platter, if I overlap the scalloped edges of the plates a bit, and once it's balanced on my shoulder, I grab a pot of coffee to bring with me and head over to the table in the back. There's no one seated there that I know, but I smile and act like I do anyway and serve everyone their cake.

The last man that I pour coffee for is dressed in a suit and has one of those Humphrey Bogart type hats on the back of his chair. He is in his thirties he looks like, but it's an older version of thirty somehow. He looks as though he has done too much living in those years, his eyes are deep and sad, with circles under them, and prematurely gray hair around his temples. He is very thin, painfully so, and his body trembles when I ask him if he'd like another piece of cake. He turns his sad looking eyes on me shaking his head wordlessly dismissing me. As he reaches for his coffee cup and brings it shakily to his lips, I see something on his left forearm where his sleeves have been rolled up, a five-digit number tattoo with a triangle beneath. I know this mark since Matthias and Harry have it as well. It's a gift from the Nazis' at Auschwitz, and now I understand the source of some of this young man's sorrow and trembling. Has he only just left there? I reach down and grasp his hand, the one that is not holding his cup, and he looks up at me again, this time in surprise.

"Wilkommen aus America. Alles gut hier. Ich verspreche." He doesn't even blink.

Finally, he snaps alert and whispers softly, "Sprechen Sie Deutch?"

My German is somewhat broken, I am not precisely fluent, but I can speak it well enough.

"Ein bisschen. Aber mein Portugiese ist besser oder vielleicht Italienisch."
I offer to speak in either Italian or Portuguese hoping to find some
common ground.

To my horror, his eyes fill up with tears. Now I've done it, gone and
traumatized some almost murdered Jewish man, who is obviously Lost
and by the looks of everyone at this table, alone. I feel the need to
apologize, although for what exactly I am not sure. Surprisingly, he
doesn't let go of my hand, but only looks at me.

"Sono Italiano" he whispers over a swallowed sob, revealing his birth
nationality.

"Do you have a place to stay tonight?" I ask switching to his home
language of Italian, which I am better at anyway. I pull up a chair and sit
down. He continues to hold my hand.

He shakes his head wordlessly.

"Do you want to come with me? I have some people I think you'd like to
meet. Our home isn't fancy, but it's a place to stay and I think you'll find
you have a lot in common with all of us there. What do you say? I'm
Sonnet, by the way." I awkwardly turn our hand holding session into a
form of a handshake.

"Bar," the man replies slowly. Has it been a while since anyone has asked
for his name? "And I would like that very much."

"All right then Bar, I'm going to run across the street and get my laundry
and then I'll come back in and get you. Does that sound agreeable?"

Bar simply nods. I clean off the empty cake plates and return them to the
kitchen where a second round of volunteers have already begun washing,
and walk out through the heavy glass doors. I don't bother folding my dry
clothes, but carelessly toss them into my baskets where they will wrinkle
freely, and push the baskets into the backseat of the Blue Beast. I'm not
keen on anyone seeing my driving firsthand, but I figure someone from

82

over seventy years ago won't be in the position to judge. I suppose it's possible he would have had a car back then, but I can almost promise he hasn't driven it lately.

When I get back, Bar is right where I left him, sitting in almost a dejected fashion in his chair. His back is ramrod straight and proud, but his head lowered in a way that appears submissive. The inconsistency of his pose is incongruous. I tell Jim to keep a look out for Rose, reminding him of her hair color and her eyes that look like mine. I also tell him I am taking Bar home with me, and he doesn't look too pleased with this turn of events.

"Now Sonnet, I am always one to embrace everyone, you know that. But even I don't invite strangers home to my house the day I meet them. That's not smart thinking. Why don't you let me find a place for him to stay? He'll be fine here, there's room and a bed and everything."

"He'll be fine with me too, I promise. I want him to meet Matthias and Harry, and I'll be plenty safe. You know how many people live in my house, and if he's a crazy ax murdering psycho you can be sure to tell me you told me so."

"Not funny. I still think this is a very bad idea, Sonnet. You call me the minute you get home, you hear?"

"Yes Jim, I hear," I hug him tightly. "And I will." Drat. That'll mean a trip across to Gladys' to use her phone. She'll keep me all night, plying me with expired cookies, powdered lemonade, and pictures of her grandchildren. If anyone's going to kidnap me for all eternity, it's Gladys, not Bar.

When I collect Bar he is as quiet as ever. Silent as we leave the soup kitchen. Silent as we walk to the Blue Beast. Silent as I unlock the passenger side and open the door for him. Silent still as I get in myself and turn the key. Thank goodness for small favors, the van in front of me has moved and it's an easy thing to pull away from the curb and onto the street.

"How long have you been here?" I ask glancing sideways at my passenger. He sits nervously and stares straight ahead.

"Today. Just today," he answers, tonelessly.

"I've been here two years. My family is Lost too. You'll be safe with us."

I don't know what I was expecting as far as a reaction, but more silence wasn't it. We drive on.

"My family was Lost as well," he finally answers, softly. "But we didn't travel last together. We were too far away from each other at the camp. I pray they traveled somewhere though, even if it is not with me. As long as they got out. That's all that matters."

"Yes," I say, just as softly. I can barely hear myself. "Yes, that's what matters." Suddenly what has happened with Rose seems less important. I am not the only one to have lost someone they loved. And I have had fourteen years at least to come to grips with never seeing my sister again. This poor man has had one night and has lost his whole family. I know already that we will be his substitute, a pitiful one at best, but we will be his new family. For this is what the Lost do when we can do nothing else, we take each other in and understand one another. And so the circle continues, loss and the dawn of a new day, the holding of hands in a soup kitchen, the lies we tell everyone else. *Oh, this is Bar, my cousin*, I will say to Penny or to Micki or to Gladys. *He's with us now.*

Chapter 10

After parking the Blue Beast almost exactly where I had stolen it from my driveway, Bar helps me carry my laundry baskets up the steps and waits for me while I fumble for my house key. By the looks of things, no one is home, but no one ever looks home even when we are. The broken blinds block a surprising amount of light, and the dated (so I've been told) dark, faux wood paneling on the walls make the interior somewhat gloomy. Not to mention we are people who are used to going without electricity and so we sometimes forget to use the lights much at all. So I'm not exactly taken aback when we walk through the door and Matthias and Harry are home after all. The television is on, the only glow in the room, tuned to a game show, and my two favorite brothers in the history of the world are sitting side by side on the couch, eating microwave TV dinners. Prue would be appalled, but she doesn't appear to be home.

"Boys," I say in Italian. Matthias and Harry, of course, speak it fluently. Out of everyone in the house they speak the most languages at least 20 between the two of them. They look up at me, then at Bar, curiosity in their gazes. "Boys, this is Bar. He is Lost, has just come from Germany during the war sometime, and he's with us now. Shove over a bit and share some of that disgusting food." I nod towards them as I look at Bar and smile. My nod is supposed to convey trust, a sort of 'it's okay, don't be afraid' kind of thing. It seems to communicate well enough and with barely a hesitation, Bar strides over and takes each of the brother's hands in turn. As I leave I can hear them talking in low voices, Matthias and Harry's voices sympathetic and understanding, Bar's voice shaky but with renewed strength.

I go to my room and put away my wrinkled clothes and then remember I have to use Gladys' phone to let Jim know that I'm okay and not hacked to death by an ax. I sigh. I really, really wanted a bath tonight. My hair still has a crispy, caramel residue on the ends and I feel grimy and dirty from my shift at the soup kitchen. Plus, my nightgown is clean and smells nice, like fabric softener, and all I want to do is don it and listen to my compact disc player. Oh well. I slip my shoes back on, where I had kicked them off only seconds earlier and trudge back out of my house and across the street.

I see the cat curled up under a tree and since I'm feeling cheery enough about my driving skills I stop and give him a scratch beneath his neck. If I had wrecked the car, I might have blamed it on my furry voyeur.

Gladys' house is nicer than ours; actually, it's the only nice house on the block. You can tell just by looking that it is owned by a little old lady who has lived here forever. It is sea foam green in color, with shiny white shutters, wind chimes hang from the sturdy porch. Through the clean windows you can see a glimpse of lacy white curtains. I walk up a handicap ramp that to a sweet looking porch swing upholstered in waterproof flowered oilcloth. There is a ceramic gnome in her flower patch and even Gladys' mailbox is shinier and spiffier than the rest of the streets mailboxes. It stands straight instead of leaning off to the side the way ours does, and is painted a pale pink. I knock on the door and after some time it opens. Gladys' small face peeks through the crack in the door.

"Oh, it's you, dear!" she says, in delight. "You're just in time for a cool glass of lemonade!" Gladys opens the door wide and shoos me in. Her hair is a soft white, so white it has a tinge of blue, and is curled all around her head like a poodle. Her frame is very petite and now bent over with age and crippling osteoporosis. I always feel like a giant standing next to her. Her eyes sparkle merrily up at me.

"I'm so sorry to bother you, Gladys, but I was hoping I could use your telephone?"

"Of course, dear, help yourself. I'm just going to pour that lemonade and see if I can find some other refreshments for us." With that, she exits with surprisingly nimble speed.

I settle myself onto a flowered chaise and reach for the phone. I know the soup kitchen's number by heart, as it is the only establishment I have ever called in my whole life other than the coffee shop. It is picked up on the first ring by Jim, poor guy, I did have him worried.

"It's me, Sonnet," I say cheerfully. "Nothing to worry about, I'm all in one piece and Matthias and Harry are befriending Bar as we speak. Seems they go way back."

"All right, then." Jim's boisterous voice sounds relieved. "Thank you for working today, and remember you don't have to keep him. I'm sure he's figured out how to take care of himself by now."

I'm sure he has, I think. Aloud, I promise to stay in touch about the situation and we hang up. Gladys has returned with two tall glasses of pink lemonade, a box of crackers and what she insists is cheese in a can. Although I think the powdered lemonade is rather nasty, I do have a fondness for crackers and I find the spray cheese the most fabulous thing I've had all this decade. I stay on the flowered chaise and listen to Gladys talk for a full hour. She is after all, one of my only friends, and though she may be from an era gone by, I know this tiny wisp of a grandmother is far more modern than I will ever be.

She pulls out a fat fabric covered photo album and I flip through it while she tells me all about her past and her family. It's as though her whole life flashes before my eyes and I feel a pain in my chest when I think about how I don't have this. These cohesive memories that line up in logical order, this stability, these people who last for years and years and don't go away. I don't have a photo album, in fact the only photo of myself I have is the one Luke took of me and my guitar. I don't have pictures of myself with siblings, lined up in front of the same plastic Christmas tree every year each time looking taller and broader, their faces losing their baby fat with each passing season.

There are photographs of Gladys as a toddler standing by a doorframe that has pencil markings all over it, marking her and her brother's heights. The same doorframe, different pencil marks, years later. I want a door frame with pencil marks. I want to see mine and Rose's heights written in, year after year. I want to live in the same house as that door frame and measure my own children's growth. *Futile, self-indulgent thoughts*, I think, and I snap shut the imaginary photo album in my mind closing with it daydreams and wishes of things that could never be. But spray cheese? I can't wait to tell Prue about it!

When I leave Gladys' I don't feel like going home. I am feeling melancholy enough without hearing Bar's story. It is selfish, but I don't want to know what he's been through. I don't feel as though I can handle it tonight. Although I still want my bath and my portable compact disc player, it's too early to retire for the night. The evening is still hot from the heat of the day, muggy and humid. It makes the long strands of my hair curl up around my face as I walk. I will go to the coffee shop although I am not on shift tonight. I look longingly at the spot where the Blue Beast is normally parked, but it is gone. Israel must have driven off while I visited Gladys. He is probably angry with me for taking it earlier, but I don't regret it. The exhilaration I felt while driving was unlike anything else I have felt in recent memory. I love driving. I want to drive and keep on driving until I reach the spot where the pavement ends, where I can leave this existence behind and be someone else.

* * *

The coffee shop is quiet and nearly empty of customers when I arrive. Micki works this shift by himself since it's a slow one and as a result, the dulcet tones of elevator music waft down from the speakers. There are a couple of college students with laptops, studying over their mochas, occasionally glancing up at each other and saying something or laughing. There is a frazzled looking young mother in exercise clothes, buying frozen smoothies for her rambunctious brood, probably on their way to the health club down the street. They make their purchases and leave, the children dribbling icy pureed strawberries down the front of their clothes and onto the floor as they walk. I wipe up their sticky trail with a napkin after they leave.

Micki is on the phone and so I help myself to a mug behind the counter and fill it with coffee and hot chocolate milk. As an indulgence to my moodiness, I top it with whipped cream. The guitar in the corner by the tiny stage seems to beckon to me and so I set my beverage beside me on the floor, and pick up the instrument. My skirt is too short to tuck my legs under me the way I normally do when I play, so I simply hook my shoes behind the cross section of the stool and balance the guitar on my lap. I run through the song catalog in my brain, discarding Johnny Cash, Pat Benetar, Bonnie Raitt, and Elvis Presley. I start with Stand By Me and when that is over I keep strumming, changing chords until I somehow segue into Unchained Melody. When I open my eyes, Luke is sitting on the corner of the stage.

"You are so depressing," he deadpans. "How about something upbeat?"

"Those are classics," I point out stiffly, setting down the guitar. "And I'm not taking requests. I'm off the clock."

"You're singing depressed because you are depressed, is that it?"

I would argue, but I don't see the point. Normally I would lie to spare someone's feelings, so they wouldn't feel obligated to cheer me up. But Luke doesn't seem like the sort to feel obligated to anyone. He actually looks like he is annoyed with me. My first initial pleased reaction at seeing him fades into a mutual annoyance. He has no idea how difficult my life is at the moment, and he comes here and judges me for my response to it? What a maddening person.

"I'm not depressed! I've had a hard day is all. I'm no closer to finding Rose and I'm worried. My time here isn't going to last forever." I won't let my voice shake.

"Come here," Luke says, patting the floor next to him. "What you need is a bucket list."

"A what?" I obediently slide down next to him, but I am still feeling frosty. I stretch my legs out next to his, though mine are long and gangly. His are longer and end in brown hiking boots, the edges of his blue jeans faded and frayed, the threads hanging down like spider webs like the edges of my old nightgown at home. I am close enough to smell him, and he smells like spice and soap. I wish again I had taken that bath and finished off my ginger pear bubble bath.

"A bucket list," he repeats. "It's a list of things you want to do before you die. In your case, what you want to do before you travel on. Things you couldn't do in another century. Bungee jumping, for one."

"No thanks." I shudder. I've seen that on the television. "I drove," I confess, feeling shyly boastful.

"Definitely a bucket list item you can cross off. Not bad, Gray. What else?"

There are so many things I haven't done yet, I'm at a loss for words. Where to start?

"Have you flown?" Luke prods.

"No! And I've never taken a bus either."

"Sky diving!"

"No!" I laugh. "Dye my hair."

"Get a tattoo."

"Surfing."

"Been to a zoo."

"E-mailed someone."

"Try to aim a little higher on the excitement scale, Gray. Ridden a bike."

"Gone to an art show."

"What? How did you go from tattoos and surfing to an art show?" He cocks one eyebrow up.

I point next to his head where a poster is taped up to the wall advertising an art show. "I was running out of things to suggest," I admit. "But I have never been to one and I am certainly not getting a tattoo."

Luke squints at the poster. "It's tomorrow, right around the corner at the gallery. Fancy schmancy." He turns his soap and spice scented self towards me. "Pick you up at eight?" He doesn't wait for an answer, but unfolds his legs and before I can recover from my surprise, he is gone.

Chapter 11

I have never had so much trouble sleeping as I have had the past few nights, since Rose's appearance and subsequent disappearance. My reliance on Nightfall pills is not ideal and are as addictive as any other drug which can lead to withdrawal symptoms if you take them too long. Despite the pills, I have trouble drifting off and staying asleep until morning. Staying awake is never an option, especially this late in the game, when we could potentially travel on at any time. I know it's coming, I feel it, and yet I can't pinpoint why I know. I believe there must be a trigger of sorts, something to gauge our time and distance, but I, like every other Lost, cannot find the pattern. It's as though we've been given a 5,000 piece jigsaw puzzle with a palm full of key pieces missing. If I could find those pieces, I could put together this frustrating puzzle of a life.

There are theories, of course, and they vary from something as simple as a headache that proceeds travel, to something as complicated as the alignment of the moon and planets. There are even links to the earth's gravitational pull, or ancient Mayan calendars and their predictions. For me, I simply get restless. I do get headaches before we travel, yes, but it's probably more to do with not sleeping than it is with predicting travel. The spot on the back of my neck becomes stiff and sore, my body feels weary, and yet my head is buzzing and my thoughts are all over the place. I feel that way now in bed after my bath, my hair still damp, my feet tucked under my nightgown. I pick at the frayed hem that reminds me of Luke's jeans.

When I had arrived home after making my bucket list (of sorts) with Luke, I had said my goodnights to everyone, eaten dinner in my room and gotten ready for bed. I have been here ever since, braiding and unbraiding my hair, changing the compact disc in my little round player and thinking of things. My thoughts race from time travel, to my sister, to Luke, and even the art show. I wish I could call Penny and ask her if what Luke proposed was a date. I suppose Meli would know, she and Will must have started out somewhere. Then I stop myself, Luke and I are hardly going to end up that route, it's only an art show. Although I am alone, I blush furiously. It's just that I've had no practice with this sort of thing.

Henrique used to try to hold my hand back in Portugal at school, and once he tried to kiss me but I ducked just in time to avoid his red lips and one of the other kids had come running up just in time to cause a distraction. After that, I avoided him as much as possible. But Luke isn't like Henrique. Henrique smelled like chicken feathers and soiled clothes, not like soap and spice. I am in over my head. With that realization both delicious and frightening, I drift off.

I sleep long and hard, much past my normal waking hour and I only awaken when Prue marches into my room and unceremoniously yanks my blankets off.

"Family meetin,'" she barks. "Up with you!"

I want to pull my pillow over my head and ignore her, but experience has taught me that will end in disaster. Most girls get to go through a lovely teenage rebellion, disrespecting and lazy, full of eye rolling and tantrums, but most girls haven't been raised by Prue.

"Yes, ma'am," I mutter halfheartedly. When I sit up, my head aches the way it always does after too many nights in a row with Nightfall pills. I feel hungry though, and the smell of sizzling bacon leads me to trade my nightgown for a T-shirt and gray sweats and sluggishly I pad barefoot out of my room.

I had almost forgotten the existence of Bar in my foggy morning state, but smile when I seem him seated between the brothers, sipping orange juice. He wears the same suit and his hair is neatly combed. His hands though, shake in their grip of his juice glass. I fix a plate with pancakes and extra bacon and sit down across from them.

"All right, let the family meeting begin," I say, trying to sound cheerful, though the sight of Bar makes me inexplicably sad. I am the last to arrive and the last to eat.

Everyone glances sideways at each other, looking like they are trying not to look me in the eye.

"What is going on?" I say.

Finally, Will clears his throat.

"We think it's time to split up, Sonnet," he says gently, placing his hand over mine. I chew in confusion, not responding. "We all know small groups of only two or three Lost tend to travel a bit less. We've been here two years and we know our time here is growing to a close. Meli and I want to put down roots, at least as much as we can. We're going to move out."

"We talked about this a little," Meli interjects, her eyes meeting mine. "Remember?"

I don't remember, but it may have been the other day when she barged in on me soaking in the bath.

"But there's no guarantee that you will stay here any longer," I object.

"Yes, but we have to try. I'm going to have a baby." Meli smiles and pats her stomach. "Can you believe it? And you know how much I hate traveling anyway. If we can just put it off until the baby comes at least...I just think it will be better."

"Oh." I feel foolish for not coming up with a better response, but I'm so surprised. Will moves his hand from where it had rested over mine and clasps Meli's instead.

"That's not all, my dear." Harry sighs. "Matthias and I are going away too. We're going to take Bar and help him find out what happened to his family in Germany. In this day and age, there's a good chance we can put together the pieces and help him say goodbye. If we travel too soon, we won't get another chance like this. We can use the internet, the museums, and all the modern knowledge of the Holocaust. We have to try, you understand."

I nod dumbly. Losing Meli and Will was hard enough, losing my favorite brothers is painful. I want to feel anger at Bar, but that would be like striking out at a child. So I muster up a small, pitiful smile and swallow back the ball in my throat.

"Anyone else?" I ask, looking around at my shrinking family. Everyone's faces are long and serious. My gaze lingers the most on Israel searching his flawlessly smooth chocolate skin. If he leaves me, I shall lose it. He reaches across the side of the table with his long arm and tousles my head, mussing my braid and calming my heart.

"That's enough belly achin'," Prue says, briskly. "What's done is done and can't be undone. Boys, I'm making you food for your trip. Meli and Will, you too. Everyone outta my kitchen, now scoot!"

I manage to shovel in the last of my bacon as Prue whisks my plate away. What just happened here? I somehow lost most of my family in one fell swoop. Although we know losing each other is always a possibility, no one has ever made the choice to abandon me. Unless you count my mother. This hurts almost as much.

"Why do you have to go, Harry?" I whisper. We are the only two left sitting at the table as everyone else has dispersed. "Someone else can help Bar."

"No one else understands, Sonnet." Harry's voice is firm and he looks a little as though he might be disappointed in me, his surrogate granddaughter.

"I'm sorry. I'm just being selfish, I know. I just don't want to say goodbye yet, that's all. You know we'll never see each other again." That goes without saying, but I say it anyway.

"Nothing's impossible." Harry smiles, the folds of his old skin wrinkling up like tissue paper.

I'd rather scowl, but I manage a halfhearted snippet of a smile instead.

It takes less than an hour for Prue to package up several bags of food, a train schedule to be found, and the goodbyes to start. One nice thing about the Lost is that we travel light. Of course I cry hugging Matthias and Harry, but I surprise myself by getting misty over the loss of Will and Meli too. They are not the easiest people to live with, but I know their idiosyncrasies by heart. I'll miss Meli's talkative nature and dramatics, and Will's monotone steadiness. Evidently they have the opportunity to live in someone's mobile home a couple of counties away, in exchange for taking care of the property. They have been planning this for a while at least, and now I feel guilty for feeling taken aback when apparently Meli had been dropping hints all week. That'll teach me to pay attention when people talk, even if I'm up to my ears in bubbles.

When it comes to Bar, I don't know what to say. I feel a little angry with him for putting me in this position, but really it's my own fault for bringing him home. It will be good for Matthias and Harry to have something to do besides watch game shows. I shake Bar's hand and try to smile genuinely enough. I would have liked for him to be my pretend cousin, and I wish with all my heart that I could somehow know how his story turns out.

What little enthusiasm I can fake is depleted, and I immediately head for the sanctuary of Emme's apartment. It's a walk that normally takes me a half hour, but I find myself marching so briskly I make it in twenty minutes. It's as though my feet are on the verge of escaping, or running away. I have been gone only minutes and I already am dreading entering back into my little brown house, made bigger by the absence of loved ones. Israel will be happy to get his own room though, he always said Harry's snoring sounded like an elk bugling all night long.

I barge in the way I always do once I reach Emme's front door. She greets me warmly and hears my sob story over tea and blueberry muffins.

"Ah, luv, you'll be just fine. Goodbyes happen all the time, you aren't cursed and you aren't the only one it happens to. That's life, that's all." She winks at me, while piling her wavy hair on top of her head and securing it with a clip.

"I know." I sigh. "But I'll miss them! Harry and Matthias were the only sane ones in the house! Well, if you don't count their compulsive game show addiction."

"What you need is a distraction. Forget your sorrows for a while."

"I'm not getting drunk if that's what you're suggesting," I grumble, picking apart my muffin until it's nothing, but a pile of crumbs with a faint purple hued.

Emme laughs.

"Oh!" I say, remembering. "I do have something of a distraction coming up tonight." I tell her about my bucket list with Luke and how we are going to the art show.

"Mmmm," she contemplates, her eyes sparkling. "And is this Luke a handsome blokc?"

"I hadn't noticed," I lie. Lying is a gift of the Lost – we all excel at it. I barely even flush.

"I see," Emme responds and I can tell by her smile that she does. "Well, handsome or no, we're going to get you ready and knock his knickers off!"

"Emme!"

"I meant socks! Knock his socks off!" Emme laughs so hard she has to hold her stomach and tears come to her eyes. Evidently my look of horror is hysterical. I flick a blueberry at her.

"All right, all right," she gasps for breath, "I'm done...really, I swear. Anyway, what are you planning on wearing? Because I can guarantee we will go with the opposite of your plan."

"Ha ha, very funny. I was going to wear what I'm wearing right now." I look down and inspect my clothes. Clean and barely wrinkled.

She narrows her eyes as she inspects my gray T-shirt and jeans. "No, you're not. Art shows are something you dress up for, Sonnet. There'll be hoity-toity rich people there, appetizers and wine. Blimey girl, women will be wearing dresses and heels, and men will be all polished up and respectable like!"

"No way am I wearing heels," I promise.

An hour later, I am wearing heels.

"I look ridiculous," I complain, as I walk back and forth in Emme's tiny living room. My ankles still toddle and wobble and I feel like I am ten feet tall: not in a good way either.

"You do look ridiculous." Emme agrees, hands on her hips. "But that's because you're wearing baggy pants and frowning. Stand up straight and smile!"

I stick my tongue out at her instead and as payment for my sassiness I promptly fall over and crash to the floor.

"Serves you right!" Emme giggles, "You're the worst pupil I've ever had."

"I'm the only pupil you've ever had. Are you sure these are the lowest heels you have? And the most plain?"

"They're ordinary black pumps, Sonnet! For goodness sake, I wouldn't wear those things to the grocery store, they're so boring! But if you really don't like them, I do have some four-inch sparkly light up ones," she teases.

"No, thanks."

I look down at them. They are ordinary black and I suppose I'd hardly notice them on anyone else, but on me they seem conspicuous and like they're crying out for attention on my feet.

"But don't worry, they won't look boring when I get you into the dress I'm thinking of. Come on now, stop stalling. We still have hair and make-up." She yanks me to my feet.

"I hate make-up," I mutter. Make-up makes me think of Harry and Matthias who would be appalled at me wearing the stuff. I never bother, mostly because I don't want to buy any, and also because my eyes are striking enough without lining them or darkening my lashes. I've never tried lipstick either, unless rubbing burst berries on my lips as a pre-teen in Portugal counts. I doubt Emme would count that.

Emme leads me to her bedroom and yanks out a deep red dress from her closet. It is very beautiful, with small straps and a satin feel to it.

"You're three feet shorter than I am. How's this going to work?" I demand.

"It's too long on me. And I'm hardly three feet shorter, drama queen. A few inches. It will show off those long legs you have."

I don't want to show off my long legs. I want to wear my jeans. With sneakers. But I obediently step into it and let Emme zip up the back. I turn to face the mirror.

"It's tight," I object.

"Is not!"

"Is too! I can't hardly breathe! I want some of those appetizers you promised me would be there! How am I supposed to eat, drink, and move?"

"Good grief, you are such a big baby. I don't know why I put up with you. Pull up your big girl nappy and stop whining. Really. Take it off while we work on your hair and face."

I grumble through the whole hair process as well, making Emme threaten me with a curling iron. After that, she applies enough make-up to glamour up an entire circus and when she leaves to make us iced tea, I wipe almost all of it off. I leave a thin line of dark eyeliner, the first layer of powder, and the mascara which make my eyes look huge. Oh, and the gloss on my lips which is a light shimmery pink color and doesn't taste half bad.

I put the hated dress back on and step back to analyze my appearance. I don't look like a girl anymore, and the reflection looking back at me is one I've never seen. No one has ever seen this half girl, half woman before. I can't help wondering what people will think. I can't help wishing I could still hide behind my jeans and T-shirt.

"All righty, luv." Emme steps back and admires her work. "That'll do. Now all you have to do is walk home in those heels and then try to look like you haven't been walking at all when this Luke picks you up."

"Oh fabulous," I grumble. "Give me back my clothes and I'll carry these instruments of torture in a sack." I gesture to the heels which are already pinching my feet.

She bundles up my clothes and fancy shoes for me and gives me a kiss on the cheek as I go through the door. "Emme," I pause, my hand on the doorframe, "Do you think we'll travel together? I don't want to leave you too. We've both been here a long while. It's time, I can practically feel it."

"Feel it?" Emme frowns. "I never feel a thing."

"It's just a restlessness, that's all. Like things are fading away, but moving faster at the same time. I can't hardly sleep and I feel like I only have a few moments left in this time before I disappear altogether, you know?"

"Not really." She laughs. "You really are a drama queen tonight, Sonnet. But you're right, we've both been here long enough and I expect us to move on soon. Nothing to be afraid of though, luv. It's not exactly our first rodeo!" She winks. Emme's American expressions spoken in her British accent always make me laugh. "Now get a move on. I want to hear all about tonight first thing tomorrow! You're working in the morning?" I nod. "I'll come by then first thing. Well, not first thing, but before noon, all right?"

"All right." I sigh, hefting my sack over my shoulder and starting down the stairs. "Do I look as ridiculous as I think I do?" I glance down at my sneakers which don't exactly go with my red dress.

"Absolutely!" Emme cheers. "Now get out of here!"

Chapter 12

Coming home to my half empty house is just as terrible as I knew it would be. The television is switched off since there's no Matthias or Harry to watch it. Will and Meli's room is empty, with the door standing open. My dad is nowhere to be found, as is Prue, which means they're manning the food cart somewhere. If they're smart, they'll be on the same block as the art show, but my embarrassment of them keeps me from wishing it. It isn't as if I'd change them, but they are a hard pill to swallow at times. And Prue would probably demand I take off this tight dress and wash my face. I hope we don't run into them, Luke and me.

I'm feeling nervous for what amounts to my very first date of sorts. Then I feel out of sorts for feeling nervous because really, what do I have to be nervous about anyway? Luke is older than I, a man of the world really, who knows what I am and knows there is no hope of a future, and is only taking me out as a farewell of sorts anyway. He just e feels sorry for me, a Lost little child who has never even e-mailed someone...much less bungee jumped or flown.

In the midst of my wandering thoughts, Israel comes through the door looking tired after putting Matthias, Harry, and Bar on a bus. Evidently he also went grocery shopping as he is loaded up with brown paper sacks. I grab the one that looks like it is about to slip out of his grasp, and we carry them to the kitchen table to put away. I wait for his reaction to my appearance, since I even put on the dreaded heels.

"Prue wanted almond paste. This look right to you?" He holds up a can of something.

"Sure, I think so." I move closer.

"Well, she practically cleaned out the fridge for the boys," Israel continues, his head deep inside the refrigerator as he puts away the eggs and milk. "Can you hand me the cold stuff since I'm here?" He peers over the door expectantly.

I hand him a block of cheese and clear my throat.

"What? Did you say something? There's an ice cream in that other sack, can you hand it to me?"

I consider chucking it at his head. He didn't even blink when he saw me. Is anyone that unobservant, especially normally astute Israel?

"I didn't say anything," I mutter.

"Yeah?" Israel shuts the freezer and fridge doors and looks at me with his eyebrows raised. Finally he's going to notice how grown up and pretty I look. "Well, you should be saying something."

"What?" I say looking confused.

"Don't pretend like you don't know. Did you think I wouldn't notice?" Where did you take the Blue Beast?

"Of course not, you notice everything," I reply sarcastically, and cross my arms over my chest. Suddenly the V of the neckline seems too low and I am uncomfortable in my skin. Not that Israel has noticed.

"Well?" He pushes. His eyes are concerned and narrowed. He stares at me and yet he doesn't even see me. "Where did you go?"

"I went to do laundry," I answer. "Maybe you've noticed I'm out of clean clothes?" I gesture halfheartedly to my dress. He doesn't move his eyes off mine.

"Do you understand how much trouble you would have gotten in if you'd been pulled over? Do you have that kind of money to pay that fine? Because I don't! And I don't know if you expected me to come bail you out for driving without a license because let me tell you, I'd probably let you sit there for a while first. That was really irresponsible, Sonnet." He looks at me like he's chiding a little girl for sneaking a cookie or a puppy for biting his pant leg. I feel like a little girl now, and I resent it.

"You're not my parent, Iz," I shoot back. "You're hardly any older than I am! Don't boss me around."

"I'll boss you around whenever I feel like it, Sonnet." He steps away from the refrigerator and moves towards me. I back up. "That is my car and it took me hours of blood, sweat and tears to get it. If you want to learn to drive, I'll teach you, but for goodness sake, don't presume to take it. What if I had an emergency that I needed to get to?"

"You're just an intern. I daresay they can get along without you there helping them save lives, Mr. Hero." That sounded much less petty and immature in my head. Now I am behaving like a little girl as well.

"Yes, I'm just the intern. The intern who needs to learn as much as he can so that he can take that knowledge with him when he leaves! Do you understand how important the education I am getting here is? Do you understand that if we leave here and end up somewhere poor and full of disease that I can help? That I can bring back knowledge of antibiotics, penicillin, cleanliness, surgical procedures?" He slams his big fist down on the counter, making me jump. "Sonnet, if we go back I can make a difference! I won't have to just sit there the way I used to as a boy and watch everyone I love die! I won't be powerless. I won't be impotent. I'll be useful. I can save people."

I simply stare at him. I didn't know this was why he works so hard, why he stays up late at night, sometimes doesn't come home. "I didn't know," I say weakly. "I just thought you liked medicine."

"I hate medicine," Israel replies, passionately. "I hate watching people suffer. I hate blood. I hate mistakes. I hate second guessing myself. I hate the responsibility, but I do it for us. For everyone we will meet who might need me. I do it for you. I won't stand by and watch anyone else die if I can help it."

I don't know what to say.

"How did your family die?" I ask softly. He has never discussed them with me before. I get the feeling it's now or never, in terms of finding out.

"Cholera. One of the worst ways to go. My mum, father, sisters and brothers. I was the only one who survived it." He rubs his face tiredly.

"Now do you see why I am finding out as much as possible about this century? Why I work so much? Why I'm angry you took the car?"

"Yes," my voice is small and miserable. "I'm sorry, Iz." I move towards him and wrap my arms around his waist. He holds me and rests his chin on my head the way he always does. I feel his hand on the small of my waist through my satin dress. I have long forgotten my dress now and even my night out.

There is knocking on the door.

Israel pulls away and lets me go. He looks even more tired now and sinks down in a chair at the table. I go to answer the door, tripping on my way over in the blasted heels.

"Hello," I tell Luke as I swing open the door and let him in. I'm relieved to see he too has dressed up in a starched burgundy colored collared shirt and slacks. The color of his shirt and my dress even match well. I had a fear that he would be wearing his frayed jeans, and I would feel like an overdressed idiot. He looks at me and whistles.

"That's some dress, Gray." He clears his throat. "You look stunning."

Aha! Stunning! That was the word I was hoping to hear before the fiasco in the kitchen.

"Really?" I find myself turning around like a show-off. What is wrong with me?

"Yes." His face is wreathed in smiles. I can smell his familiar scent of soap and spiciness. "Very much so. Are you ready?"

"Mmhmm." I start to walk towards him, but am stopped by Luke glancing over my shoulder with his friendly smile.

"Luke Dawes," he says, extending his hand to someone behind me.

Suddenly, I am sandwiched in between him and Israel .

"Israel Rhode." Israel clasps his hand but his smile is not as ready as Luke's.

"Ah. You, um, live here? With Sonnet?" Luke asks.

"Yes."

"Ah," Luke says again, looking uncomfortable. "I didn't meet you when I was here the other night."

"I was probably working."

"Ah."

"Yes."

"Well!" I chirp in. "I might be gone late, Iz. I'll see you when I get back, okay?"

I practically shove Luke out of the doorway and speed walk down the rickety steps of my porch.

Luke catches up and takes my elbow. "He looks like someone you won in a raffle," he says. "Bit intimidating, don't you think?"

"Who, Israel?" I laugh. "I guess so, when you first meet him. He's grumpy because I stole his car. He's not so bad once you get to know him."

"Car thief, huh?" Luke pretends to look impressed. "You're a mystery, Gray. Speaking of cars, this is mine." He stops in front of a silver pickup truck and opens the passenger door for me. I sigh, looking at my feet and tight dress and wonder how to climb up in a ladylike fashion. Finally I manage to struggle my way up and in. Dressing up is for the birds, I think. Luke crosses in front of the pickup and gets in the driver's side.

Driving is a wonderful miracle; I think as we ride along. It takes me forever and a day to walk to the coffee shop, and we are there in less than ten minutes in Luke's car. He parks nearby and opens the door to the truck for me again, helping me down by holding onto my elbow. I almost step on his foot in my heels, but he doesn't seem to notice.

Inside, the small place is bustling with people. The artists stand proudly by their work and everyone mills up to compliment them. There are caterers in their pressed black and white uniforms with large platters of wine and tiny bits of finger food. I help myself to olives and cheese squares on a frilled toothpick, but leave the wine alone. I am unsure that I could pass for the legal drinking age, and besides I grew up drinking wine like water. In the time periods I grew up in everyone drank wine, but I don't see the attraction of it. Luke doesn't take a glass either, but keeps one hand on his plate of appetizers and one on my elbow. I'm not sure if he's afraid of losing me in the crowd or if he's simply being chivalrous. He leans over and whispers something in my ear. I am distracted by the noise around me and by having him so close to me. Because of that I have to ask him to repeat what he said.

"There's something I want to show you after this," he says. "Something I thought of when I was going through my photos this morning."

"What?"

"I'll show you later. Just have some fun. Here, have some of whatever the world this is." He offers me his plate.

We do have fun. The people are loud and friendly and it isn't difficult to make small talk. I recognize some as regulars from the coffee shop. We wander through the room, looking at all the paintings and photography. I tell Luke that his skills with a camera are better, and mean it. He holds onto my elbow the whole time, and I feel secure, grown up and wanted. Two hours go by and it feels like half that time. Finally, we've seen every painting, every piece of artwork, and every photo. We've also spoken to everyone who looks approachable or familiar, and eaten several plates of appetizers. There is nothing left to do, but end our night and cross the first thing off my bucket list. I feel very accomplished indeed.

"So, what did you want to show me?" I ask, after climbing back in the truck. I kick off my heels and breathe a sigh of relief, wiggling my toes.

Luke starts the truck and pulls out of the parking space. "I was looking at some photos I took this summer, mostly still-lifes and landscapes. I spent some time out on the edge of town, photographing these old dilapidated buildings and farm houses. There's quite a few out there that are just falling apart, roofs caving in and windows boarded up, things like that. Abandoned places like that make for great shots. You'd be surprised at how many people want shots of old Americana. The most expensive shot I ever sold was one of this field that used to have a house. Now there's nothing left but the chimney in the middle of a field of wildflowers. Anyway, I remembered this one house had some garbage around it, and I thought maybe tramps were living there. So I got a couple of shots and got out. It got me thinking that if Rose is staying somewhere, it could be she's playing house somewhere like that."

"That's a possibility," I agree. "It's not unheard of for the Lost to do that if we can't find a place. I think that's a great idea, Luke." I'm getting excited. "Can you take me there?"

"Sure. Aren't you working tomorrow?"

"I mean tonight! Please?"

"Gray, it's late!" Luke laughs. "And it is REALLY dark out there. No streetlights, no electricity. Nothing. You don't want to go out there tonight."

"But it's on my bucket list!"

"Breaking and entering is on your bucket list? You really are a little criminal, aren't you?"

"Please?" I say again.

"In those shoes?" He glances down at my feet. "This isn't town living, Gray. The places I'm thinking of are way out there and you'll break an ankle in the dark."

"No I won't, Emme made me practice until I could walk in these things on a tightrope!" I boast. Of course, I am completely lying. I almost turned my ankle twice in the art shop and had to grab at Luke to steady myself. I'm certainly not fooling him. He probably has bruises the exact shape of my fingers on both his arms.

He contemplates in silence as he drives. But I have already noticed we are not turning towards my house; I've already won.

Thanks to the miracle of automobiles, we have left the paved streets behind us for country gravel roads in less than the time it takes for me to rummage through his glove compartment for a flashlight and develop a plan.

Chapter 13

Our first trek out of the truck and into the darkness is fruitless. We explore a rundown shack of a house that has no recent inhabitants other than bats, mice, and raccoons. Walking in darkness in heels is every bit as difficult as Luke forewarned. I finally take them off and carry them, hoping against hope that I don't step in something questionable or disgusting. Our flashlight beam isn't the brightest, but it does illuminate enough to know that Rose isn't here and never has been.

"There's another up the road a couple miles," Luke says, starting up the truck again. I toss my useless heels behind my seat. My stomach growls, and I wish the art show had something more substantial to eat than olives, cheese, and fruit in the shape of flowers.

The truck bounces along the gravel road and we sit in silence. I feel elated to be doing something to find my sister and scared both at the prospect of locating her or not locating her. How will I convince her of who I am? How will she react? Will she come home with me? What if I'm wrong and it isn't Rose after all? What if the only person we find is a crazed serial killer escaped from prison who buries us under the floorboards, never to be seen again? My imagination has never been my friend in stressful times.

"There!" Luke leans forward in his seat, hunched over the steering wheel as he peers ahead in the darkness. "Did you see that? It looked like a light in a window."

I lean forward too. If there was a light, it's out now.

"Maybe it was the reflection of your headlights," I suggest. We are close enough now to see the outline of a two story house. It's definitely abandoned, and half of it has collapsed from the weight of a fallen tree that still leans crazily into the rubble. There are junked cars in the field next to it and their shapes are eerie lumps that loom at me. I expect them to suddenly jump up and reveal their true forms of ogres, giants, and trolls, but they are only cars.

"Don't park too close," I whisper. "Here's good." I suddenly feel as though I don't want to drive up with our yellow headlights and scare her, if indeed she is here.

Luke stops the truck obediently and kills the engine. My heart is in my throat, but I get out. The dirt, weeds, and rocks hurt my feet, but I don't slow. I feel a premonition that I will find Rose here. It's not like the nervousness of the last house, where we crept along with Luke whispering in an exaggerated voice, and me laughing when a bat flew over our heads. I knew instinctively Rose wouldn't be there, and it was only a fun game we were playing. I am not having fun here and we haven't even reached the house. I keep my eyes straight ahead, and I too feel as though I see the briefest flicker of a yellow light, like a candle or a weak flashlight beam as it passes by a window. It is gone so quickly that I can't be sure. I blink hard and keep walking. This time Luke takes my hand instead of my elbow. I lace my fingers through his and hold tighter than is probably necessary.

"Hello!" I call out weakly. I clear my throat and call again, this time stronger. Only the silence of the night and my own echo responds. Gingerly we reach the house and I reach out my hand to try the door, which I realize is silly as half the house has collapsed and we could just as easily go through the gaping holes in the walls if we wanted. Somehow it seems disrespectful to do so. If there were a doorbell, I would ring it. It's no surprise that when I turn the old knob, the door obediently creaks open. Luke shines the beam of the flashlight inside. Directly ahead of us is a staircase, to the right is the broken wing of the house where the floor is littered with boards, beams, and broken glass. To the left is a small room with two doors. Past the stairway is a hallway, but the collapsed section of the house has reached it as well and it is nearly impassable. Here and there we see pieces of furniture, they loom and list to the side the way the abandoned cars did outside. Their shapes are misshapen, lumpy and unrecognizable until the flashlight beam hits them. There is clearly a chair here, a small end table there, and a bookshelf with broken and missing shelves over here.

There is a book open, lying face down as though the page where someone stopped reading is being saved, on the couch. Some of the pages had fallen out and lie on the floor. There is a line of cleanliness down the middle of a table, through the dust, as though someone's finger had drawn along it as they walked by. Without knowing why, I shiver.

"Hello!" I call again, ignoring my cowardice. My voice sounds stronger and clearer than I expect it to. "Is anyone here?"

"Rose!" Luke adds his voice to mine. "Rose Gray, are you here?"

"Through those doors or up the stairs?" I whisper to him. There is obviously no one here in this room with us, although the book and the line drawn through the dust suggest otherwise.

"Through the doors." He jerks his head towards the first one.

"Great, a closet," I mutter once I get up the courage to open the door. "No one here but moths."

We try the other and it leads to the kitchen. Luke shines the light around to reveal an old stove, a rusted and filthy kitchen sink, cans of unopened food on the floor where they had apparently tumbled out of the pantry and a broken chair lying on the floor. I could be wrong, but it doesn't feel as though anyone has set foot in this kitchen for years and years. And yet, I still feel a presence in this house, a sense of being watched, a feeling that I am not the only one holding my breath and listening.

"Do you think the stairs will hold?" I ask as we enter back into the living area.

"Beats me," Luke replies, as he shines the beam of the flashlight up the staircase. It must be my imagination working overtime again because I think for a moment that I see a flash of something moving in the dark. I take the flashlight from Luke and without a word, I begin the climb first. The stairs seem as though they should shake and tremble beneath us, like the fragile things they appear to be. They hold our weight well enough though and barely creak with our footfalls. The more I climb, the more my flashlight illuminates and I can see the top of the stairway. The hallway to my left has doors to what I presume to be bedrooms over the kitchen area. There is a gaping hole to my right where the tree had crashed through causing most of the roof to cave in. The cool night air comes through it and lifts my hair, causing goose bumps on my arms and drying the nervous clamminess on my body. We obviously can't go to the right, and so I round the short corner and reach out for the knob to one of the bedrooms. My fingers curl around it and I grasp it and try to turn.

It's locked. I can hear a scuttling sound, like something scraping the floor or a body pushing itself away in a hurry.

I look over my shoulder at Luke. He shrugs.

"Hello?" I call softly though the closed door. "Is anyone in there? I won't hurt you. Please open the door."

Silence. Nothing but silence.

I rattle the knob. Still nothing. I press my ear to the door and listen. Is it my imagination or do I hear breathing on the other side? Similar to the feeling I would get as a little girl after a nightmare when I would huddle under my blankets and swear I could hear the breathing of a monster under my bed. I try to stop my own breathing, but the harder I try the more shallow and loud it seems and the more my heartbeat thuds in my own ears.

"Maybe we should just come back tomorrow," Luke says in a normal voice. Does he want the person behind the door to hear him? "Bring the police even."

"No!" I shoo him away and put my ear again to the door. My fingers have rested all this time on the knob and as if guided by instinct I attempt to turn it again.

This time, it turns.

The door creaks open. There is no one there.

Chapter 14

The letdown and disappointment hits me like a ton of bricks. My breath that I've been holding is let out in a rush. My eyes take in the scene before me, a dingy mattress on the floor with a ratty blue blanket, a dresser with broken drawers hanging lopsided or fallen out completely. There is a box that looks to be filled with half packed and then forgotten knick knacks, and a plastic crucifix on the wall. The closet door is partly open and there is a broken window letting in the night air. I rub my eyes tiredly with all ten of my fingers.

"Are you all right?" Luke asks in concern.

"I just don't know where she could have gone," I reply in frustration. "Didn't you hear her in here?"

Luke looks surprised and shakes his head. "No, I didn't hear anything. Sorry, Gray. Want to get out of here?"

I nod, wordlessly. The sense of Rose being here has diminished now, although I cannot shake the feeling of a presence in this room. Someone was listening to me the way I was listening to it like an ear pressed to the inside of the bedroom door to match mine on the outside. A single piece of pressed wood between us, so close I could almost hear her heartbeat, almost feel her breath, and yet as far away as I have always been.

Back in Luke's truck we are silent for several moments. I feel foolish for thinking it would be so easy to find Rose, yet I also feel strangely as though we came close, though I have nothing substantial to base this feeling on. I wonder why this man is chauffeuring me around on my fool's errand. I steal a glimpse of him from under my eyelashes as he drives. His hands are both on the steering wheel, fingers drumming a bit as though he has a song in his head. He has taken off his tie and it sits obediently between us on the seat of the truck like a tiny quiet passenger.

"Well, it's possible she was there and was scared of us." Luke says.

I don't think he actually believes that, but it is nice of him to placate me.

"We could go back in the daylight," he continues. "Might not be so intimidating that way."

"I suppose breaking and entering with a flashlight wasn't the way to go," I agree morosely. I turn my attention to the window and watch the moonlight flit in and out through the trees, a slim slice of white in the blackness. The way it dances and flickers makes me remember other nights long ago, where candlelight was the norm. The way the flame would skitter and prance about if there was a breeze or if you breathed a little too close. The moon between the pines looks like that to me.

Steadily the shape of the trees gives way to more and more housetops and buildings, and before I know it Luke has pulled up to the curb outside my house. I pick up Emme's shoes in my hand and am still thinking of our strange night as I pull the handle on the passenger door. It seems sticky and so I shove hard. I hear a thud and a muffled exclamation as the door hits something solid before swinging the rest of the way open. I jump out and peer around the door to see Luke sprawled on the sidewalk, scowling at me.

"Gee, Gray, I kind of thought you'd appreciate the chivalry of a man opening the door for you." He rubs his chin and narrows his eyes as I look down at him. "If you're one of those feminist types you could have just said no thanks, and saved me the broken body parts."

"Sorry," I laugh offering my hand to help him up, "I didn't see you there."

"You could wait to forget about my existence at least until I've walked you to your door," he grumbles grabbing my hand and almost pulling me down to him as I haul him up.

"Don't fret, big man."

"I'm not fretting!" His scowls get bigger, if that's possible. "I've never fretted in my life. You really have a way with words, Gray. No one else has managed to insult me quite so much, and with such finesse."

"That's me." I try to curtsy wearing this blasted tight dress. "Full of finesse, insults and harebrained schemes. I'm also available for birthday parties and holidays."

"I'll remember that." We have reached my steps and I wonder suddenly if he is planning on coming in. Will he sit uncomfortably on my couch while I serve powdered lemonade? Will we make small talk? What am I supposed to do now? It's nearly midnight, and Prue will be exhausted waiting up for me.

Speak of the devil, Prue yanks open the front door before I can reach out for the knob. She glares at us in her ruffled nightgown, one hand on the door, the other on her hip. Her foot taps impatiently as she stares Luke down.

"Young man, you had better hightail it home now. It is extremely late and some of us need to work for a living. Not all of us go 'round, snappin' pictures and callin' it a profession. Some of us have to actually get up at the crack of dawn to start the bread risin.'" This is a complete and utter fabrication, seeing as how Prue doesn't serve breakfast and therefore has no need to start her bread dough rising anywhere near the crack of dawn, but I'm certainly not going to point this out. She looks like a disgruntled mama bear in pigtails.

"And thank goodness you do!" Luke smiles from ear to ear. "I'd be skin and bones if it weren't for you Prue. Now when you going to give up this hard working lifestyle and marry me and just cook for one?"

Prue smacks him smartly, but the corners of her mouth are quivering in an attempt not to smile. I stare closer at her; is she blushing? Prue, blushing? What a day.

As I open my mouth to wish Luke a pleasant evening, the headlights of a car pulling up practically to my front steps almost blind me. The engine of the intruding vehicle idles while I hear the sound of first one, and then a second, door being opened and slammed shut. I can see the illuminated shapes of what appear to be two men seemingly arm in arm coming towards us, but I cannot make out who they are.

"What in the world?" I murmur.

"It's the police," Luke answers and then under his breath, "It looks like your father got himself a ride home."

I almost find myself wishing that my date (if that's what Luke is) could be exceedingly less chivalrous and just leave me to my state of mortification. Mortified is the only emotion you can feel when your own father, drunk of course, is escorted home by a cranky policeman. You don't really need company to watch you process your mortification and go through the final stages of embarrassment, excuses, faked casual laughter, and forced inane chatter. But that is what I am putting Luke through at the moment, and quite possibly all at once.

"Well, the police here certainly do take their streets seriously, don't they?" I chatter on, forcing my voice to sound light, as we lower my father's inebriated self to the couch. He is barely conscious. He stinks to high heaven, and he is humming a song under his breath. The cop had threatened us nicely and made sure we heard several times that he won't show such kindness and unparalleled generosity on his part if there was ever to be a next time he discovered Noah Gray drunk in public. I assured him several times there wouldn't be a next time.

"Here you are, sir." Luke props up my father's head on the only throw pillow we have. It's a round chenille that I bought at the same yard sale I found my favorite monogrammed washcloth.

As a thank you, Dad hiccups.

I'd like to give him a good smack, and realize that I don't have a mother to turn into the way daughters do in times like these. Instead I am turning into Prue. Such a lovely thought to cap off my utterly lovely evening.

I look at Luke and wish desperately that he would leave. It is too much to have him here, feeling sorry for me as he must, and probably wondering frantically how he will ever get rid of me now. Strangely odd Sonnet Gray, with her pesky time traveling habit, dead mother, ghost of a sister, and now her thoroughly pickled father. What must he think of me?

I'm more exhausted and drained than I thought because as I steal a glance at Luke he is looking at me in a way that does not look like pity. It is a soft glance, a warming of his eyes really, a flash of a smile, and it almost feels as though my very bones are turning to liquid. I shake off the notion to bring myself back to the present, and to make myself feel better, I tweak my father's nose a bit harder than necessary in what is disguised as a gesture of affection. It really is a painful twist that makes him yelp, but it makes me feel much better.

"Just leave him," I tell Luke and head for the door. He really has no choice but to follow me. "He'll be fine." *He always is.* That is the part I don't say, but I might as well since we both hear it anyway.

"Thank you for the art show, it was lovely." I smile, or attempt to. It feels wooden and stiff. "And thank you for trying to find Rose. And for," I gesture toward the couch, which is emitting a peaceful snoring sound, "that."

"It was most interesting." Luke chuckles. "Maybe we can do it all again sometime."

I don't take him seriously and to show I don't, I push him lightly out the door and say goodnight. What genius would want to do this all again sometime? He is either terribly masochistic, ridiculously lonely, or a glutton for punishment. I simply cannot come up with a fourth alternative for wanting to be near me.

When Luke is gone and Dad is tucked in, Prue presses a mug of hot chocolate in my hands. It is as though I am nine years old and it will cure all that ails me, and then she sends me off to bed.

I dream.

I am eight years old and sitting beneath a stone wall. There is a dog baying somewhere nearby and the whole world seems flat and gray through my blue eyes. I am lonely. The children here don't like me. I am slow to learn their language and I seem odd to them; I don't find the same things amusing and I laugh in all the wrong places at the wrong times. I still look for my little sister everywhere we go because I still remember her.

I wake up with a start. I did remember her at that age. My own memories, and not the stories repeated that make me wonder if I remember, but actual solid images. The frustrating thing now is the more time goes by, the less clear those images are until, like a dream, the edges blur and become fuzzy like clouds. In my mind, I attempt to stare and concentrate and make it come into focus, but the clouds come faster and faster, blurring my vision and taking with it any clarity that once was there. I want to fall asleep again, to dream and remember some more, but it's useless. I lie in bed, tired but awake until the break of dawn.

* * *

At work in the morning, I feel that restlessness that comes with having been too long in one place, and I find myself giving Micki notice again. He ignores me as usual and asks me to re-do the entire chalkboard menu behind the counter. He likes it when I redesign it because my handwriting is pretty. His would be too if he learned to write in a monastery with monks who wrote bibles by hand and spent days on just one letter. My hands cramp in memory.

I am balanced precariously on our tallest bar stool when Emme stops by for her favorite beverage, scalding hot tea in a double cup.

"You look like hell, luv," she greets me cheerily.

"I've been having trouble sleeping," I grumble erasing my C in the word cinnamon and starting over. I had gotten too ornate with it and it looked like Ginnamon. "And you're awfully perky for the morning."

"It's Joe's birthday," Emme replies, blowing on the cup of tea that Micki hands her. "I'm going shopping for a gift. Want to come?"

"I'm working."

"Take her," Micki sticks his nose in the conversation, "She keeps glaring at the customers anyway."

"I am not!" I protest. "I'm concentrating, not glaring!"

Micki and Emme exchange glances that seem to commiserate with each other and completely irritate me.

"Really, I can handle it. Go, have fun," Micki pushes. "I'll even finish the menu."

"You write like a four-year-old," I argue.

"I'm the four-year-old who signs your paycheck, so get lost."

Get lost. Just another modern expression that always confuses me into silence. I suppose that in order to convince everyone that I am not glaring and grumpy, now would not be the time to complain about how much I despise shopping.

"Fine." I climb down and hand over my chalk to Micki, along with my apron. "Try not to spell cappuccino wrong, boss."

Outside, the day is almost chilly. It's that time between the late summer and the early fall where we have gone from using the air conditioner to turning on the furnace in the morning. I was too fuzzy headed this morning to grab a jacket, so I pull my sleeves down around my hands and hug my arms to my chest as we walk.

"Couldn't you have brought your mum's car?" I ask pretending to have chattering teeth.

"You really are in a mood," Emme retorts. "You know I don't drive that killing machine. It could chop me up four ways from Sunday. I hate automobiles." She shivers.

"Well, I love them! I pinched Israel's car the other day." I say proudly. "Driving is easy, and I love it!"

"Well aren't you feeling brave," Emme looks suitably impressed. "I bet Israel wasn't too pleased though."

I shrug remembering when he came home and bawled me out even though I looked so nice. I could wear a bird on my head and he wouldn't notice. Unless I was wearing the bird as I drove off in his car, now there's a thought.

"He wasn't. He's been awfully crabby these days anyway. I can't do anything right." I hug myself tighter.

"He's just focused, that's all. He takes life seriously."

"And I don't?"

"Calm down, Miss Tragedy." Emme laughs. "Quit being so prickly. What put this bee in your bonnet?"

I sigh in frustration. "I'm just tired and stressed out, I guess. I keep seeing or feeling Rose all around me, but I can't find her. My dad was brought home by a cop last night and half my house walked out on me." I am feeling glummer by the minute here. Aren't best friends supposed to cheer you up?

"Aww, come 'ere, my little fashion disaster!" Emme pulls me into an embrace, right there in public. She's such a short little thing that my chin nestles in her strawberry colored curly bun atop her head. She squeezes me tight and says, "Being eighteen is rarely a picnic no matter what day and age you're living in. This too shall pass, isn't that what they say?"

"I'm sure eighteen wasn't a bed of roses for you either?" I say trying not to pry into Emme's past.

She snorts. "You have no idea."

Given Emme's line of work and the stories she could probably tell if she were so inclined, I don't want to know anymore. Nevertheless, she keeps talking.

"Joe was not even one year and we were living in some God- forsaken Norwegian village. He was always such a sickly thing getting croup, pneumonia, and all sorts of illnesses those first couple years. Kept thinkin' I shouldn't get attached to him. Didn't want to grieve too much if we lost him altogether. I swear, we should have just had a live in nurse with us. There was this old granny who'd come by and give him herbs, and tinctures, and he finally started getting a little better that year. Still coughs a lot though, even now." I had noticed that actually. "And he's a little undersized for six. 'Course, being us and being what we are, who the heck knows what his real age is anyway." She sighs. "I'd keep him little if I could, so I probably shouldn't complain. Anyway, that village was tiny and let me just say, business was slow!" I roll my eyes. "I wasn't exactly Miss Popularity with the village ladies. That old granny was about the only one who'd have anything to do with me." She pauses, remembering.

"And your mum?"

"Hmm? Oh yes, Mum was there helping out with Joe and taking care of the house. She planted a garden, but of course we ended up travelin' on before it ever sprouted. Someone in that village ate a lot of turnips that next year."

"Helping out with Joe?" I repeat. I'm starting to put two and two together and I don't like the sum much.

Emme looks at me sideways, wearing a brightly knit turquoise scarf accented with her cold pink nose. We do a strange dance of watching each other sideways as we walk in a straight line, while she unwinds her scarf and pulls it over her head and ears. I suddenly have the feeling she is blocking out my last question.

"You're so naïve, pet." Her words are a little harsh, but they are said with a loving tone. "What kind of boy wants a whore for a mum?"

"Don't call yourself that!" I stop walking abruptly and grab at Emme's arm sharply. "You know that's never mattered to me and it wouldn't matter to Joe. I can't believe you never told me."

"Oh Sonnet, of course it would matter." Her eyes look flat and expressionless now as she looks at me. "It's better this way. And I don't have to stop loving him any less, or be around him any less. It really is better. Come on, there's that lovely toy shop, let's go in!"

In an instant, the fire in her eyes is back and she is like a little girl as she pulls my elbow and drags me across the street to Ramone's Toys and Trinkets. She claps in glee at the train set that decorates their front window and pushes open the door merrily. A bell tinkles from over our heads and like magic, a man appears at our side as though he has been conjured by eager shoppers. Emme certainly is eager. She spends an obscene amount of money as she picks out huge lollipops, a stuffed bear, and a set of blocks. She also holds up a walkie-talkie that she says will give Joe and Bea endless entertainment, and finally throws in the train set from in the window. At one point, I open my mouth to remind her that he could get attached to all of this, and then must leave it, but I cannot say it. I cannot remind Emme of the realities of her little Lost boy. It isn't as though she doesn't already know the unfairness of it all.

Chapter 15

We walk back from our shopping spree laden down with bags in boxes and boxes in bags. Emme is fresh faced and excited for her purchases as we make our way back to the coffee shop. I can't help but cheer up a bit, as Emme's childlike exuberance is contagious. The wind has whipped itself into a frenzy however, and my fingertips feel frozen to the plastic handles of the shopping bags, and we still have a couple of blocks to go.

"Let's play Best and Worst to keep my lips from frostbite," I suggest heaving my bags up and over my shoulders like Saint Nicholas. Best and Worst is a game just about every Lost child has played at one time or another. It's a game where you state the best places and worst eras you can imagine waking up in.

"Mmm," Emme wrinkles her button nose the way she always does when she's thinking. "Best: Cancun. Worst: The Black Death."

"Best: Discovering America. Worst: Marie Antoinette's court."

"Best: The abolition of slavery. Worst: On board the Titanic."

"Best: The nativity in Bethlehem. Worst: The Trail of Tears."

"Best: The Wright brothers' airplane. Worst: Vietnam in the sixties."

"Best: You know that scene in every Robin Hood movie? The one where they're gnawing on gigantic turkey legs? That. Worst: The Great Depression."

"Yeah, I've had those turkey legs, and they weren't that great," Emme answers. "It was like gnawing on shoe leather rather than poultry."

"Please tell me you didn't actually meet Robin Hood!" I stop in my tracks.

Emme laughs. "Pretty sure he's a fictional character, genius. Did meet a lot of friars back then though and maidens in long frocks. The castles aren't nearly as romantic as they look, let me tell you. Bloody cold and full of rats."

"All right then. Best: Elvis Presley's tour bus. Worst: Marilyn Manson's tour bus."

Emme laughs again. "We're here. Ugh. What are the odds of you taking all this stuff back to your place to hide?" She manages to balance a box beneath her chin, and free her left hand to open the door to the coffee shop. Wedging my knee in the opening, we both somehow get inside without dropping anything.

"Pretty good as long as Israel comes to get me. I'm not going to walk it all home, that's for sure." I spent most of my shift shopping, but it is still daylight. I wonder if he'll be up for picking me up. Sometimes he abandons me to walk the sunlit streets and fend for myself when it isn't an evening shift. Plus, I don't think he's completely forgiven me for stealing the Blue Beast.

"Can I talk you into wrapping it all, too?" Emme pleads, her eyes sparkling.

"Sure, as long as I can write Love, Auntie Sonnet on all of them," I agree. "And your Bambi eyes don't work on me, so shove off. I'll see you later. Come by tonight, I'm sure Prue has something we can stick some candles on for Joe. Bring him and Bea, we'll have a party."

"Perfect. Thanks, Sonnet. You're a good friend."

"I'm your only friend. See you later."

After Emme is gone I line up all her packages in a row on the front counter that faces the street. There are bar stools that swivel and look out into traffic. It's the favorite place for little kids to sit and spin in circles while their moms and dads drink coffee, and I sit and spin now as I wait for what I hope will be the massive rectangle of blue that is my ride home.

"Thanks for the ride," I tell Israel meekly as I climb in the passenger seat. All Emme's gifts are piled up in the back.

"You're welcome. Who are all these for?"

"Joe." I want to tell him that Bea isn't Joe's mother, but it isn't my secret to tell. "They're coming over later. Do we still have ice cream?"

"We should have since Matthias isn't around to eat it in the middle of the night." Matthias was a bit of an ice cream fiend.

"How was your day?" I ask again meekly. I still feel guilty over the theft of his car and our conversation concerning medicine back in the kitchen.

"Busy," Israel answers stopping for a red light. "You?"

"Fine."

"How was the rest of your night last night? With, what was his name, Larry? Luther? Lucifer?"

"Luke. It was fine, nice actually. Well, until the end. I think he thinks I'm nuts for chasing after Rose, plus when he brought me home the cops were bringing in Dad."

"Well, I'm sure he isn't much of a loss."

"You didn't like him?"

"Well, he's not my type, but I guess if he's yours..."

"I don't even have a type!" I feel my face flushing. Israel's smiling which means he was egging me on. "Well, he doesn't much like you either. He said you look like something I won in a raffle."

"What does that mean?" He scowls. "He looks like the cover of a hunting and fishing catalog."

"What does that mean?" I can't help but laugh. "I don't think he hunts or fishes!"

"You know," his scowl deepens, "All that flannel, and scruff, and stuff."

"Well, you're one to talk with all your scrubs and scruff." I reach over and scrape my knuckles against his five o'clock shadow. Normally Israel is shaved and smooth, but you can always tell when he's working too much by the length of his prickly facial hair. Instead of laughing with me, he bats my hand away like a fly.

"We're home," he says gruffly and almost runs over the curb as he parks. He leaves me to carry in all the packages myself. I wish he had tried to open the door for me just so I could plow him down flat the way I did Luke; only with Israel I'd do it on purpose.

Prue takes it literally when I ask her to put candles in whatever she can find and put together at the last minute. By dinner time there are candles in the fish casserole, pepperoni calzone, chocolate pudding, and an entire loaf of raisin bread. Where she got all the candles I'll never know, but I just hope the same cranky policeman doesn't show up tonight along with a fire marshal. Since it's an official party now, we are all looking our best and even Dad is looking bright eyed and put together. I haven't spoken much to him since the police incident. His baby face and clear, fresh skin never show a trace of his nights. His bow tie is straight and triangular and he's wearing his favorite argyle cardigan. He looks more like a college professor, than a tipsy pickpocket.

Prue is wearing her best apron, the one she wears for special occasions. She likes it so much I have even caught her wearing it over her nightgown. She'd never admit it, but I think she wants to bring it with her when we travel next.

Israel has gone to shower and says he won't be able to stay for the party. I am wearing my plaid skirt and my T-shirt with the horses on it in honor of Emme. She will absolutely hate it, but Joe will approve.

When the doorbell rings I pull it open with panache, expecting to see the birthday boy on the other side. Instead I see Luke. I drop my arms in a flash from the ridiculous pose they had struck a mere second before.

"Oh," I say. "You're you."

"I am?"

"Yes. I wasn't expecting you. Sorry." I want to say 'what's up?' in a casual tone, but I can't bring myself to say such a modern slang expression in anything that passes for casual.

"Can I come in?" He looks a little bit awkward, like he's regretting coming or perhaps like he doesn't want to be here at all. Trust it to me to make a man feel awkward within seconds of arriving at my door.

"Of course."

To make up for my lack of graciousness, I open the door wider and smile at him. A real smile, full of what I hope is warmth and good cheer. Well, actually I hope it's full of beauty and mysterious charm, but warmth and good cheer is more realistic. Whatever my smile is full of it seems to have the desired effect and Luke relaxes his shoulders immediately and comes in to our party. I forget to ask him why he's here, but instead get him a glass of ice water and an empty plate, which if I know him at all, he will have piled high with Prue's cooking in no time.

The next time the doorbell rings it is Joe, Emme and Bea and we all yell "Surprise!" Joe is delighted and bounces like a kangaroo through the living room. He is awestruck by the sight of all the gifts wrapped by me, all with borrowed wrapping paper from Gladys. Most of it is pink and very feminine, but he doesn't notice. Once Emme says he can open them, he starts tearing through them at lightning speed. He is happy enough with the bear and the lollipops, but he is enthralled and enamored with the train set. Within minutes he has Luke sprawled out on the carpet with him, putting it together.

"Such a lot of presents for a little fellow." Prue sniffs. "He'll hardly be able to play with all that, now will he?"

"Aw, that's what big sisters are for," says Emme, not missing a beat. Her voice doesn't waver, and she sounds as happy as ever. Nothing in her voice or demeanor suggests anything but a proud older sister looking on as her little brother grows up. I steal a glance at Bea and she is every bit the actress as well, adopting the part of mother when she should be grandmother. Bea is the one who says no when Joe asks for more chips, and the one who reminds him to chew with his mouth closed.

Israel comes downstairs and says hello to Bea and Emme, his car keys in hand. He has taken to keeping them on him at all times now, I've noticed. He tousles Joe's curly red hair in greeting and stiffly nods at Luke, who still sits on the floor amidst a complete train wreck, literally. Luke twitches his right arm as though he is about to offer his hand, but thinks better of it and nods back.

"Sonnet is there another plate?" Israel asks me.

"I thought you had to work?"

"I changed my mind. I can't miss this, right Sport?" he swings Joe up by his knees and dangles him like a pendulum.

"Right!" Joe squeals in delight from upside down.

"Right," I mutter. "Sure. One plate, coming right up." I get his plate and since his hands are still full of brand new seven-year-old boy, I go ahead and fill it with the foods I know he likes. Since I'm still a little on the outs with Israel, and it would make sense that I'd fill it with the opposite of his favorites. Fortunately for him, my waitress/barista instincts kick in before

I can help myself. I bring him a plate of Prue's delicacies, and then I find myself being held against my will as Emme combs out and braids my hair.

"Not too elaborate," I instruct as she yanks a section of hair and the comb gets caught. I wince. "This isn't Regency England anymore, it's the twenty first century and a pony tail will do just fine, thanks."

"A lump of clay doesn't tell the potter what to make it into," Emme points out, although it's hard to hear what she's saying as her mouth is full of pins.

"I don't even know what that means. Ouch!"

Since my head is being forced to stay in one agonizing position, I stare straight ahead and see the whole group. It feels strange with so many missing, as though if I squint enough or turn my head quickly I could just get a glimpse of Harry sitting next to Matthias on the couch with the remote control in his wrinkled hands. If I concentrate, I could catch a blur out of my peripheral vision that would be Meli walking briskly by on her way to the kitchen. But our group now, small though it is, still fills our living space, and it's still a lovingly flawed little family of sorts.

Bea is talking with my father, who is sipping from a mug, and Luke is unwrapping a lollipop for Joe. Prue is almost asleep on the recliner, and she jerks herself awake every couple of minutes when her eyelids begin to droop closed. Israel is putting in the batteries for the new walkie-talkie. It's started raining heavily outside, and the darkness of evening has fallen. You don't have to see the drops to know they are big and falling fast and in sheets. If I tune out the noise inside my house, I can even hear the splashing sound they make as they hit the porch. It's not a night to be outside, and with a start, I think of Rose. If she is out there in that abandoned old house, she's cold, wet, and must be miserable. I had meant to go back out there today, but between work, shopping with Emme, and planning Joe's impromptu birthday gathering my chance was lost.

It's almost as though Luke hears my thoughts. He looks over at me as Emme pins in place what I hope is to be the last of the headache inducing pins, and gives me a reassuring smile. It is almost as though he's telling me it's okay, that she's not there, and never was. The look also says she's someplace better and we'll find her soon. My imagined translations of Luke's smiles help a little and now that Emme has relinquished the comb, I get up and stretch my legs and go to serve the ice cream with candles, of course.

That night after Luke, Emme, Bea, and Joe have all left, Israel went to the hospital to work for a couple of hours. Dad and Prue go to bed, and I stand in the kitchen and shake out the very last Nightfall pill into my palm. It's ridiculous how quickly I've gone through this bottle. When was the last time I slept deeply without help? I know without looking that there are violet colored circles under my eyes, but I also know without aid, I won't be able to sleep with my family. I can feel in my bones that we are traveling soon, and now is not the time to chance it. I swallow the last pill before going to bed.

It's a murky kind of place that I slip into, but it isn't fully sleep. It isn't dreaming that I'm doing it's more of a pondering and remembering that my brain does as it whirls around in my head.

I am thinking of being a child again, that same fireplace hearth and of my mother and of Old Babba. I was so little that I could fit very comfortably under the small wooden table that we ate at. I have draped two blankets over the top and fashioned myself a fort of sorts. I have my doll in there, and a snack of dried fruit in a little clay pot that I pretended to stir and make into something else. I drank imaginary tea from a thimble that I shared with my doll, and taught her not to slurp and to blow on it properly. I played very quietly because I had already been scolded once for being too loud and for bothering my little sister. I heard Old Babba come into our kitchen and Mother greeted her. I pressed my fingers to my lips to keep the groaning sound from coming out and causing me to be scolded again. I hated that old neighbor lady of ours, but last time I said so, Mother swatted me on the backside and told me not to be saucy. I continued to play with my thimble, my doll, and our pot of fruit. I didn't begin listening to Old Babba until she became too loud to dismiss and ignore.

"You'll bring nothing but trouble to this place, Carolina," she said. "You and that girl of yours."

I wonder what kind of trouble Old Babba was afraid of my mother causing. And me? What could a child of not even five cause to happen? Was she just a meddlesome busybody leaving venomous words in her path, not caring who she insulted and accused? Why did my mother put up with her?

My whirling thoughts are brought to a sudden halt when I hear the screech of tires outside my window. I see the familiar lights of the Blue Beast as they turn into our driveway. They shine right into my window and onto my bedroom wall. I wonder what the screeching was all about, and since I'm not sleeping anyway, I leave my bedroom and tiptoe down the stairs. Israel is taking off his jacket when I reach him and I give him a quizzical glance.

"What was the noise out there?"

"I don't know." He rubs his five o'clock shadow. "Thought I saw something. Too big to be Gladys' cat, must have been a stray dog or something. I was afraid I was going to hit it so I ended up hitting the curb instead. How was the rest of the party? Joe have fun?"

"Mmhmm."

"You look exhausted." Israel stares at me concerned. "Are you not sleeping?"

I shake my head. "I feel like a zombie. I'm sure I'll fall asleep eventually. I'll probably not get up until noon tomorrow."

"Well, get some rest." He heads towards his bedroom. "Goodnight."

"Goodnight." I sigh and head back to my respective bedroom as well. I walk to my window to peer out through the sheets of rain still falling. Everything is dark except for one dim street light near Gladys' house. It illuminates her side yard and her sweet little fencing. A shape that is surely what Israel almost hit with his car appears in the light too, the shape of a slim woman wearing a soaked red dress. Her hair is ghostly white in the light and plastered to the sides of her beautiful face, and dripping down her back. Her feet are bare, and she is standing in a pool of water as she stares up at me in my window.

Chapter 16

Once when I was about twelve, I came upon a deer and her little baby drinking from a pond. I was up in a tree at the time, and I had a perfect view of them. They didn't know I was up there, and I sat there for the longest time just watching and admiring the way their red dappled fur shone in the sun. I so desperately wanted to get closer to them, but I was torn. If I left my perch in the tree I would have to take my eyes off them, and there would be no guarantee that once I could look again they would still be there.

Now was like that time, but in place of the sunlight and deer, I am staring breathlessly at shadows and Rose. She doesn't move and neither do I for what seems like the longest time. I don't think I am breathing. Finally, I lift my hand and press it against the glass where the condensation has proven I am indeed alive and breathing.

The second I move, Rose winces as though slapped. I see her feet step backward, out of that pool of dim light that bathes the sidewalk. She nearly disappears in that step, but not quite and with my heart in my throat I can no longer wait motionless. I whirl away from my window and thunder down the stairs. My house is quiet and dark and because I don't bother flipping a light switch, I nearly trip on an end table as I round the corner at the bottom of the stairs. My toes throb from the collision, but I don't stop running, and throw open the front door stepping onto my porch.

I suddenly stop, willing my eyes to adjust to the dark focusing on the streetlight and what lies beyond it. I cannot make out any shape, any woman standing there, only Gladys' fence and her ivy that crawls up it in picturesque curlicues. I am sorrowed but not surprised to know she is gone. God knows I want to sink to the porch and cry there in the rain, but I won't let the sorrow defeat me. Instead I cross the street more cautiously choosing my footing, my eyes always several yards ahead of my feet.

The rain is still coming down in sheets, soaking me instantly. My nightgown is drenched and cold, and the varied coins that I have sewn into the hem over the years clank against my ankles. They feel heavy like they could drag me down, and there is enough rain collected in the street that it splashes mightily with every step. I wrap my arms around myself for warmth, and step exactly into the spot where Rose had been only moments before. I stay there soaking in the light from the lamp, trying to feel her essence, her thoughts, her plans, anything. It seems obvious now that she doesn't want to be found, and yet isn't she making herself known? Have I really stumbled upon her twice or three times now without her knowledge? That seems too incredible to be true, and yet why would she continue to hide from me?

This is maddening. I am soaked. It is so dark. Why did I have to move into such a poorly lit community? This is the only street light for nearly two blocks. The shadows Rose has disappeared into are all around me. She could be anywhere, even four feet from me, watching.

I call her name but my voice comes back to me, void and fruitless. I walk calling aloud, until my throat hurts, and the shivering takes over. I continue walking and calling until I can call no more.

Then I go inside my house where I pick up Israel's jacket off the back of the couch. I put it on, wrapping it nearly twice around my frame. I slip my arms into the sleeve and savor the warmth for only a minute. Then, my thoughts repeating an endless refrain of *please, please, please*, I dip my hands into the pockets. My fingers wrap around the contents and I pull out the car keys.

I debate the wisdom or folly of stopping to wake up Luke and ask for his company. For that matter, I could have brought Israel or even Prue or Dad, surely he has a right to this as much as I do. I feel as though my sanity is reaching a breaking point, and it's as if I don't want there to be an audience when I finally come to my own conclusion. This shroud of mystery surrounding my sister is going to disappear like the mist tonight; I will make it so.

My resolve doesn't keep me warm and although my arms and chest feel better in Israel's lightweight coat, my legs and especially my feet are chilled through. My bare feet work the pedals of the Blue Beast, my frozen toes clutching at the pedals. It would only have taken another moment to run upstairs and get my shoes, but of course, I was in no state of mind to be pragmatic. My hair is still halfway braided from Emme's handiwork, and the rest taken out after she left. It drips down my neck wet with sweat and rain. I find the dial for the heater and crank it up as I turn out of town, the way we had gone when Luke took me to the empty house. I felt Rose's presence there as surely as I felt his next to me.

I find the way with surprisingly little trouble. It's as though I'm following the trail of breadcrumbs left behind from a little girl who wanted to be discovered. The road is bumpy but straight, the moon playing peek-a-boo with me through the pines the way it did before. The familiarity of that comforts me somehow. Other than that, the darkness is oppressive. If I thought my street was dark, it was a well-lit crystal chandelier compared to this heavy blanket of black. It had taken me a few moments to find the switch to the headlights of the car, but when I did they shone like a beacon, slicing through the night's ebony cloak ahead.

We pass the first house Luke and I had broken into. It sits, dejected and deserted, like a lonely child at the playground that everyone has run off and left. I can make out the overgrown yard and the caved-in barn next to it as I drive by. She isn't there. I know where she is.

The next house is my destination, and it is dark, still, and silent. I kill the engine, and see the same dead tree sitting upon the same tumbled down side of the same house. The same sunken porch is right where I left it, and I can even see the tire tracks of Luke's truck. There is no hospitable light, no flickering candle or lamp to welcome me.

The butterflies in my stomach are doing unbearable flips and somersaults now, I search Israel's glove box and backseat to no avail. There is no helpful flashlight for my search. I leave the headlights of the Blue Beast on, shining brightly, mere feet away from the front door. The lights are spotlighting my destination, the front door, the door to my sister. I'll make her see she has nothing to fear from me, that she can leave this place, and come home to her very own father, and live happily ever after.

It will happen. I can make this happen. If only I could leave the car.

It will happen.

It is so dark and I am so very cold.

I have finally left the warmth of the car, leaving behind with it what seems to be all my courage and resolve. I am a strange mess of emotions as I turn the knob and push open the rusty, drafty front door. My stomach feels as though a hurricane is going on inside it, I am nauseated and shaky at the premonition of being so close to Rose that I almost touch her. I would not be able to explain to Luke or Israel or Dad why I know she's here; she simply is as am I. We are breathing the same air, holding our breaths in the same places, as we find the valor to step forward and claim each other. The only difference is that I can't see her, and yet I feel she sees me from somewhere in the dark.

I speak and I astonish myself by sounding very steady and sure. Inside I am a quaking mass of jelly but to anyone listening, I am granite firm and stable. "Rose? Rose Gray? It's Sonnet, honey, I'm here to take you home. Rose?"

My steady, firm call echoes eerily in the stillness. The air feels thick with the hush that is nothing calling back to me. Nothing answers me. Nothing responds to my invitation.

I begin the climb up the staircase.

The stairs and what lies at the top of them is beyond the reach of the radiant headlights of the car outside. Five more stairs and I will be engulfed in darkness, swallowed by shadows of things I cannot see. Four. Three. Before I can lose what is left of my courage, I take the last two at once and am at the landing. My left hand grasps the old wooden rail with a desperation that I know turns my knuckles white even if I can't see them. My other hand is clenched in a fist so tight that my nails make jagged half-moon shapes in my palm. It isn't the darkness that is scaring me any longer; it's the sound I can just barely make out. A soft whisper that at first sounds like a breath. A breath that becomes my name.

Sonnet.

"Yes!" I call. My voice is loud and painful to my ears.

Sonnet.

I nearly run to where I think I hear the voice. If my blind sense of direction is accurate, it's the room with the mattress that I had been in earlier. The one I was sure had Rose on the other side of the door when I was with Luke, though he had heard no one. I fling the door open with such power that not only does it grant me entry, but it ricochets back again and slams shut with me on the inside. I can do nothing but stand still for a moment and let my eyes adjust to the dark. There should be a window, but instead there is only tiny slits of light on the wall. There are now boarded up planks of wood, where the broken window had been the last time I was here. The mattress I can just barely make out, but there is no one atop of it. There is the crookedly hung closet door, and it looms at me. It is only a door, not a person. Not Rose.

With my heart beating so loudly and my breath so labored it is a wonder I can hear anything at all, but I do.

I hear the unmistakable sound of a key in the lock of the door that had slammed shut behind me and, the scratching sound of a deadbolt being slid into place. The next sound I hear is the very, very soft sound of someone's dreadful laughter.

Chapter 17

It has been hours. I know because the moonlight that was visible through the slats of the planks nailed to the window became sunlight hours ago. It has also been hours since I bothered banging on the door, or kicking, or shouting, or whimpering. The rest of the time has been spent staying awake, which is getting more and more impossible by the ticking of my body's clock. I am terrified to sleep; yet I want to sink into that blissful oblivion more than anything. My body aches, my head pounds, and everything that dwells within me from my kidneys to my lungs feels as though they are stuffed with sand weighing me down from the inside out. Even my hair feels heavy and what a lovely pillow it would be...fanned out around my face and sleep...

Stop it, Sonnet. Your family is far from here. This is no time for slumber. My thoughts take on a stern, reproaching tone, as if I were my own mother. I stretch my fingers, clench and unclench, watching my knuckles, and chewing my nails, anything to stay awake. I stand. I sit. I don't lie down. And to keep my mind busy, I remember.

My favorite monk at the monastery, was young, surprisingly so. In my small child's mind, I had imagined monks to be old and wizened, stooped over and wrinkled. But this monk was young with baby fat in his cheeks which were as smooth as the perfectly carved statue I played with on the floor. I never knew his name, at my age I never thought to ask. I was still young enough to make friends with anyone who would have me, and names, ages, or genders didn't factor. Prue had fallen ill the moment we'd arrived here and had been in bed ever since. Dad was around, but not around for me. We had awoken to the sound of a flock of birds and our faces pressed to the very dewy grass. I remember opening my eyes, knowing I would not see what I had fallen asleep seeing, but instead something new, some place new. I could tell by the wet grass and new smells that things weren't the same. Would it be nice? I wondered. Would I like it here?

I spent so much time lying there, my eyes squeezed shut, imagining my new surroundings - a castle with a princess? A farm with horses for me to ride? Suddenly I became aware of breathing on my face. I lay still, pondering if this hot stinky breath could be Dad or Prue, and then I heard a snort. With startled reflexes my eyes flew open of their own accord, and I was face to face with a huge cow. I screamed like a baby and woke up Prue and Dad.

We were in a field in the middle of Spring, and I later learned it was twelfth century Spain. After the initial shock wore off and after I had apologized most sincerely to the cow, we walked until we found the monastery. They welcomed us politely enough. Visitors who were lost, and hungry were not uncommon. We could speak their language, but not that much conversation went on in that place, and we blended in as seamlessly as we always had. The lies dripped from our lips as easily as they had dropped from our own Lost ancestor's. I didn't even feel guilty for lying to monks, though oddly enough I felt guilty for not feeling guilty.

My favorite monk was silent as a tomb, but he didn't ignore me. He took me along as he plucked sweet potatoes in the garden or as he painstakingly copied the Bible, letter by Latin letter. I had learned to read by then, but my letters were terrible. Prue had no patience for teaching me and she would bark corrections at my funny shaped words, and tell me I was wasting paper. But this monk wrote every bit as slowly as I did! He took all day to copy one beautiful sentence. He would decorate each and every curlicue, every hole and every loop. When he saw my interest, he handed me my very own quill and ink and let me practice copying what he wrote and drew. It entertained me for hours, working in silence side by side; the only noise or sounds between us was the scratching on the parchment. Gradually, Prue got better and the monks tired of Dad's constant sampling of their wines. We spoke of moving on, finding our own place to live. I cried that when we finally left, and I embraced my monk friend. He gifted me with the quill I favored, and I had it sewn into my nightgown. Eventually it snapped in several places, and the feathers all but disintegrated into my hem.

I hear a rooster from a farmhouse that can't be too far away. If only I could crow as loudly, maybe someone would hear me and come pounding up the stairs to my rescue. Instead the only pounding heard is that of my frightened and panicked heart. The laughter I had heard as the door locked last night still chilled my blood and echoed in my mind. The rooster makes me wish for Prue's rooster stew. I must be hungry if I am salivating at the thought of that chewy, tough bird. She used to make rooster stew in Portugal. Henrique loved it. I didn't, but I'd give anything for a big steaming bowl of it now.

"Father says we must be grateful for the way the Lord provides no matter what," said Molly. The daughter of the missionary was my age, but far nicer and sweeter than I would ever be. She had seen me make grimaces at the stew, and watched me pretend to gag. No doubt she was hoping not only to keep me from punishment from her father, but also from everlasting punishment from our Heavenly Father. Molly was forever trying to save my soul, since it was obvious I wasn't putting in much effort myself.

"Yes, Molly." I sighed. I forced some of the greasy, chewy lumps down my throat. Dad wordlessly passed me some fiery hot powder made from ground peppers that transforms the taste of everything. I dumped a liberal helping into my stew and could no longer taste anything as my tongue promptly felt as though it had burst into flames. Coughing and sputtering, I pushed back my chair from the table and reached for the water which was kept in a large ewer in the kitchen. It was almost bone dry and so with my eyes watering, I rushed out the door and down to the river still hacking and wheezing. I knelt down, my long skirts dragging in the mud, my hated corset making it difficult and painful to bend at the waist. I drank mouthful after mouthful of warm river water from my cupped hands. Finally, I had to come up for air, pushing the wet, snake-like tendrils of my disheveled hair away from my face. I saw Henrique standing nearby, watching. Henrique was always watching, and the thought of being alone with him always sent shivers up my spine. He was most likely harmless, but he was the sort who tortured insects and frogs and pulled apart worms with his teeth. All in all, he

was not someone I wanted to be left alone with at the side of a river with no witnesses.

"Drink?" I offered. Which was ridiculous because I didn't have anything with which to give him a drink in besides my own hands, and that was certainly not a possibility.

"No, thank you." He moved closer. I debated splashing mud in his eye and making a run for it. "You look nice today."

I didn't look nice that day. I hadn't washed my hair in weeks and it was a hot summer. However, Henrique had no standards. I wore a skirt and a corset that while despised by my aching lungs, did wonders for my fifteen-year-old figure. Therefore, I evidently looked nice. Nice to chop into small pieces and add to his rooster stew, I thought.

"Umm, thank you. I'm heading back now. Don't want anyone to think I've choked to death!" I said flippantly. I hesitated briefly seeing as how Henrique was in my way if I wish to end up back at the missionary's house. I gathered my spunk and marched past him, head held high and the urge to cough still in my throat and lungs. He didn't follow me back to the house, but I knew he stood there watching as I left.

That next day was the day we met Israel. Matthias and Harry found him while they were out fishing. They knew straight away he was Lost: he had no horse with which to have brought him to our desolate spot. The boatman who typically brought us any visitors had been ill and bedridden, and the village nearby did not know him. He was a stranger with no logical story to excuse his manifestation in our location. That is something I learned later about Israel; he does not lie as readily as the rest of us do. Of course, being so unapproachably tall, intimidating as he is, it makes people question him less. He can glare or offer some noncommittal response or simply say nothing at all and very few men will press him for answers. He was tired and wounded (from what I still don't know to this day) and so hungry he ate all of Prue's rooster stew left over from the night before. He had next to no contact or conversation with me but I found him interesting and I wanted to be *near him. I was immersed in my studies and in my avoidance of Henrique, and thus had little opportunity to get to know our resident stranger.*

Later, after we had gotten over the discomfiture and awkwardness at being thrown together in life, we would begin to spend longer periods of time talking. He disregarded my questions about his life thus far, but of course, I talked and talked enough for the both of us. Molly was terrified of him and spent most of her time trying to repent of her fear, which she considered ungodly and un-evangelistic. By the time we left Portugal and traveled on, Molly and I had grown apart, Henrique had disappeared, and Israel was one of us.

I was so pleased to have left corsets behind.

* * *

The sunlight which had peeked through the boards in my window so forcefully and cheerfully had faded to the duskiness of twilight. I am alone in the dark once more. To the best of my knowledge without a watch to tell me differently, I have been locked in this room for nearly 24 hours. It has been nearly double that since I've slept. I am nauseated from the need to relieve my bladder but I refuse to give in and do the unthinkable on the floor like an animal. The minute I do that I will know I am officially a prisoner.

My thoughts are jumbled and running together. Nothing is rational or logical. My memories are blended with my dreams, my imaginings, and snippets of television or movies I've seen. I have gone from thinking and remembering to singing. Whatever comes into my frazzled brain: bawdy Irish drinking songs, Spanish love songs, Elvis Presley, children's limericks set to tune, hymns, Christmas carols, The Supremes. I sing softly at first, then louder, no longer caring if someone sits on the other side of that door mocking me.

My throat begins to hurt from the singing and from the shouting I had done earlier. I had beaten my fists against the door until my knuckles were bruised. In a house that was falling apart how could one old door defeat me? I had kicked, pummeled, and pushed the planks that boarded up the one window, but the screws and nails used were long and the wood thick and heavy. There were splinters under my fingernails from digging at the wood and trying to pry them away from their fastenings.

My head has gone from pounding to being listlessly quiet and rather empty feeling. I am not thinking at all any longer. My mind is a black hole from which no thoughts echo. I am so tired that I no longer even want to throw up from my aching bladder, but simply want to give up and put my head down. The only thought far off in the distant regions of my brain, is that if I sleep I may lose my whole family.

Will they sleep without me? I wonder. Have they already? Did they travel without me last night, as they lay in bed, while I was traipsing through this haunted house looking for ghosts? Are they hundreds of years in the past looking for me frantically? Prue a mess of worries, Dad searching for a bottle as frenetically as he looks for his daughter. Israel penetrating the surroundings looking for the tall girl with the light eyes who used to be his friend. Will they grieve for me the way they grieved for Rose? With arms around each other, will they say, *I do hope she found a home with Gladys?*

Now my head slips down, down, down. Down to the old smelly mattress beneath me. It's no longer me who wars with sleep. I don't war with anything any longer. I give up and give in. The comfort of my decision makes the corners of my mouth turn up in a slight smile. Quietly, I hear the faintest of all scratching noises. If the room hadn't been so silent for so very long, perhaps I wouldn't hear it, but I do. As quickly as it started, it's gone. I want to spring to my feet, but my feet don't oblige. My legs buckle under my weight, and I am back down on the mattress once more. I try to call out, but my throat is parched and my words unvoiced. It takes everything I have for a moment just to stand and wobble like a fawn or a newborn colt to the door.

The knob turns as easily as if it had just been oiled.

Chapter 18

I skim down the dark stairs as though I am a weightless ghost, and I feel as though I may be. Sonnet Gray, dead in this lifeless house, doomed to haunt it for all eternity. My feet barely skim the floor at the bottom of the stairs as I fling myself at the front door, and out into the night air. The first thing I see is the sun coming up over the trees, the second is the Blue Beast sitting quietly where I left it. My foggy brain doesn't register the fact that the headlights are no longer shining like a symbol of hope, instead they are cold, silent, and dark. I give a little cry as I realize suddenly what that means, the car is as good as deceased. I killed the battery, and without another car to jump start it, the Blue Beast will stay right here, silent as a tomb.

My fingers which had already grasped the door handle to the car eagerly only seconds before flex and release, and I slide my tired body to the ground. I debate just staying there for the rest of my life which seems quite short and pointless anyway. I am too tired to fear whoever locked me in that room, and whoever let me out. My brain is too weary to form any type of plan. Lying in the mud seems a very viable and intriguing option, but if Prue and Dad have managed to stay awake and wait for me, I cannot keep them any longer.

That is the only fuzzy logic that gets me to my feet again. I relieve my aching bladder behind a tree and then rummage in the Blue Beast for nourishment. I find a can of almonds in the console and the bottom inch of a bottle of water that had rolled under the driver's seat, and I make short use of them. Feeling somewhat better, at least somewhat less sick, I begin to walk.

I think I am walking like a drunken man or like a woman balancing on a tightrope. Lean, correct, stumble, over correct. I weave around the road in aimless patterns and I know I am doing it, but I am powerless to straighten myself out. My feet drag, which hurts the soles of my bare feet, but I cannot find the energy it would require to step higher.

The sun rises illuminating more of the road ahead of me.

Once I look back because I think I can hear the softest sound of someone calling me, but all I see is that hateful house, getting mercifully smaller the farther I walk away.

The road I travel on is going to intersect with another road just up ahead, I can see the road signs and the way the two roads make a cross at their juncture. It is only a few yards away from me now, and I can hear the rumble of a car approaching where the roads meet. I begin to make out its shape, its fuchsia color, the smallness of a two door little hatchback. I see it nearing the cross, and I know that if the road I travel on has a stop sign, then perhaps the road the fuchsia car travels on does not. It will speed by and not look my way.

I call out frantically and attempt to run trying to be at the cross at the same time as the car, but it is fruitless. If the driver of the fuchsia car sees me, a dirty girl in a long tattered nightgown, he will think he sees a ghost.

Am I a ghost?

I walk.

I miss driving. I miss the speed, the way the machine hugged the curves, the way my hand would dangle out the window, and I would feel so glamorous and modern.

I continue to put one sore foot in front of the other. My toes are dirty and my heels bruised. I realize eventually when I do not stumble into town, or anything that remotely resembles a town, that I have gotten myself lost. I am Lost and I am lost. I laugh out loud. What a dunce I am. I must be the worst heroine in history.

When plotting your next escape, Sonnet old girl, try to remember to turn left at the abandoned scary house, and not right. That'd be great. Thanks.

I decide to sit down and let someone find me. Isn't that what we learn as little children? If you are lost, stay put and let Mum and Dad find you. Well, I think crossly, dear Mum isn't coming and Dad can't seem to find his own way home these days, much less find me. Prue doesn't drive, Bea and Emme won't know where to look, Israel has had his car stolen by the girl in question, and Luke...Luke should know where to look!

I have to believe that Luke will know where to look.

I send him what I hope are telepathic messages to turn left and not right after he's searched the house. Will the someone who locked me in and then let me out try the same thing with him? Is it only I that is being messed with emotionally, and as I look down at my feet, physically? Is Rose traveling with a sociopath? Or was Rose never there at all?

I lean against a tree trunk on the side of the lonely dirt road as I ponder. My body feels heavy again, and my hopes of reaching town on my own without sleep have diminished. I can't do this anymore. No one can stay awake forever.

I am realizing this when I hear the motor of a car, and see the dust billow up on the road, coming closer and closer. An expensive looking car pulls up beside me. It is silver and the windows are tinted black. I hear the driver's side door open and slam shut with excessive force. I know I should be very happy about this change of events in my circumstances, but I am simply too weary. I don't even stand; I simply watch as my rescuer comes around the large car and to my side.

My eyes are too heavy to really focus and the form of a person swims before me, blurry and fuzzy around the edges. His voice, when he speaks, sounds distant and remote.

He also sounds angry, I realize with a little surprise, and although I am having trouble with my ears making sense of his diatribe, he appears to be cursing.

"Get in the car," Israel says, slowly and with measured fury. Without so much as a soft word in my direction, he lifts me bodily and deposits me on the soft seat of the car.

Chapter 19

"Start talking," Israel demands as we speed off down the dirt road. "Now."

"Thank you for finding me, Iz," I whisper. "I'm going to sleep now."

"Oh no, you're not. Talk! What is going on? What happened to you?"

In my head, I explain it all coherently, Israel understands, and we go home. But I cannot seem to make my lips work properly or form articulate sentences. I mumble something, but I am not even sure what language I speak it in, if it's a language at all and not just gibberish. I think it may be Spanish. Israel glances over at me in alarm.

"Just hang on then," he says. "We'll be home soon. Everyone is out looking for you, even Matthias and Harry. We're all going on too little sleep. Just hang on until we can all be together, Sonnet. Don't sleep without us. Don't travel without us."

I nod in obedience, but my eyes are already shut fast and it would take an act of God to open them.

"She's only been asleep for ten minutes," I faintly hear Israel say. My body has been pulled out of the car with very little care and ceremony. If I ever wake up fully I plan to correct Israel's manhandling and lack of gentleness. As I lay like a sack of bones in Israel's arms, I feel several hands on me. One on my cheek, another on my wrist, and one feels like a complete set of arms around my waist.

"Ten minutes is all she's getting," I hear Prue's bark. "Get her in the bathtub."

"Bath would be nice, but later please," I mumble.

My requests are ignored, and after we get to the top of the stairs through the narrow squeeze of the bathroom door, I am dumped awkwardly in the hard, cold porcelain tub.

"Ouch!" I rub my shins and sit up.

My finally open eyes are met with five other pairs, all staring at me. Prue looks so angry she makes Iz look like a teddy bear, Dad looks like he has been awake even longer than I have, and Matthias and Harry have clearly been crying.

"I'm very glad to see you," I say and then I promptly burst into tears.

"You had me worn to the bone with worry and grief, child." Prue turns on the water. It is frosty cold, and I yelp. The iciness stops my crying. "What did you mean going off with the car? We had no way of knowin' where you went, when you'd be back. We've been up all night waiting for you!"

I consider pointing out that I've been up for two nights and then some, but I think better of it. I sit meekly watching the tub fill up around me, the water turning warm, the edges of my nightgown darkening and billowing out in the tiny pool. The water is already turning grimy and dirty.

"I was looking for Rose," I say stealing a glance at Dad as I say it. He does not react. "She was here. I thought I knew where she might have gone, so I found the car keys and went after her. I went to an old house where I thought she was staying, but I got locked in. I couldn't find a way out until this morning, and then I started walking and got lost." I am too tired, and too confused to say anymore.

Prue doesn't even appear to be listening, she is scrubbing my hands and elbows with a bar of soap. She turns off the water, lets it drain, and then fills it back up again. It will take more than one bath to get me clean again, especially wearing this nightgown.

"Israel came and got us when you went missing and we came straight away," says Harry. His lip quivers like a small boy who is trying to be

152

brave and not cry. "We didn't know where to look so we went to the soup kitchen, checked with your friends at the coffee shop. Just got back here a bit ago to check in. So relieved you're back, honey."

"Thanks, Harry. I'm sorry I messed up your travel plans."

"Aw, you didn't mess anything up."

I feel my eyes closing again, but Prue splashes water on my face.

Really, as far as a rescue and welcome home committee, my family is not the top of the line.

What feels like a torturous number of hours later, is really less than one. I am clean, my hair shampooed, my nightgown thrown in the laundry, although it may not be salvageable. I am wearing clean clothes, I have obediently eaten scrambled eggs and toast, and I am at last in my bed. Emme has come over, and embraced me ferociously, and left again. Finally, someone who doesn't yell at me to show they care. No one has forced more explanations from me, though Israel looks at me from underneath hooded, suspicious eyes. He holds his tongue for now, but I know instinctively that when we wake I am going to be drilled with questions.

Everyone is almost as exhausted as I am and they all are as happy to drop into their beds, but Harry and Matthias leave for their new home first. It is not even twilight, but it no longer matters, if we all sleep together we don't care what time of day or night it is. Dad tucks me in like a little girl and I am touched by this rare demonstration of sentimentality.

"You scared me," he says from his perch on the side of my bed. "Don't do that again. Please."

"Yes, Dad," I promise and put my hand over his. His trembles just a bit. With his free hand, he reaches up and smoothes his eyebrow. Then he reaches over and brushes my hair back from my forehead. I feel pleased and honored to be the recipient of his nervous habits somehow. "I just wanted to find Rose, and be together again, like it used to be."

"Rose is gone, Sonnet. Your mother is gone. I couldn't bear it if I lost you too." I realize then that he is not slurring his speech and that his eyes are clear and focused on mine. Has my disappearance sobered him?

"Yes, Dad," I repeat and blink the tears from my eyes. "I'm sorry. Do you feel it coming?"

I speak of traveling. That feeling that has been lingering in my mind and emotions for days now. To my surprise, he seems to know exactly what I'm referring to.

"Yes," he says. "It's coming."

I sleep.

I sleep like the dead and it feels so lovely that when I feel strong hands shaking me awake hours later, I squeeze my eyes closed tighter and mutter a threat. The hands are persistent and I can't ignore them much longer. I open my eyes and scowl at Dad.

Besides the worried and nervous look on his face, the smell is the first thing that clues me in. An odor of cabbage and cold humidity wafts by my nostrils, like the smell of dank heavy fog mixed with old vegetables. The aromas, though not entirely pleasant, match my surroundings, and I'm not in my bedroom. It is not my house, my town, or even the same century I fell asleep in. There are cobblestones beneath me, hard and unyielding. I am curled up against a wall, and on inspection it seems to be a very large building on a very English looking street. London, I'd wager, not because I am an expert on architecture or geography, but because of the frowning mustached man looming over me. He is quite obviously British, from his well-trained mustache to his bowler hat and walking cane. If that hadn't been enough to tip me off, his accent certainly convinces me.

"Get up then, miss." He pokes me with the tip of his cane. "There isn't any loitering in this neighborhood. This is a respectable neighborhood, and I'll thank you, sir," he turns his attention to my father, "To stay out of it."

Dad only blinks, touches his own mustache indifferently, and nods.

The man makes a humphing sound and continues his walk down the street. He tips his hat to a smartly dressed lady with a parasol as they pass, and the woman frowns at me, stepping farther away from my vicinity as she walks by.

Wonderful. Corsets. Just my luck. My ribs ache already at the very real memory of whale bone cutting into them. I stand with a sigh.

"Prue and Israel?" I ask Dad.

"Here." He nods. "Been up a little bit. Went to find things out, thought we'd let you sleep as long as possible."

"Thanks." It's very cold, there is slush on the street, and I jump from one foot to the other to keep warm. My head feels foggy, I'm still not quite awake. I feel the encroaching thoughts of reality coming, and I ache to keep them at bay. I do not want to deal with them just yet. I do not want to think of the coffee shop, Luke, or Emme, Bea, and Joe. I do not want to think of anything at all. Though I am determined to stick my head in the sand, or the slush as it were, I am incapable and tiny images of the past wander through my head the way your whole life flashes before you when you die. In a way, I feel as though I am dead. I am certainly dead to Micki, to my customers, to Jim and everyone at the soup kitchen, and to Luke.

Although I have known him the least amount of time, my chest aches with a dullness when I think of Luke Dawes. The way he would show up uninvited at my house, our silly little date, the way he humored me by taking me to that old house to look for my invisible sister. The way he doctored up his black coffee until it was unrecognizable and then scowled at me over it. His big feet stretched out in front of him, lined up with mine as we sat together. If he truly believed my story, he will know I am not dead, but traveling. Will he miss me? I wonder.

Dad takes my arm and begins to steer me towards the street. Though the wind does not blow, the air is still cold, and I wrap my arms around myself with Dad's hand in the crook of my elbow. I am wearing what I put on to go to sleep in last night which was at least a hundred years in the future, judging by the fashions on the corseted lady, and I must look a sight in my second best nightgown. Of course my feet are bare, as are Dad's, and they feel nearly frozen trudging through the slush as we cross the street. I feel strangely uncurious about our surroundings, about our new home here. I don't care that it may be exciting to live in England so long ago, I don't care that we could have landed somewhere much worse. I want instead, to pout and be sullen over the loss of my old life. The loss of Elvis Presley, Gladys, the Blue Beast, and cheese in a can. Who wants to live in a century without frothed milk, art shows, and Stevi Nicks? Not me. I refuse to look around me and admire the architecture, not yet anyway. It feels disloyal somehow.

We are headed in the vicinity of what I know now to be Prue. She is standing at the other end of the street, not alone, and as we approach I can tell she is arguing vehemently with the person. Home sweet home is my Prue.

"It was bloody well your fault, boy, and you know it!" Prue berates a boy, maybe twelve or so, who looks quite terrified. He is hopping from one foot to the other, as though he is warming up his legs in order to take off at a moment's notice. Either that, or his feet are as cold as mine, though I doubt it in his boots. I eye them longingly. It is usually Israel that begs, borrows, or steals clothes for us all in times like these and I mentally beseech him to hurry before frostbite kicks in.

"I didn't mum, not exactly!" he wheedles. "I didn't mean to knock into you like that, I didn't! It's just now I've lost them veg and if I don't bring something back to show for my trouble, my employer is going to have my hide! It was your fault as well as mine, mum. You gotta help me by paying for your share!"

Although I don't know what this boy is blathering on about, I have to give him respect for taking on the likes of Prue. He's either remarkably brave or extraordinarily stupid.

"That's a laugh, boy, you came runnin into me! Me, an old lady! Now you want to exploit me for the damages!" Prue snorts and humphs and makes a general show of her displeasure. I haven't figured out her game, but she's playing at something, I'd bet on it. "Do I look like I have any money?" She gestures to her nightgown, with her favorite apron tied on top. The boy reddens up and looks away.

"Well, I can't go back empty handed," he mumbled. "Gotta have some story at least for why I lost all the veg. Can't just admit I knocked it in the river, can I? Cook will kill me if the master doesn't beat her to it." He looks quite miserable. Even his feet quit their incessant dancing and he holds still morosely, staring at the river to his left as though willing his missing vegetables to bob to the dirty surface. It must be the River Thames and it looks like nothing so much as slow moving sludge, as thick as cake batter and dark as chocolate in places.

"Cook, eh?" Prue narrows her black eyes. "A good cook, is she?"

It's the boy's turn to snort. "Who? Gertie? She's real good, mum, real good if you like the taste of coal!" He bursts out laughing and slaps his knee at his own joke.

"And why doesn't your employer hire someone better for his meals then, eh?" She presses. Ah, I'm beginning to comprehend her wheeling and dealing now.

"Like who?" The boy looks suspicious. This small talk was not solving his problem and his feet begin hopping again.

"Like this poor woman you ran down and accosted," I cut in, adopting a strong British accent without even thinking. I join him in the feet dance in order to get my blood flowing and stay warm.

The boy widens his eyes. "You must be joking, miss. I can't just bring her back to the house!"

"Why not? You practically injured this poor old woman and now you're refusing her care and attention? Why, it's the least you can do! I witnessed the whole thing and I'm sure there's a policeman nearby who would be quite interested in the story. In fact, I'd wager that missing vegetables is the least of your criminal worries, young sir." I feel a little bad for him, but the lies drip easily off my tongue. I am freezing, and not going to let a chance of sitting by a fire somewhere pass by me without a fight.

The boy swallows visibly, his Adam's apple bobbing up and down, as he weighs his options. "Right then, mum. Miss." He bows my way. He even offers his arm gallantly to Prue.

"Oh, I don't think so, young man," I continue my stern voice. "I will personally accompany you, along with my father, to assure this unfortunate woman meets no other calamity at your hand." I hold my head high and wish I had a long skirt to swish majestically or a parasol to rap him on the head with. It is difficult to assume the identity of a snobbish gentlewoman with bare feet and all the wrong clothes. My manner seems to have the desired effect however. The boy sighs, but nods and we begin to walk together. Youth is no match for arrogant patronization no matter how confident the youth in question.

"Israel?" I whisper to Dad as we walk.

"Always go back to the beginning," he replies. A Lost rule if there ever was one. The rule is if you get separated after traveling, continue checking in at the spot where you woke up. I picture Israel wandering the streets of London in his pajamas and have to stifle a giggle. Dad's sleeping outfit is nondescript and doesn't seem too out of place wherever we go, a goal that most Lost women try to emulate with their white nightgowns. His dark pants and white button down shirt are surprisingly timeless, although very unfinished they could seem as though he was simply interrupted while dressing, thereby neglecting a coat, shoes, and hat. I groan when I think of my soiled and tattered nightgown back home. I have been in this century before, and surely had coins and money of value sewn into the hem. What a comfort they would be to me now and the things they could buy like hot bread with butter, lodging, and shoes.

As we walk, the sun continues to rise, the river continues to give off that cabbage-y smell I noticed before, and the city comes to life. People begin to emerge from their homes and businesses fling open their doors. I feel conspicuous in my cold feet and silly clothing, but other than a few odd looks, reminiscent of the corseted lady from earlier, I am ignored. The boy, Oliver, walks at a steady, brisk pace; whether to keep his body warm or to get to his destination, I don't know. He certainly goes to great lengths for his employer. It is quite a jaunt for a vegetable supply, but perhaps Gertie of coal cooking fame is particular with her groceries.

I keep my eyes searching for Israel as we walk, but we reach our end at a large house without having seen him, and enter through the back. Oliver leaves us in the kitchen where a large, rawboned woman, presumably Gertie herself. She eyes us suspiciously and stirs a spoon around a pot. Oliver had scurried out with nary an explanation for our manifestation in her kitchen, and when it seems that the anticipation has gotten to her so that she cannot bear it another second, she whirls around and brandishes her spoon.

"What's this all about then? You that brat's family? You expectin' me to feed you, are you?"

"On the contrary," I reply, rising as gracefully as I can considering my frozen muscles, which had only just begun to thaw out by the kitchen fire. "We are unrelated to the boy, but we do expect a hot meal and hospitality, as I'm sure the lord of the house will no doubt, concur. My father and I have surrendered our modesty and dignity to see this dear lady to safety after your kitchen boy nearly ran her down. We have been through a frightful adventure this morning and would like tea, please. Immediately." My words are not only for Gertie, since I have heard Oliver's footsteps returning and have seen a large shadow fallen across the hallway floor. My words are also for the ears of the master of the house.

Gertie eyes me thoughtfully before lowering her spoon. Whether or not she believes my ridiculous impersonation of a genteel lady caught in an unsavory episode is hardly my concern. What would Oliver's employer think? His retort answers my unspoken question.

"Gertie, hot tea. Madame, if you'll permit me?" A tall, willowy thin man steps into the kitchen and offers Prue his arm. "I have rung for the doctor, but in the meantime I must ask you to lie down and rest. Please forgive my impetuous Oliver, what his manners lack he makes up for in energy.

As far as you go, Sir, Miss," he nods the way of me and Dad, "I shall return shortly to sort this out. Oliver is bringing blankets to warm you and do not hesitate to ask Gertie of any nourishment you may require." He escorts Prue out of the room, bowing a bit as he does so, his heels clicking together as he dips his head.

When they are gone, Dad and I accept tea from a grudging Gertie and blankets from Oliver. My shivers subside and the tea feels like molten lava running down my throat. It's heavenly. Real English tea, Israel will be so happy.

"Who is your employer?" I ask Oliver in hushed tones as he settles by the fire near me.

"That's Sir Halloway, Reginald Halloway. It's just him who lives here in this big old house. Has a son, but he don't live here anymore. He's a ne'er do well," Oliver leans in to whisper this bit.

"Ah. And what exactly is a ne'er do well?"

"Oh you know," he waves his hand, "He's a scoundrel is what he is. Gambles away Daddy's money and spends it on the horses, booze, and the ladies." Oliver wiggles his eyebrows suggestively at me, and I have to turn my laugh into a ladylike cough.

"Sounds frightful," I reply, sipping the last of my tea. "I will be sure to avoid him at all costs. Thank you for warning me, Oliver. You're a good lad."

"You could certainly say so to Sir Halloway," he suggests earnestly, scooting closer. "You know I didn't mean to run down that old woman, don't you? She about came outta nowhere and plowed me down, that's what she did!"

I bet she did, I think to myself and probably threw the vegetables in the Thames for good measure. Thanks to Prue's ingenuity I have a belly full of tea, a warm blanket, and a hot fire. No matter that it may not last, I will take the gifts as they come, one at a time. I fully expect Prue to weave a story that will worm her way somehow into this house, but I don't expect Dad and me to be quite so lucky. Like Cinderella, our magic will wear off soon enough and we will be exposed for the frauds we are. If we can secure Prue a position though, and buy enough time for Israel to find clothing and shelter, our time here will be well spent.

"I'll put in a good word for you," I promise. "Whatever good it may do."

He smiles a smile that is full of sunshine, good humor, and at least a couple of missing teeth. "I like you. You make me think of Lady Halloway. She was tall like you, and had dark hair too."

"And what happened to Lady Halloway?"

"She ran off with the livery man," Oliver explains, matter of factly. "Terrible scandal it was."

"Oh lovely," I retort sarcastically. "I remind you of a scandalous trollop, is that right?"

Oliver chokes on his tea. "No, no, miss! Course not! I just meant she looked like you is all. Bout your size and coloring, that's it, miss. Begging your pardon, miss."

"No harm done, Oliver." I smile. I reach over and pinch Dad hard on his leg. He has been sitting, sipping tea, probably wishing for something stronger, and not listening. "Did you hear that, Father? I'm the same size as Lady Trollop, I mean, Halloway. Isn't that interesting?" I turn my attention back to Oliver. "I suppose Sir Halloway was dreadfully angry, and gave away all her things?"

"No, it's the opposite, miss. Why, he kept everything! Keeps her room a shrine to her, he does! Housekeeper tries to convince him to clean it all out, but he says no. It's a shame, it is."

As imperceptibly as possible, I nod towards the door that Prue had been escorted out, my eyes on Dad.

"A dress," I mouth, though in my head I added, "And hold the corset."

Chapter 20

With mumbled explanations that are intentional in their vagueness, Dad has exited the kitchen in his shifty quest for dresses, and I am left with Oliver and Gertie. Gertie has taken to ignoring me, either because she does not like me or because she is embarrassed to have spoken so harshly to someone who may or may not be a lady of high standing. Oliver on the other hand, prattles on about this and that. Although I had taken him to be about twelve when first we met, I would now place his age younger. His gawky limbs are newly elongated, I'd wager, and he hasn't grown into them yet. I remember those years, as I was a tall, lanky ten-year-old as well.

"You do seem a smart lad, Ollie. You don't mind that I call you Ollie, do you?"

He beams, his missing teeth a mischievous asset to his mouth. He nods.

"Well, Ollie, I'm sure I cannot perplex you if I tried, you being so very smart. What is four times two?"

He responds correctly.

"And what is the name of the third month of the year?"

Again, correct.

"And the date, Ollie? What is the date today? Don't forget the year now."

Oliver scrunches up his face thoughtfully. "Well, the year, that's easy. It's 1887. And I know it's December...I think it's the twentieth of December? Is that right, miss?" He looks very anxious.

"You are a sharp lad! Well done, Ollie!" And well done, Sonnet, I think to myself.

"And I'm sure you could spell the name of our dear city, now couldn't you?" I am certain it's just old London, but I would like to be very sure.

"L, O, N, D, I, N." Ollie grins.

"Close enough," I smile. "Listen, I think I hear your master approaching. We must look very busy and angelic." I wink at him. So much for my haughty lady impersonation, my new friend is simply too appealing to not want to be his friend. And I will need a friend in time.

"Please come this way, miss," says Sir Halloway as his reed thin frame reappears in the doorway of the kitchen once again. "Your father?"

"Looking for you it seems," I adopt my regal, snooty bearing and up my accent a notch. "He was quite cold and quite concerned for our mutual friend, Mrs-"

"o Broin? Yes, she's with the good doctor now. Seems she is fine; nothing a rest won't cure. Won't you tell me though of what you saw? I do want to be quite sure that Oliver is reprimanded appropriately."

I accept the offer of his arm and together we leave Gertie and Oliver.

"I expect, good sir, that Oliver was simply being an exuberant boy, on his way to run an errand for your cook. He merely wasn't looking where he was going and combined with such a large armload of vegetables, accidentally knocking into Mrs. O'Broin. She had just exited a doorway, you see, and neither of the two saw one another until the unfortunate collision happened.

You know, my dear Sir Halloway, I do believe Mrs. O'Broin is quite frail and elderly. I am so very concerned for her constitution and also for her future, you see. If only I could demonstrate my Christian duty by taking her in myself, but I'm afraid I am only here on holiday and must return to my home tonight. Time simply doesn't allow for me to act upon my urging of charity and generosity. I am so glad she has fallen into your capable hands! I am sure with your kindness and Gertie's nourishment, she will make a full recovery, and perhaps even be a welcome addition to your lovely home!" I attempt to squeeze his hand as it guides my elbow, but since I am still wrapped in a blanket it is easier imagined than done.

Still, my preposterous words have had the desired effect. Sir Halloway agrees to keep the mysterious Mrs. O'Broin for as long as she is indisposed. Oliver is off the hook as well, and we have reached the front door of the large house. I adjust my blanket and wonder if Dad has had enough time to acquire anything of value while I spouted silly propositions and distracted Sir Halloway.

"I have had my driver pull around. He'll take you home." Sir Halloway bows once more, his heels clicking together sharply again, and even kisses my hand.

"Ah, there's my father now." I grab Dad as he approaches, looking suspiciously bulky under his button down shirt.

"You don't mind, old fellow, if I bring along the blanket for the ride?" Dad holds up the blanket he had been given which is now folded and if I'm not mistaken, stuffed with any number of items. I'm praying for shoes. His smart English accent is quite adequate, and I want to throw my arms around him suddenly and hug him tight for trying his best.

"But of course. Good day to you, sir," the bow once again, "Miss."

We leave hastily, not wanting to give Sir Halloway the opportunity to become wary of our story, and so we could get our stolen goods to the carriage where we can inspect them properly.

"Place of residence, sir?" asks the driver, a nondescript man with gray hair and a pot belly.

I stifle an urge to laugh.

"America, the twenty first century," I say. "And be quick about it!"

"What'd she say?" the driver asks Dad, incredulously.

"Nothing. She's been out in the cold too much. Take us, oh, that way." Dad gestures towards where we came from earlier this morning.

I climb into the carriage and as I do so I glance up at the house we are about to leave. Someone stands in the window at the second story and I pause long enough to blow a kiss towards the person.

Prue has secured herself a warm bed, and food within an hour of traveling. It must be some sort of record.

When we are unceremoniously dumped off where we started from I am uneasy to not yet see Israel. I am being unreasonable in my desire to all be together so early, I know, but I cannot hold back the feeling that if we are not together something bad will happen. So much bad can happen in an unfamiliar place, and an unfamiliar time. We can be arrested, hurt, taken advantage of as well as any number of other things. Although made of sterner stuff than most, the Lost bleed red the same as all others.

"I'm done waiting," I announce several hours later.

The sun has gone down or rather what there was of it that wasn't obscured by clouds and fog of gray. We have sat by the road, leaving only when we felt pressured by passersby and only then to go a short distance. Israel has not returned, and I am itching to do something, go somewhere. I worry about Prue, without a friend in that large house, lying through her tobacco stained teeth. I worry about our Lost comrades, Iz especially, but Harry and Matthias too back in modern America without me. I worry about Dad, who has wasted no time in shoplifting something to drink and is halfway to smashed. So much for sobriety.

The neighborhood we are in appears middle class, not elaborate and wealthy like Sir Halloway's, but not destitute and poor the way I know London to be in several areas. Most of the people we see are servants running errands, working men, ladies in corsets who aren't exactly the leisurely affluent, but perhaps close enough.

166

"Definitely done waiting," I repeat.

Dad responds with a soft belch. We are mostly hidden in an alley way of sorts where we have a good view of the place we woke this morning. I am about to walk away from Dad when Israel appears, like a mist the way he always does.

"Food," he says shortly, tossing a bag towards me. Since I am not exactly the athletic type, I of course drop it, and I glower at him as I bend down to clean it up.

"I was worried," I say shortly and then tear into a roll with my teeth.

"Sorry." Israel rubs his eyes and yawns. "This place is a maze. I think I spent half the day lost. The other half was trying to blend in." He smiles awkwardly. "Didn't work out so well."

I swallow my massive bite of bread and smile a little. I eye another roll longingly, but evidently Lady Halloway had a more willowy figure than I and without a corset I could barely do up the buttons of the blue dress Dad pinched for me. I'm not sure the stitching could handle another roll.

Israel yawns again before asking, "Where's Prue?"

"She was in a warm bed sipping tea and bossing the rich around last time I saw her," I roll my eyes indulgently. "I'll go check on her tomorrow or the next day. I think she can charm her way into the household, but my story of being a noteworthy gentlewoman wasn't going to check out so Dad and I hit the road pretty quickly."

"That must be some sort of record," Israel muses.

I laugh. "That's what I thought. Of course she's been here before, so that's an advantage. She told me she worked for a rich Victorian lady once. Oh my word, do you think she could actually run into her first husband? Or was it her second?" My eyes grow large at the thought, and I stop chewing on my second roll for a moment.

"Who knows? Stranger things have happened. There are some sausages in there, fish them out, would you?"

For a while we eat in silence. My dress is warm (especially since I left my nightgown on underneath the full skirts, partly for warmth and partly because I have nowhere to stash it) and the blankets we kept from Sir Halloway are helpful as well. All in all we are cold, but only because the dampness in the air has a heaviness that seeps into your bones. Dad had stolen a coat and shoes for himself, and Israel is fully dressed as a dapper Englishman too. I don't ask where he got them, but I certainly hope we don't run into a naked, six and a half foot tall, angry man anytime soon. Israel looks rather nice, especially in the hat, though I want to tell him so, I don't.

"And as for lodging?" I finally ask through bites of cold sausages. I lick the grease from my fingers.

"You're looking at it, at least for tonight."

I want to sigh melodramatically, but I know Iz has done the best he could for today, and besides we've stayed in worse surroundings than a dirty alley in the streets of London. Just once though, I'd like to wake up in Buckingham Palace.

"Can we build a fire?"

"Not here. Area gets more run down if we walk farther we could stay there. A few more huddled around a fire won't be noticeable."

"Yes, please."

"Can your dad walk?" Israel glances over at Dad who is snoring away serenely oblivious to the cold and huddled in a little ball with his contraband bottle grasped tightly against his chest.

"It would be tempting to leave him, but I suppose if we wake him, he can walk."

"Go on then." Israel helps himself to the last sausage.

"Thanks," I mutter.

After a few moments of shaking and shouting in Dad's ear, we finally rip his bottle away from him, and he stirs enough to apologize and agrees to join us. The weather becomes frigid, and even with my blanket wrapped around my head to protect my ears, my teeth chatter. I start talking to keep the cold at bay.

"Did you know it's almost Christmas? Ollie said December twentieth though he didn't seem quite sure."

Israel frowns. "I know. We don't usually lose two months like that."

I snort and sound just like Prue. "What's two months in the grand scheme of things? We just lost a century and a half!"

"I know, but I still don't like it."

"Do you ever get the feeling we're supposed to figure this out? This whole traveling, lost in time, sort of thing? Like it's maybe really obvious and we just haven't put the pieces together?"

"All the time, Sonnet, all the time. Share the blanket, would you?"

We walk the rest of the way in silence, huddled together under the woolen blanket. It makes for strange walking, trying to find our sync and not stumble around the way Dad unfortunately is doing. I match my steps to Israel's and once we find a rhythm it starts to be successful in an ungraceful sort of lurching way.

I tell him his new clothes smell funny.

"What? I can't hear a word you're saying."

I remove the blanket from where I have it wrapped around my face, only my eyes peeking through.

"I said you smell like pipe tobacco. I think whomever you stole these clothes from was a big smoker."

"I didn't steal them, I borrowed them."

"Uh huh. Smells nice actually. Like cherry and smoke."

I may imagine it, but it feels as though his arm around my waist tightens just a bit and the fingers of his hand move slightly, almost like an unexpectedly strange caress.

"I'm glad you're here," I whisper from under the protection of the muffling blanket.

We don't have to go far to reach a different section of London altogether that is seedy and teeming with people. They are either huddled in groups around fires built in iron trash containers or walking briskly. We are ignored for the most part other than the ladies of the night who call out or whisper offers to Dad, which turns my stomach. Israel, they only widen their eyes at, and I don't know if it's out of fear, respect or curiosity. Maybe all three. There are children too, playing in the street or sleeping on their mother's lap, but it's mostly the prostitutes who are swarming about in numbers so large I can hardly fathom it. I think of the girls who used to come into the coffee shop, the ones with tight pants and low cut shirts and provocative eye liner, who were only playing silly children's games, texting boys and flirting. I think of them paired up with these girls, who are old before their time and hardened, what a contrast they are. The slums are worse than any I've seen in any other time, that I tell Israel I want to stop. It seems as though the farther we go, the worse it gets, and I'm reticent to discover anymore. This is bad enough.

"Stay here," Israel instructs, propping Dad up against a wall. "I'll borrow a light."

He is back in no time, with a torch made of garbage and lit up with the glowing warmth of blessed fire. I watch him as he makes a small bonfire in the metal circular bin that we are near. The flame lights up our three faces, making us seem ghoulish in the orange reflection. The yellow radiance that dances across Israel's dark face makes for a Jack-o-lantern effect and I tell him so. He bares his teeth at me in good humor.

I laugh at the sight and therefore am unprepared when I am knocked to the ground by the force of a person jumping out of the shadows.

It's Emme.

Chapter 21

"I can't believe you're here!" Emme squeals with such delight that I throw my arms back around and hug her for at least the fourth time since she knocked me to the ground.

Joe and Bea have come to join us and I am startled by the sight of my Dad now lying on the ground with his head on Bea's lap. She even strokes his hair lightly, and I wonder what I haven't noticed when I'm too busy thinking of myself.

Joe has gleefully accepted the offer of my blanket and has mummified himself right by the fire and gone to sleep. Israel lays next to him, not out of the desire to be near a kicking, snoring six-year-old all night I suspect, but out of a desire to protect him in a precarious neighborhood.

"I can't believe *you're* here," I answer. "I really thought I'd never see you again."

"Guess we were close enough after all, huh?" she continues happily. "When we got here I absolutely hated myself for not taking you up on your offer to live together. I felt like such a dope, setting myself up for traveling without my favorite family! I'm so glad we got a second chance."

"Me too. And you look adorable, by the way."

Emme looks down at her dress which is pink, her favorite. "Isn't it pretty? I'm so glad to be back in England!"

"You look like a fairy princess. In a corset."

"That's what the boys call me, too."

"The boys?" At first I think she means Harry and Matthias, and then I grimace. "Oh. Those boys. You've been here, what, a day? For crying out loud, Emme."

"Don't be disapproving, Sonnet. You have Israel and your dad and even Harry and Matthias. I have a middle aged mom and a little kid. Someone has to bring in food and clothes."

"You're right, okay." I kiss her cheek, nearly sacrificing my eye in the process as it runs into a feather poking out of her jaunty pink bonnet. "I'm sorry. I just wish you wouldn't. That's all."

"Let's go to sleep. We'll figure out what to do in the morning."

I agree and together we settle down, our arms and legs akimbo, mingling with the arms and legs of four others.

It's a long, restless, cold night, but we sleep as best we can.

* * *

"I think my eyelashes are frozen solid. I'm afraid to blink," Emme says when the sun finally makes its lazy way up in the sky. She does look a little blue.

"I know. What the heck happened to October and November?" I blow on my hands and stiff fingers.

Dad has gone, along with Bea, they're looking for opportunities and places to sleep that are better than the street. Joe is still sleeping and Israel is too, his arms wrapped in a bear hug around the little bundle of blanket that is Joe. I'd admire his fatherly leanings if I didn't believe it was more for warmth than for anything else.

"Is it December then? As much as I love London, I do wish we'd been dumped off in June instead. Are we in time for Boxing Day?"

"Boxing Day? What, is that the English Christmas?"

"No, silly, they have Christmas too. It's just an extra holiday is all. I'm all for extra holidays, aren't you?"

"If they involve turkey and mashed potatoes, definitely. I'd like to stick my toes in mashed potatoes and gravy right about now. Emme, what are we going to do here?"

"Feeling worried already, ducky? Cheer up, this is London! The possibilities are endless!"

"I need to go check on Prue today, make sure that Sir Halloway hasn't kicked her to the curb. I appealed to his sense of Christian duty, but I think he was only humoring me in case I actually turned out to be somebody."

"You are somebody, you're a time traveling witch! You can foresee the future, tell fortunes! Hmm, not a bad profession now that I think of it." Emme wiggles her eyebrows.

"Except I don't know a thing about anyone in particular. What am I going to foretell?"

"Oh, there must be something you can think of. You're better at history than I. Anyway, come on, I need to make water."

"Make water?" I wrinkle my nose.

"Pee. If you're going to live here you have to learn the slang, chickadee. Can I leave Joe with Iz, do you think?"

"Sure. There's no better protection than a giant. Help me up, my joints are frozen solid and I'm not sure I can bend my knees."

We find a solitary spot to take care of personal hygiene business and then wander off with no particular destination in mind, other than the vague, gnawing hope of breakfast. My stomach growls. The streets are quieter now than they were last night, though the dank feeling of depression and poverty seem almost worse in the garish light of day. In the dark, you imagine some of it, but in the sun, there is no imagination necessary, it really is as bad a slum as your mind's eye thought it might be.

There's garbage in the street and once we almost get hit in the head with something gloppy that someone drops out of their window over us. Judging by the smell, it wasn't something edible.

"I'll need to find work," I say. "I don't know that I can make a living with singing here."

"Mmm. You must have other skills. Can you sew?"

"Crookedly."

"Cook?"

"Terribly."

"Perhaps you'd best find a rich man to marry you then!"

"Yes, that's the ticket. An excellent plan, Emme, thank you. Always helpful."

"Here's a bakery, let's go in." Emme points at a dilapidated shop with a crooked sign advertising breads and biscuits.

"Wait."

The dingy store with its dirty windows reminds me forlornly of Luke's photography shop and my step falters. I remember the day we sat there, eating squirrel pie and talking of Rose.

Rose. Where is she now? If Emme traveled the same night we did, couldn't Rose have as well? Not if she was as far away as the abandoned house, but hadn't I established quite nicely that she wasn't there after all?

"What is it?" Emme asks impatiently.

"Just thinking. You haven't really asked me what happened night before last. I mean, night before last a hundred and some-odd years in the future."

It's Emme's turn to wrinkle her nose. She does that when she's thinking. "Well, I suppose I haven't had much time, have I? Besides, I knew you'd tell me if you wanted me to know."

"I do want you to know. Mostly because I want you to explain it to me," I answer ruefully. I tell her all about that night, about seeing Rose in the rain, stealing the Blue Beast, finding myself locked in the old house, and finally so many, many hours later walking until Israel found me. I even tell her about the laugh I thought I heard when I was in the room. "You're giving me goose bumps, Sonnet," Emme says when I'm finished with my lurid tale. "Do you really think someone locked you in and then let you out? Why? That seems a little harsh a punishment for a trespasser."

"I know."

"If it was Rose you saw and you were right about her living there, maybe it was her who locked you in."

"Why?"

"You may have scared her. Maybe she has no idea you're her sister. Maybe she thought you were a deranged lunatic stalker." Emme shrugs. "I don't know. How did Israel know where to find you?"

I frown. "I don't know. I didn't think to ask."

"Well, let's think on it some more after a biscuit. There's a ridiculously cute boy in that shop, and I'm going to get us a free breakfast if it's the last thing I do. Come on, come flirt with me." She pulls on my elbow.

"I can't flirt! My flirter is broken. Seriously, you'll stand a better chance if I just stay out here."

"Fine then. Stand in the slush. I'll try to save you some crumbs."

Emme saves me more than crumbs, she's managed to use her feminine wiles to convince the young man working at the bakery to give us anything

that was broken or had fallen apart or had burnt. We end up with a paper sack of ugly looking biscuits that taste much better than they appear.

"I'm going to stop and ask for directions if I want to find Sir Halloway's house again," I muse. "No wonder Israel got lost yesterday, this place really is a maze."

"Really? I find it quite logical."

"Oh, please. You're just happy to be back in England and you're every bit as lost as I am. What do you think it costs to rent of those carriage-y thingies? You know, one of those ancient taxi services?"

"More than you have, plus some. We're going to have to walk it. Maybe we'll pass a shop with a sign out front advertising 'singing girls wanted!'"

"Yes, that sounds very likely. Right after we pass the one that says 'free rides to Sir Halloway's!'"

There's no choice really but to walk and nothing else to do anyway, and so we walk.

Chapter 22

The directions we get from an old man seem to make sense, and Emme and I follow them to the letter. It begins to rain, but it's only a light drizzle that makes our hair curl and it stops as soon as it had started. The basic layout of the city is beginning to seem slightly more logical than I had first believed. We spent the night in the East side of London, the poorest side, but most likely also the most hospitable to the Lost. Sir Halloway is in Mayfair, or at least the old man seems to think so, and it's a few miles away. Once again, with nothing else to do, we decide to walk there.

We end up finding the place, not because of my stellar memory of the building, but because I catch a glimpse of the stern, potbellied driver who had driven me back to East London the night before. Knowing I didn't make the best of impressions on him I don't make myself known to him, but we do follow him discreetly for a block or so and he leads us directly to Sir Halloway's house.

"Oh, this isn't that exciting, Sonnet." Emme looks disappointed. "He isn't that rich after all."

"No?" I lean my head back and stare up at the home. "Seems rich enough to me."

"Middle class, at best." Emme yawns. "Probably has a few servants. Underpaid ones most likely. Probably behind on his bills, and has creditors after him. Bet his floozy wife was a spend thrift." She nods knowingly.

"You can get all that from a house?" I ask incredulously. "My, you're good. Maybe you should hang up the shingle for Fortune Telling."

"I do quite well with my chosen profession, thank you," Emme responds primly, petting down her pretty pink dress and then giving me a wink.

"Ugh. Whatever. Let's go in. I'm really anxious to see Prue."

We ring the bell, after lifting our skirts daintily to climb the steps. Emme is daintier than I naturally, I almost trip but I blame the boots Dad stole for me which are far too big. For a tall girl, I have little feet, a claim that Lady Halloway could not boast. That sudden thought stops me in my tracks.

"Oh my word, Emme, wait! I can't show up wearing his wife's dress!" I am appalled at myself and my stupidity. I want to scurry off like a wayward little girl, found out by her elders or playmates. I glance around frantically for a tree, a bush, anything to hide behind.

Emme regards me with amusement.

"Goodness, girl, settle down. It's not like Sir Halloway is going to answer his own door. He won't even be home, and if he is he'll be sipping sherry in his library. Come here and quit looking like a silly nut."

"Really?" I creep back towards her. "Are you sure?"

"Yes, of course. Look smart now."

The door swings open and sure enough, to my relief and Emme's credit, there is a maid on the other side. She regards us with a look of expectation on her young face.

"We're friends of Prue's," Emme says. "Can we see her please?"

"The old lady? Aye, I expect you can, though that crazy bag having friends is news to me." The maid laughs at her own cleverness. Evidently she recognizes us for commoners and is not concerned with the impression she makes. She does not blink at my dress though, and that, at the moment, is all I care about.

"We'll find the way," Emme says, bossily, as soon as we are admitted into the home. "Go back to work, girl."

The maid gives her a look that could melt a glacier but stalks off and we are left to ourselves in the foyer.

"What was that all about?" I speak softly.

"Working girls," Emme winks. "We understand each other but I can't say we respect each other, is all. Up the stairs we go," she whispers cheerfully.

I follow her dutifully, my heart still in my throat at the possibility of running into Sir Halloway while I wear his runaway wife's stolen dress. Emme peeks into doorways and listens and tiptoes and is so light on her feet that she practically flits around, while I am preoccupied with not making heavy boot stomps on the floor, giving away our location.

"In here." Emme beckons me over to a door and I hurry to her side. She flings it open.

"Surprise!" Emme says happily.

Prue is sitting up in bed and looks delighted to see us, or as delighted as I've ever seen Prue look, which is to say smiling all the way to her eyes.

"Oh, my girls, come in, come in," she whispers like a small child trying not to get caught. "Shut the door. How are you? How are things out there?"

"Chilly and damp and too far away from you," I say.

"Wonderful and glorious and so England-y!" says Emme. I roll my eyes at her exuberance.

I sit down on the bed and squeeze Prue's hands. "How are you? Is Sir Halloway buying anything you're selling, you old liar?"

Prue bats away the notion that anything less would be possible the same way I've seen her bat away flies from her food cart. "Just a matter of time, girl. I slipped something special into Gertie's breakfast that she served the mister this morning so now I'm just waiting for it to take effect."

"You poisoned Sir Halloway?" I can't help myself and gasp.

Prue glares at me. "I ain't stooping to murder. I just made him a little sick is all. 'Sides, that woman's cooking is awful enough on its own.

Probably kill him herself if I gave her enough time. I'm just hurrying her termination along faster."

"You've always had the imagination in this family, Prue," Emme winks. "That's why you and I get along just fine."

"Well, I wasn't expecting to see you again, that's for sure. I suppose it's nice that I am. Seeing you, I mean." As far as emotional displays of vulnerability, that's about as mushy as I've seen Prue in recent memory.

"Do you want me to braid your hair?" Emme asks and picks up the brush on the table by the bed.

"That'd be nice. Sonnet, you can rub my feet, that's a good girl." She settles herself comfortably and stretches out her feet.

"How do I always get stuck with the feet?" I complain.

"Because we've seen your hair styles," Emme points out. "Right now you look like a flock of eagles made a nest in your hair."

"Hey, I just got here! It's not like I own a hairbrush at the moment, much less shampoo or a fancy little bonnet like yours." Emme's bonnet is pink to match her dress and pinned at a flirty, saucy angle on her strawberry waves. "Besides, eagles don't flock."

"I haven't been here any longer than you and I managed to make do and not look like I just crawled out of a grave. Don't glare at me, I'll brush yours out next."

"Oh, will you please?" I mutter. "Prue, I can't massage properly if you keep being so ticklish!"

Like a group of giggling girls at a slumber party, the three of us pass away an hour or two, listening for steps on the landing. I prepared to jump under the bed at a moment's notice if Sir Halloway walks in on us. When Emme and I take our leave, Prue's hair is plaited around her head the way she likes it, mine is brushed into submission and pinned up like a proper Victorian lady's would be, and my hands smell like feet.

"Home again, home again?" asks Emme, cheerily as we wander back the way we came.

It has begun to drizzle rain again, causing humidity and curly hair once more and I bemoan my poor, smooth hairstyle which barely got a chance to live and thrive in this weather before it died an untimely and sudden death.

"Home, street home," I agree, and we pick up our pace.

"I need to talk to you," I tell Israel once we finally get back to our dingy little alley way. He has brought us all two dried apple pies and for a while there is nothing, but the sound of munching and happy bellies growling. I report to everyone that Prue is well and fine. Dad has been successful enough at a day of pick-pocketing to have a pocket full of shillings and a couple pound notes that he oddly enough, turns over to me. Is this a step to temperance, I wonder? More likely, he just doesn't want to be caught red handed.

The last thing I want to do after mine and Emme's long walk is take another walk, but I want to talk to Iz alone. The shock of traveling has worn off for the most part, and I need to let my mind go back to America and what happened the night before we left. I need to know just how he knew where to find me and also if anyone had bothered to ask Luke where I might have gone. Luke knew about the old house, and he should have known that's where I was. Why wasn't I found sooner?

182

Once we're away from the others, I ask these questions. Israel's face is as guarded and unreadable as ever, and he pauses before answering me.

"We did go to Luke's shop that first day, but it was closed down. I couldn't find him. I tried the coffee shop, and Prue mentioned places she had seen him before but no luck. Then we tried the next day and he was there, but he said he hadn't seen you. He said you'd been trying to find Rose, and he started suggesting places to look, but we'd searched them all. We tried the soup kitchen, tried Penny, even went to her house, went and found Harry and Matthias. At one point, he and I separated and he went driving like a bat out of hell. Met up later at the house and that's when he mentioned the abandoned house you two had went to on your date."

"It wasn't a date. I don't think." I object.

"Whatever," he answers shortly. "He was upset he hadn't thought of it before. He had walked all the way from his house to tell us because he said his truck had died. I borrowed Gladys' car and found the old house. It was pretty easy to know which one since my car was sitting in front of it. No one was there obviously. I checked the whole place, so I left and kept driving. Eventually I saw you leaning against that tree like a ghost."

"You were mad," I interjected. "You were like an avenging angel or something. I was hoping for hugs and you threw me in the car like a sack of potatoes."

"I was mad? Of course I was mad!" Israel looked at me and glared and it was that night all over again. "You keep running off searching for someone we don't know is really there, and you refuse to ask for help. We slept all that first night without you, not even knowing you weren't in your room. We could have traveled without you, and never even knew what happened. Do you think your dad could handle that again, after Rose?"

"I know," I say miserably. "I'm sorry. I wasn't thinking. I just knew she was out there and I kept missing her, and it was making me crazy. I thought if I could just catch up to her and make her see...make her want

183

to be with us. I didn't know I'd get locked in that awful place. I stayed awake so long, hoping you would do the same for me."

"Well, we did. Anyway, when we got back, you probably didn't see him, but Dawes was there. He didn't say anything, just watched to make sure you were all right, and then walked back into the night."

"He must have felt bad for not thinking of the house sooner. I wish I could have talked to him before we left." I stop walking and sit down on the cobblestones to give my feet a rest. The stolen boots are rubbing raw blisters on my heels and they sting. I pull them off and wiggle my toes in relief. "Did you see the book?"

"What book?"

"On the old couch in that house. And that line drawn in the dust, like someone had been there?"

"No, I was a little busy looking for you or your dead body, whichever I found first," he answers drily.

"Well, it was creepy. I may have been wrong about Rose being there, but someone definitely was."

"Someone who locked you in?"

"Yes, and then let me out. Which was even stranger."

"You were deliriously tired," Israel points out, but he doesn't sound as though he believes what he's suggesting any more than I do. "Maybe it was never locked?"

"It was locked," I say firmly standing again. "And then it wasn't. And I was too upset and hurting to try to find the person. I just wanted out of that house. I didn't realize I was walking the wrong way until later. Then I just gave up, and I was almost asleep when you found me."

"Well, we most likely will never know what happened."

"I suppose you're right. And my chance to find my sister may be lost forever." I am glum and my voice reflects that. "Let's change the subject. What did you do today? Have you any ideas for lodging?"

"Yes, but you aren't going to like it." Israel starts walking again, back the way we came, towards our makeshift family. I step back into my boots, not bothering to lace them up and run awkwardly to catch up. The heels of the too-big boots slap against the ground.

"What do you mean I won't like it? Whatever does that mean?"

"I met a young doctor. He has his own practice not too far from here. He treats the poorest and lowest, some of whom don't even pay. It's a bit of an underground thing really; not many know he's there and that's the only way he can keep it going, otherwise he'd be swamped with patients. This district is abominable and rife with disease and crime. He came from a wealthy enough family, but they cut him off when he married a Chinese woman. That's how I got him to trust me and offer me a position."

I raise my eyebrows. "What? I'm confused."

"Well, besides my medical knowledge which he could put to use too."

"Yes, besides that."

Israel looks uncomfortable. "Well, I had to appeal to his sympathies. So I made it seem as though we had more in common than we actually do. Besides being young doctors, I mean."

"I don't follow, you don't come from a wealthy family, and you aren't married to a Chinese woman."

"She doesn't have to be Chinese; I'm already the ethnic minority here, remember? She only has to be white in order for me to have that social difficulty in common with him."

I stop walking. "You didn't?"

"I did. I saw my chance and I seized it."

"Me?" I squeak.

Chapter 23

"You have got to be joking." It's the only thing I am capable of saying and I have repeated it three times in as many minutes.

Israel looks irritated. "You've got a better idea then?"

"No. But-"

"There's just barely enough room in his little house for us. This doctor, he's really excited about some of the things I had to teach him, especially about germs. He wants to know more. Their house is small, but there's a back room we can take. Your dad can come too."

"Sounds cozy."

"Quit complaining. Who knows how long we'll be here? It could be just a few weeks."

"It could be years."

"Well, then we can take it one day at a time. We can always figure out a better plan later." His voice is beginning to sound irritated. "But we can't just stay on the streets of London. The place is filthy, winter is coming on fierce, and there are Bobbies all over the place." Bobbies being the police.

We have reached our little party again. The fire burns brightly in our receptacle, Joe is practicing what looks like ninja moves in the firelight, and Bea and Dad are watching him, bemused. Emme is gone.

"Fine," I blurt out. "If no one else figures out a better plan, we'll go with yours."

I cannot believe what I have gotten myself into. Israel's pretend wife. My head spins.

"Where's Emme?" I ask Bea. She is dressed now in the garb of the period, a pea green coat that is buckled over a long brown dress. Dad must have been busy today, I think. We're such a bunch of criminals it makes me sigh aloud.

"Out. Working," Bea either looks embarrassed or worried, I'm not sure which it is. Her mouth turns down in a neat little bow shape. "I asked her to come back tonight and stay with us, but I don't know if she will. She says she met some women who were going to take her to a…" Bea's voice trails off. "Well, anyway, a place where she might be able to live and work both."

"I think they call them houses of ill repute in this day and age," I keep my voice light and teasing to candy coat my crass words.

Her bow of a mouth turns back up a little. "Well, it's a start. I'm trying to get her out of that work, but you know how Emme is. Nobody tells her what to do. She's stubborn and independent."

"What will you do here?" I ask. I don't know whether family members can stay in those places that Emme is thinking of, and I hate to think of Joe growing up in such an environment.

Bea waves her hand through the cold air. "I can sew and that should be marketable. There are factories if I can't get on in a shop somewhere. It just might take a little time is all. I wish we'd arrived here in summer; the nights are too cold for Joe to be sleeping outside." Without a doubt, she looks worried.

"It is cold," I agree. "Nice that ladies these days wear all those glove and hats and things, keeps them warmer, I imagine. Too bad we don't have any of them." I cup my hands and blow into them. The heat from my breath warms them for about a nanosecond.

"Yes, we do look like paupers compared to some of the gentlewomen we've seen, don't we?" She looks down at her coat and fingers a tear in the fabric.

188

"Well, I miss my overalls and my Budweiser cap."

"No one else does," teases Joe, cutting in on the conversation.

"Hey, you little monster!" I tickle him ruthlessly. "Naughty little children don't give fashion advice. Go finish your candy and rot your teeth, it'll serve you right." I push him off my lap and still wheezing from too much laughter, he leaves to join Israel.

Israel. I feel butterflies in my stomach. Am I mad to have agreed to such a crazy scheme? Sonnet Rhode? This whole idea is preposterous. What was I thinking? I glance over at him. He's talking in hushed tones to the boys. I can tell he's telling them of our plan, or rather his plan. My plan, by default only. I'd like to point this out but my lips seem glued shut for all of eternity.

Emme does come back and seems pleased as punch with Israel's plot to have a faux marriage with me, and so do Dad and Bea. Emme's eyes widen at the idea.

"Fancy that." she smirks. "You're finally getting married. I always thought it'd be you and Israel actually. I'm never wrong."

"You're always wrong, smarty. You said you were going to marry Johnny Depp."

"Yeah, well," she tosses her reddish hair over her shoulder, "I ran out of time is all."

"Sure. Pull up a cobblestone and go to sleep."

Now it's dark and cold, and we have run out of miscellaneous kindling for our fire. The smoke that drifts by my nostrils feels like my only heat, and I breathe it in deeply. I have kidnapped Joe for a little extra body heat and we curl up together like two pink shrimp. Emme is behind me, her arm around my waist, and now we are three.

Sometime in the middle of the night I feel Joe move and scoot over to be with Bea. The front of my body chills instantly with his absence. Uncomfortable, I sleep once more and dream of Luke Dawes.

* * *

I am awakened by an insistent foot nudging me in my shoulder. A concerned and wary looking face peers into mine. He looks relieved when I yawn. He has a bushy, salt and pepper colored beard that comes to a point nearly four inches below his chin. He is wearing the uniform of a Bobbie, the British police.

"Come now, miss, up you go!" he barks. "Off the streets. Thought the lot of you were dead for a minute there. Find something to do besides scare innocent people to death, would you?"

"Sorry." I smile, ruefully. "We're all fine." I motion to the others which consists of just Emme and Joe now. Iz, Dad, and Bea must have awoken already and are off goodness knows where. Emme stretches and opens her eyes. "We just are in need of a place to go to, sir."

The man rubs his beard. "Well, you can't stay here," he repeats himself. "Isn't safe. Don't like stumbling upon bodies first thing in the morning, not nowadays. You say you two girls don't have anywhere to go?"

"Of course we do!" Emme scowls at me. "We're just fine, officer. Just had a bit of a rowdy night is all. But it isn't as though we haven't got a home. You don't need to worry about us."

Stubborn and independent? Isn't that what Bea described of her headstrong daughter? I sigh. Any hope I had of a nice Scotland Yard hero whisking us off to a lovely home and a bath is dashed.

The officer looks skeptical. "Well, see that you do. Move on, I mean. Name's Walter Andrews. You remember that name if you ever need me. Miss," he nods briskly towards me, "Miss," nods to Emme, "Young sir," this is directed towards Joe who has awoken and stares up at him with owlish eyes.

"Yes sir, I mean, no sir, I mean goodbye, sir," says Joe and salutes smartly.

"You protect these young flowers," Officer Andrews continues to Joe.

"Yes, sir! I know all sorts of ninja moves, sir!" Joe proceeds to leap to his feet and demonstrates one.

"Ah. Yes. Certainly." Officer Andrews looks bewildered but properly impressed at the flying feet and hands. "That will unquestionably do the trick should the occasion call for it. I don't want to see you three here again. Am I clear?"

I nod embarrassed, chagrined, and put in my place, as the homeless penniless girl I am. A stand in for Israel's wife is beginning to sound better and better.

"You could have seen if he was offering help," I scold Emme after the officer leaves.

"He wasn't. He just wanted us to move on. We don't need help, we're doing just fine on our own." Emme brushes off her pink dress and licking her fingers, tries to comb down her son's hair.

"My back begs to differ." I frown, twisting from the waist and feeling my joints pop.

"Oh, it's our last night here. By tonight you'll be in a real house and I'll have Mum and Joe taken care of too. Come on, let's walk and try to find everyone."

"Are you going to live in one of those...you know, one of those places?" I can't help feeling the worry come through in my voice even though I know Emme will resent it.

"Sure. It's not a palace, but it'll do for now. I'll move up, Sonnet, you'll see. Maybe I'll be someone someday. But I have to start somewhere."

I don't have a response to that, and so we walk in silence for a while. Joe stops long enough to pee on a tree, (ah, the joys of being a boy) and then he merrily skips ahead, feeling no cold in his bones and no sorrow in his little heart. Somewhere between his age and mine, I seem to have grown old.

"This is where we woke up," I point out when we pass the spot.

Emme looks around, interested. "Mum and Joe and I were further down a ways. See that ugly blue store front? Over behind that. I knew it was England even before I opened my eyes, smelled just how I remembered." She takes a deep breath and spreads her arms wide as if embracing all of London.

"Like cabbage and steam?"

"Pretty much!" She laughs.

"We might be walking in the wrong direction. Maybe we should stay put a while. This is the beginning, at least for me." Go back to the beginning, Dad said.

"Right, luv," Emme agrees. "But I'm hungry. Give me some of your dad's money, and I'll get us some breakfast and bring it back."

Joe sits with me on the nearest bench. He's a bundle of energy, swinging his legs back and forth and talking a mile a minute. I am only half listening as my mind is wandering off to places unbidden. My thoughts are of what I left behind, what is coming next, and worries about Emme, Prue, and my sadness over Rose. I am mindful of his musings, but when I hear the words that come out of his mouth next I am so shocked I nearly fall off the bench.

"Hullo, Mr. Dawes! Did you bring me some breakfast?" Joe chirps.

For what seems like a maddeningly large amount of time, everything stands still. I feel as though I'm trapped in a dream, can't speak, can't move, and can't even seem to blink, as I stare at Luke. Luke, in a shabby eighteen-hundreds style overcoat and hat, his hair as floppy as ever underneath, his whiskers even more stubbly than normal. He looks like he hasn't slept in a week. He looks beautiful.

"You're here." I have this terrible feeling my words will come out in a girlish squeal, but actually they are only a whisper.

"I got that impression as well," Luke says ruefully.

I somehow find my legs and stand taking a step slowly, then another one, faster, until I have reached him. He raises his arms and his eyebrows simultaneously. I find myself launching myself into the former.

"Gray," he breathes into my neck. "You don't know how much I was hoping you'd be here too."

I laugh and pull away enough to look at his face, though our arms are still entwined.

"I didn't think I'd ever see you again. I never even hoped you traveled with us. How?" I finally feel the awkwardness of our embrace and step away, my hands falling to my side.

"The night we all traveled I didn't go home," he confesses. "I was out on your porch and slept there. I didn't feel exactly welcome after I was stupid enough to realize I knew where you had been the whole time, but I was worried about you. Plus, I was way too tired to walk all the way home." He winks.

"I can't believe you came with us." I shake my head in amazement. "I guess your father isn't living a double life in Topeka. He really was – is – Lost. You're one of us!"

"Is there a special ceremony or anything I should know about? A cool robe to wear or a secret handshake or a hazing?"

"Funny. Wait 'til everyone hears. Here comes Emme!"

"Well, well, well." Emme laughs as she nears us, her hands full of hot bread. The steam from them rises up in the cold in a column. "Look what the cat dragged in! Nice to see you, Lukie my boy. Been here long?"

"Couple days, same as you I expect. Hi, Emme." Luke bends down to kiss her upturned cheek. Wait, where was my kiss? Somehow my face doesn't seem to beckon and invite kisses the way Emme's cherubic face does.

"Hullo, yourself! And the number of our family grows, just like that," Emme snaps her fingers after handing over the bread to a jumping Joe. "Here, you little beggar. Save some for Auntie Sonnet. I had mine already."

"Where have you been staying?" I ask, biting into the fresh hot bread and offering a piece to Luke.

Luke shrugs and takes the bread thankfully. "Here and there. Not sure exactly what to do or where to go. New to this, you know. I spent the whole first day in total shock and hardly moved."

"That'll never do now that you're Lost," Emme says practically. "You have to figure things out lickety split. No sitting around feeling sorry for yourself. Why, we had hardly been here at all when Sonnet here got herself married to Israel!"

Luke chokes on his bread. While Emme slaps him on the back sympathetically, I glare at her and hurry to explain the situation. Luke appears only slightly less aghast when I finish my tale.

"Unless of course, you have a better offer for her?" Emme asks offhandedly. Was she flirting on my behalf now? I'd like to smack my infuriating best friend. "I mean, you could pretend to be married to Sonnet yourself."

"Or *you* could," I snap. "It's not like you're a married woman either."

Emme waves away the ridiculous notion and doesn't even blush, which naturally, I am doing to the roots of my hair. "I'm not the marrying type. Luke knows that. No hard feelings?" She looks at Luke expectantly.

"I'll try to get over it," he agrees good-naturedly. "And Gray, you don't have to pretend to be married to me, but if you aren't going to eat the rest of that bread I'd take it off your hands."

My hero.

Chapter 24

The arrival of Luke has thrown a wrench in everyone's plans. We meet up with Dad and Bea and Israel; sure enough we all gravitate towards the area we woke up and meet up there. Dad and Bea are more thrilled to see Luke than Israel seems to be, but Iz has never been one to show much emotion unless it's his irritated at Sonnet emotion, which he displays with steady frequency and expertise.

"Well, he's not coming with me," Emme says cheerily. "Though I expect there's a market for your type, it's all girls where I'm going and frankly, I don't want the competition."

We ignore her.

"Maybe your doctor friend can squeeze in one more?" I direct this towards Israel who hasn't contributed much to the conversation.

"I'm already asking a favor bringing your dad, so no."

"That's okay, folks, really!" Luke looks self-conscious. "I'll figure things out."

"Yes, he's a big boy," Israel adds, with little sympathy. I glare at him.

"I don't want to lose track of you is all. You're our family now. We don't want to lose you." *I don't want to lose you.*

"You'll be seeing me," Luke replies. "I promise. I'll find you."

"It's time to go, Sonnet. I told the doctor we'd be meeting him by now." Israel looks down at his wrist and speaks somewhat impatiently.

"You don't even have a watch," I point out annoyed. "Fine. I'm ready."

Emme turns her face up to Luke for another of her exasperatingly frequent kisses, Bea hugs him in a motherly way, Joe high fives him, Dad shakes his hand, Israel wanders off rudely, and I am left to say my goodbye to the friend I have only just found.

"Please come find me," I whisper to his chest as he pulls me close for our second hug in one hour. "I worry about you."

"I worry about you too. Are you sure this is what you want?" Luke's eyes look over towards Israel, who stands several yards away watching.

"It appears to be my only option. And he'll take care of me."

Luke narrows his eyes. "I expect he will. Anyway, who's going to take care of me? I feel like Oliver Twist, wandering the streets. I may break out into song at any moment or at the very least join up with a boy pickpocket gang. Think your dad would let me in on his secrets?"

"Funny again. Just try to stay out of trouble and don't lose me!" Seized by impulse, I lean over and quickly kiss his cheek, as close to his mouth as my cowardice will allow. It's fast, it's light, it's meaningless, but my cheeks are ablaze when I pull away. "Bye," I say nonchalantly.

I manage not to trip as I don't wait for a response and run to catch up with Israel and Dad. I push myself in between them and link arms with each. Dad pats my elbow absentmindedly.

The walk to our destination isn't long, especially in comparison to the one I took before with Emme, and as we walk I dutifully listen to Israel's plan and story.

"Do you think you can remember all that?" He finally asks when he takes a breath and stops instructing me on every little detail.

"Something about you and me, a marriage, strife, job, dead family except Dad over here, all our belongings stolen, etc, etc, etc." I reply cheerily. "Got it."

"You better have it," he answers, grimly. "We're here."

'Here' is a bricked building with a door that you have to descend three steps down to get to before you can knock on it. It reminds me of Bob Cratchit's house somehow, or at least how I've imagined that house to look. The street is gloomy and narrow and I wouldn't be surprised to see the ghostly hearse that holds Jacob Marley's body glide by us. I'm finding London to be a sinister place and I shiver.

Israel raps on the door and it is opened to us directly. A man of medium height with sunken cheekbones and deep set eyes stands on the other side of the threshold. At first I am startled by his menacing appearance, then he smiles and it's as though his face has transformed into something light and whimsical. The eyes that seemed so dark a split second before are dancing with warmth, and he looks positively excited to see us bedraggled and destitute at his door.

"Ah, Dr Rhode! So good to see you! So good, so good indeed! Come in now, come in out of the cold, and I'll have Lu put the kettle on for tea." He sweeps us in with long arms.

I take in my surroundings with the expertise of one who has taken in many, and has practice at assessing situations quickly. The carpet is a red that once was most likely lush and bold in color, though it has faded with time and wear. The furnishings are clean but shabby. I am no expert at nineteenth century fads to know if it is dated, but I would say that it is. The lighting is a simple oil lamp that gives off a softness, but hardly any illumination, so everything looks darker than it really is without the glow of modern electricity that I have grown so accustomed to. It will take retraining myself, to keep from entering a room, and feeling for that familiar switch on the wall even if half the time I forgot to flip it when I had the chance.

"Dr Smythe, this is Noah Gray, and this is Sonnet. My wife." Israel doesn't even falter or shrink from the words. And here I thought he had a harder time lying than the rest of us.

I almost put out my hand to shake Dr Smythe's, but then remember that is probably not the greeting a woman in this age would offer. Instead I smile and drop the smallest of curtsies.

The woman he had referred to as Lu has tea in our hands almost instantly. She is petite and silent. She appears to be several years her husband's senior although perhaps life has aged her prematurely, or perhaps age has been uncommonly kind to the good doctor. I smile at her and thank her for the tea, but she doesn't lift her eyes to mine and she remains silent. Great, I think, I'll be stuck here while Israel doctors every day and night with a silent unfriendly woman as my only friend. Well, maybe she can help me brush up on my Chinese...mine is terrible since I've hardly had a use for it until now.

The rest of the evening is dull and slow. We are stuck in that place between boredom, and forced manners that you always find yourself in when spending time with new people. The doctor is friendly enough and he doesn't pry too much, but it is difficult making small talk when everything you're saying is a lie. His wife, Lu, never speaks, but since I've had practice myself pretending not to understand a language when I do, I can tell she understands us all well enough. Her eyes narrow at certain spots in the conversation, and once I saw her mouth twitch when her husband was telling us an amusing tale of life in London.

We drink tea and eat a spicy soup with a clear broth. It hardly seems to be anything more than water and spices with a few chunks of some sort of green leafy vegetables that float in our bowls, but it is surprisingly filling and tasty. I can't help but be concerned that they will able to feed us. Their place is shabby and their cupboards bare enough without three more adults. Perhaps that is why Lu is silent and pensive.

After supper and more painful small talk we can no longer hide our yawning behind our hands and everyone retires. Dad makes himself comfortable on the couch in the living area which I'm sure feels like our old house to him. Unfortunately, theirs is hard and unforgiving while ours back home was soft and could practically swallow you whole. Lu walks Israel and I up the stairs and to our room and exits again without a word.

It is very tiny, and would qualify as a closet in more modern houses, but it's clean enough and it's warm. There is a lamp and a small writing desk. The bed is small and covered in two quilts. I flop on it gratefully.

"I know this should be awkward, but I'm way too tired and I suppose we've slept in more embarrassing places." I yawn some more. "I get the fluffy pillow though." I toss the other, more flat one, at Israel.

Israel doesn't attempt to catch it, just lets it fall to his feet. He is looking...uncomfortable? Embarrassed?

"What?" I can't help laughing at his pained expression. "This was your bright idea, remember? You can remember that when you're trying to get comfortable on the cold, hard floor."

"Thanks," he mutters, finally shaking himself out of his stupor. "Can I at least get the fluffy pillow then if you're going to make me sleep on the floor?"

"Heck no. Aw, look at the cute pajamas they set out for you!" I hold them up for his inspection. They're less like pajamas and more resemble a nightgown. I stifle another spurt of laughter, but am unsuccessful and I giggle like a school girl while Israel grabs them out of my hands.

"Are you sure this isn't supposed to be for you?" he grouses holding it up against himself.

"Nope, this one's mine." I gesture to the other folded pile next to me. "I don't have quite as many ruffles." I erupt in peals of laughter again and have to hold my stomach.

"There's no way I'm wearing this. It's too short anyway. My legs will freeze. Now give me a blanket, the big one." He pulls it out from under me like a magician who yanks out a tablecloth and leaves all the place settings. I am left on the bed, trying to get my giggles under control.

"What are you doing now?" I lean over and watch Israel as he is gingerly pulling back the dust ruffle on the bed and peering under. "Looking for bogey men?"

"Spiders," comes the muffled reply. "I despise spiders."

I start laughing again and only stop when my breath runs out.

* * *

The next couple of days are long and slow and dreadfully monotonous. I help Lu around the house as much as I can, but it is obvious she is a loner and I am only in the way. I spy her with a basket of clothes and surprise her by speaking enough broken Chinese that we can get a sort of hobbled conversation going. The clothes, she says, are either forms of payments from patients of Dr. Smythe's or hand-me-downs. They are for Dad and Israel and I. She apologizes for their condition, and I thank her graciously since dear old Lady Halloway's muslin is getting a bit of a funky smell, so I am rather grateful. I am not so grateful when Lu informs me I need to be wearing a corset.

"You'll need it anyway to get into this one, it's very small," she holds up a yellow dress with a million tiny buttons. It looks like it would fit Emme, not me. Lu sees my doubtful air and presses it into my hands along with the blasted corset. "You'll look very nice," she says, and I see her smile for the first time in the three days I've known her.

"Yes, I'll make a very nice looking corpse," I agree a few minutes later as Lu yanks on the laces of the corset. "Holy Moses, woman! I can't breathe!"

As a parting shot, she pulls them another centimeter tighter and pats my head in a mothering way. "You'll live," she replies cheerfully. My, my, Lu just needed to see someone in pain for her mood to lighten. I must introduce her to Prue soon. Prue and Lu. They'll be quite the vaudeville act in my sorry life.

While standing in the yellow dress and instrument of torture that is my corset is painful enough. Trying to sit in it, with the whale bones poking into each and every rib, and my lungs collapsing in agony is even worse. I decide to walk for the afternoon and try to find Bea or Emme or Luke. I have seen Bea once the day before yesterday, along with Joe, but I can't help worrying both for Emme, who is playing a dangerous game in a dirty city, and for Luke, who is attempting to live through his first travel as a Lost. He must be so bewildered.

I retrace my steps as best I can, from the afternoon we left Luke and walked to Smythe's place. I am sure I probably walk in circles and am getting myself hopelessly lost, but it seems right. I seem to think I remember this particular storefront, and that particular cranky looking man who barks at me to buy his fish. I am almost certain this is the neighborhood we woke up in and I believe I can see the blue doorway that Emme said she arrived near. There's the store across the way that Luke said he found himself behind. I remember the smell of sweated cabbage that is the Thames, and since my breath is coming in short shallow gasps now, I think I'd better stop and take a rest. Since sitting is too desperately uncomfortable, I choose to lean against the nearest building and stare out at the water. I hear the barking of the fish man from a block away and since the day is bright and sunny – somewhat of a rarity in England, especially in rainy December – the street is bustling with people. I hardly notice when someone slows their walking and stops a short distance from me. Out of my peripheral vision I see a figure in a charcoal gray cape but that is all I see until the person speaks and I spin to face the speaker.

"Hello, sister," says Rose. "I knew you would find me."

Chapter 25

I feel calm, shockingly so. I don't feel as though my legs will collapse or that I can't breathe, the way I felt the other times I saw Rose. Instead, my thoughts are collected and tranquil, and I do not shake or feel faint. I do feel though, that my heart is beating exceedingly loud, and that my feeble ribs will not be able to contain it much longer. They may snap like dried kindling, allowing my heart to leap out like a wild, untamed thing.

"I knew you'd come," she says lightly. Her eyes avoid mine and she speaks evenly. The hood of her gray cape is low over her forehead, and I can see her blonde hair straggling out in wispy strands that blow softly around her face. She has a soft spoken voice that sounds nearly childlike.

She is close enough to touch, but something holds me back. Trepidation of some sort. Or a fear that she will disappear like a phantom or a spirit if I reach out. Will my hand pass right through her like an apparition? I won't try it.

"I've been looking for you," I say softly almost the way I would speak to a scared child or a wounded animal. "I thought I'd never see you again."

"Why would you think that?" she asks pulling her cape closer around her bird like frame, and staring out at the river. "I'm your sister, aren't I? Don't we belong together, you and I?"

"Yes." I swallow hard. "We do, but we've been apart so long. Are you" I don't know how to finish my question, are you all right, are you happy, are you really here?

"Oh, I'm fine sister." She still doesn't look at me, though she turns her head to face me. Her eyes stare blankly at a spot over my shoulder, and she brings her hand to her mouth, and begins to nibble at her nails. "You? You've been well all these years? Living with our father?"

"Yes. He'll be so anxious to see you, and so happy too." What a ridiculous understatement. "Will you," I clear my throat, "Will you come and see him?"

"Oh, not today. I'm very busy today. Perhaps another time." She pulls her hand away from her mouth then and I wince at the sight of blood lining her cuticles. She has bitten them to the quick.

"Another time? No Rose, please. Please come with me." I am confused by her attitude, and it shows itself in my shaky voice. I finally reach out and touch her arm, just touch it lightly. She moves away with an apologetic smile.

"No, no, I really mustn't. I have to finish my walk, and I have to meet my friend. I don't like to upset my schedule. It's not good for me to upset my schedule. The doctors say so. You understand."

"What doctors, Rose? Are you ill?" Is this my fate then, to find my sister and lose her so quickly to some dreadful disease? My heart begins its terrible thudding in my chest again, and this time when I reach out I grasp her arm more forcefully.

She shakes me off with unanticipated strength and shakes her head at me. "No, no, don't pull on me, I don't like it." She frowns and brushes the spot on her elbow where I had grabbed her as if the touch is implanted or seared on her cape. As if I've soiled it.

"But what doctors, Rose?"

"The ones at the hospital, silly."

"I don't understand."

"Not now," she narrows her eyes, "The doctors aren't here because they are all dead. From before, they were here before, like I was here before. You travel like me so you must know." She speaks impatiently, like she doesn't like explaining and I am beginning to exasperate her.

I don't understand, but I will change the subject if what I'm saying agitates her. "Where are you staying?"

"Home, of course. I'm always home. Sometimes home is different, but it's all right because it isn't the hospital. I don't want to go back to the hospital, but I always do." She shakes her head vehemently and her hood falls back. Her hair is dirty and stringy yet she is impossibly beautiful.

"I won't make you go back to the hospital," I promise. Again, I speak as I would to a cornered animal that I'm afraid would bolt if I were to scare it.

"Were you there?" Rose cocks her head to the side and for the first time, stares directly into my eyes. It's like peering into a looking glass. Her pale eyes are the exact shade as mine. "You look familiar. Do you know me?"

"Of course I do. I'm Sonnet, your sister. Remember?" I want to cry, but I swallow back the lump in my throat.

"Oh yes. I forgot, but now I remember." She laughs at herself. "Sometimes I can be so silly. We weren't at the hospital together; we were babies together. Yes," her voice slows, "We were babies, but you left me behind. How could you, Sonnet?" She looks devastated.

"No! We didn't mean to! We didn't want to travel without you. It just happened. We've been so worried all this time, but now you're here and we can be a family again." I must make her see. Why is she acting this way?

"Families don't leave their babies behind. I don't like you. I have to go home." She pulls her hood back up over her tousled hair. "I don't like to be late for tea. It's nice to be back where there's tea, don't you think? You can come for tea someday, but not today. You can come visit me even though I don't like you because it's important to have good manners. Doctor says so. I like to have lots of people over for tea. Lots of interesting people because they amuse me."

"All right," I falter. "I'll come for tea another day. Will you tell me where your home is?"

Rose waves her hand down the street. "I don't want to tell you the exact house, because I don't know you. You see and it wouldn't be safe, now would it? That's not sensible. There are bad people in the world, bad people here too. I met a bad man yesterday. He won't hurt me though, he told me so. He said I was a good girl. He might hurt you though."

"Why would he hurt me?"

"Because you are a bad girl! He wants to hurt the bad girls. You left behind a baby. Bad girl. You shouldn't leave babies behind. It makes them sad." Rose turns again and begins to walk away.

"Wait! Did Old Babba find you? Did she raise you?" I can't leave without at least that question being answered.

"Old Babba hated me and I hated her. I remember that. I was very happy when she died. So happy. I danced and danced." Rose closes her eyes, remembering, and begins to sway. "I like dancing. They let me dance in the hospital when I was good. We had balls every month with music and dancing and everything. Did they put you in the hospital too, when you told them you could travel through time?"

"No, they didn't put me there. What hospital, Rose?"

"Why, Bedlam, of course." She stops swaying and looks surprised that I don't know. "I grew up in Bedlam. Well, I must be off sister. You know what they say, don't you?"

"No," I whisper. "What do they say, Rose?"

"Go thy way! Let me go mine. I to rage, you to dine."

I am still standing there several minutes later. A half hour, an hour, a day, I don't know. Rose had walked away, in the opposite direction of where I came from and where I will return eventually, once I find my center of gravity again. I feel sick, sick with sorrow, sick with dread.

My sweet sister is mad. If she wasn't mad before Bedlam, she was after they were through with her. I know some history, and I am familiar with its reputation as a freak show for people to gawk at, for their crude experiments and half-baked rehabilitation attempts. If Rose had any sanity at all when they found her, they probably strapped that sanity down to a gurney and operated on it, or medicated it with horrible things. Didn't they open their doors to the public and let them come and poke fun and fingers at all the lunatics, for the price of a ticket? What had Rose endured? And could she ever recover from such a thing?

London seems to pull the Lost in like a magnet, or like a moth to a flame. This is Prue's second travel here, as well as Emme's, and evidently the second for Rose. What is it about this place that draws us here, unwillingly and accidentally? Is there a fate that awaits us in London?

Eventually, I grow cold enough that I feel as though I must move my bones or lose them to the beginnings of frostbite. I walk home as if on auto pilot, my feet trudging obediently through the puddles and over the cobblestones, until I reach the three steps that descend down to the door of Dr. Smythe's house. Our house. I let myself in and hang my cloak up near the fire to dry as it had rained on me at some point, though I hardly noticed. I do not see Dad anywhere, and am glad for it. I have not figured out what to say to him or anyone, concerning Rose. Of course I don't intend to just leave her, I will not abandon her to a life without us any longer, but I am unsure how to describe her. 'Simple' will hardly prepare Dad and Prue and Israel for the shell that is Rose.

I wander into Lu's kitchen and prepare myself a cup of tea. A week in old England and I'm officially addicted to the strong, boiling hot brew. I barely even miss toffee cream breves anymore. I am adaptable like a small puppy pulled around on a leash. I go where my unseen handler leads, helpless to object, and so I simply acclimatize.

I finish my tea and still have not decided what to do about Rose. Part of me wants to find her immediately and bring her here, by force if necessary. Could Dr. Smythe help her? Are there medications or procedures that would help her fragile mind? Or could it be that today was simply a bad day and maybe, just maybe, she isn't really the way she seemed to me: broken and empty?

Who was the friend she spoke of? Did she really dance when Old Babba died? Who was the bad man she spoke of?

Tired and desperate to turn my brain off, I go to bed before anyone in the house even comes home for supper. I wait until I hear them before I will myself to sleep and even in my dreams, I have no peace.

"She's not right, Caroline. She's unholy, that's what she is. She killed that cat."

I listen from under the table again. I have stilled my hands from playing with my doll and my ears itch from straining to listen. Who killed a cat?

"It was an accident, Babba. Rose is a good girl. Don't speak about her like that."

"She's unhinged. She's not right, you know it, and the whole village knows it! She bit that woman in the square and laughed when she bled. What child does that? You have to take her far from here! If you won't do it for everyone else's safety, do it for the girl. You still have another child, Caroline...what will happen to Sonnet if you leave Rose to her own devices?"

"Rose loves Sonnet. Nothing bad is going to happen. You'll see."

"It's you that will see, mark my words. You'll see that nothing good comes from offering solace to Satan."

I wake, cold and shivering and in the dark. It is the middle of the night and pitch black. I know from the sound of breathing from the floor by my bed that Israel has returned and is sleeping. I almost wished he snored.

The silence is menacing and threatening, and causes me to brood on the meaning of my strange nightmare.

I lean over the bed and adjust myself so that I am comfortable on my pillow and yet can keep my hand just touching Israel's chest. Just a touch.

Chapter 26

It's Christmas Day and our celebration is halfhearted. Lu, being Chinese, doesn't celebrate the holiday and Dr. Smythe tells us apologetically that since he never liked Christmas much he doesn't feel the need to impose it on his wife. It's any other day to them, and since it is their house, any objections seem crass and impolite.

So, it's off to Bea's new house we go, with simple handmade gifts tucked under our arms as Israel, Dad and I leave the Smythe's. We will collect Prue on the way and take her for dinner with us, and return her afterwardss. Emme and Joe will of course be there. All we are missing is Luke, and of course, Rose.

It's been two days since my conversation with my sister, and I have told no one. Several times I have rehearsed a dialogue with Israel in my head, but each time I open my lips nothing comes out. It's as though I need to speak with her again, feel her out, see if things are as bad as I fear, and then come to a decision.

Also, I don't know where exactly to find her again. My family has been through enough of me and my madcap searches for Rose. They haven't exactly ended well up to now.

Dad has collected enough shillings and Israel has earned a tiny salary this week so that we can take an omnibus to pick up Prue and get back home again. Prue had sent a message boy to let us know that she had secured a position with Sir Halloway three days ago and is comfortably situated. Whether or not she is close enough in proximity to us to travel with us again remains to be seen, but hopefully time is on our side and eventually we can all find homes nearer to one another. Dad has kept tabs on Bea and Joe and they are content enough in a small room in a rundown neighborhood, where Bea is attempting to do enough laundry to eke out a living. Emme is living with some other girls, I try not to think of it as a brothel.

"Prue!" I give in to a rare display of courage and pounce on her as she enters our tiny carriage, enfolding her in my embrace. "I've missed you!"

"Good Lord, child, don't smother an old woman." Prue brushes off her old coat and smoothes out imaginary wrinkles, but I can tell she's pleased enough to see me. "Well, look at you. You look like a woman, now don't you?"

I look down at my blue dress. It's a new one from Lu. I spent yesterday letting out the hem to accommodate my height and it does look rather nice I think. It's a sapphire kind of color, and the jewel tone sets off my hair and skin tone. At least that's what I think Lu told me.

"Thanks for noticing," I respond, dryly. "These two wouldn't notice if I was wearing a potato sack." I gesture to Dad and Iz.

Dad looks offended. "Didn't I say you looked nice? I thought I said so. You look very pretty, Sonny, dear." He pats my knee, absentmindedly as ever and goes back to staring out the omnibus window. He always acts absentminded when he isn't intoxicated.

Israel doesn't take the bait. "What?"

"You didn't notice my dress. Just like you didn't notice the last time I got dressed up." I may as well back him into a corner, see if a cornered mouse will take the bait.

"I didn't say I didn't notice."

"You didn't have to. You're oblivious."

Israel rolls his eyes. "Quit hinting for compliments and take the ones people offer you of their own free will."

"Well, if you'd offer one occasionally I wouldn't have to beg!"

"Children! Knock it off, you're giving me a headache." It's difficult to see in the relative dimness of the cab, but I can hear the scowl on Prue's face.

"And here I was thinking I had missed you two. Stubborn, quarreling, argumentative little brats."

"He started it," I object.

I have to strain to catch Israel's reply and I may have imagined it, but it sounds like he mutters under his breath something about him being the one to finish it.

The cab jerks to a halt and we all pile out, ungainly in our unaccustomed finery. My dress catches on the door and I nearly plow down Dad and smack into Israel, who catches me with a groan.

"Oh that's nice on a girl's ego," I grumble. "I'm not that heavy."

"I meant to say, was that a fly that landed on me? A mosquito? A feather?"

"Just your little wife. And I twisted my ankle, blast it!" I blink back the tears.

"Here, sit down a minute. Let me take off your boot."

He undoes the laces of my boot and removes it as painlessly as possible, but even so, I wince and bite my lip to keep from crying out like a baby. It feels red hot and I'm sure it's swelling.

"Help me up and we can hobble into the house." I pull hard on Iz's arm and stand.

He sighs. "I suppose this is the part where I offer to carry you?"

"Thanks, but no thanks, Prince Charming. I can make it, but you'll probably have to fetch all sorts of things for me all evening."

212

"Like what, Princess?"

"Oh, you know! Ouch! Cookies, ham, drinks, the paper, my pipe, cookies, my slippers, and cookies..."

My list continues on as he loses patience with my slow motion shuffle the way I knew he would and he sweeps me up intolerantly in his arms.

Several hours later I have officially eaten more cookies than Joe, I am pleasantly relaxed by a glass of hot spiced wine, the fire is burning nicely in the tiny fireplace in the tiny two room home, and we are about to open gifts.

"To Emme from Sonnet," reads Prue. As usual, being our matriarch and also the most bossy, Prue hands out the presents, and we all wait obediently and quietly. As a little girl, the more I clamored and begged, the more she ignored me. We have all learned that lesson and so we sit, hands folded meekly on our laps and not a peep crosses our lips, not even Joe's, who of course, has the most gifts.

Emme opens her package to reveal a large sugar cookie in the shape of a high heel shoe that I cut out painstakingly with a knife, cursing the lack of easy cookie cutters. I have given everyone the same thing, though a message written in icing on each is personalized and so is the shape of the cookie. Emme's says 'You'll always be my Fairy Godmother,' and it's a sort of homage to the night she dressed me up and made me wear her pretty shoes. Emme smiles at me and promptly eats the stiletto.

Our assortment of gifts is silly and simple. No one has money to buy anything real, and so it is food or something sewn or written on paper for everyone. Dad has homemade cards that are surprisingly poetic. Mine is a poem about a little blue bird that flies away, but never strays too far. I think it is a metaphor for me and the sweetness of the sentiment chokes me up a moment.

Prue hasn't gotten anything for anyone but she barks out an order to come see her at Sir Halloway's and she will have homemade cake for everyone. Just be sure to come in the back and wait until dark, she says.

Our lovely time is momentarily interrupted by a tantrum of Joe's, who evidently had gifts in mind the size and description of the ones he got for his birthday not so long ago, and years in the future. Suddenly a typical little boy, he is unimpressed by large sugar cookies and a tiny set of marbles and a homemade card. Red faced, snotty, and finally worn out from crying, he falls asleep with his head in Emme's lap. We all remember being Lost at such a young age, and no one minds his temper and anger.

Dad opens his cookie from me, which is in the shape of a bow tie, and Prue opens her's, which is shaped like a teapot. Bea's is shaped like a sewing machine, although it's terribly done because it was an impossible shape to make. She holds it upside down while smiling at me ever so politely. I am suddenly anxious for Israel and his cookie, but he laughs long and loud when he sees it.

"To my favorite husband," he reads holding up the ball and chain shaped cookie.

Everyone laughs and I don't even blush, but revel in our contentment and joy of the night. All too soon, it is nearly midnight and we have to leave. Israel will be up at the crack of dawn, and Prue says Sir Halloway's favorite meal is breakfast, so we must get her home.

Before I know it, I am snuggled up in bed and thinking of Rose and how I can get to her. Despite being what I think of last, I do not dream of her, and I sleep peacefully without stirring at all even with a throbbing ankle to keep me up.

* * *

The day after Christmas, Boxing Day, dawns bright and uncharacteristically sunny. I limp down the stairs still full from our holiday feast the night before, and decide to skip breakfast and instead resolve to find Rose again. If it takes all day and if I have to pound on every door I pass, I will find her and bring her home. Dad deserves to know his daughter is alive. And if she needs help, we will help her. My will resolved and my mind made up, I set out.

My familiar barking fish man is not around today, perhaps it's too early in the morning or perhaps they haven't been caught yet. To keep my ankle from swelling and to keep the pain at bay, I stuff my boot with snow every block or so. I am nearly alone in the streets, but whenever I pass someone, I make it a point to ask if they've seen anyone who matches Rose's description. Person after person shake their heads no, until finally a girl around my age nods her head. Her head is bonneted in some sort of hat that looks like a blackened mushroom, and it bounces as she nods.

"Yes, miss, I think I seen her. Real yellow hair? Pretty, but needing some tending? Sure, she's been around here a bit. Wanders by at around two o'clock every day she does. Comes outta that there doorway, in that house over there. See the one there? With that bush in front? That one? That's old man Tate's house and no one seen him in a month or two. She his daughter or something?"

"Something like that." My she's good at finding abandoned homes to call her own, I think to myself. "Thank you, you've been very helpful."

"Have I now?" The girl holds out a grubby gloved hand, expecting payment for her information. Her fingers poke out, and I don't know whether the gloves are designed that way or if they are simply falling apart and full of holes.

"Not that helpful," I reply wryly.

The girl leaves in a huff, and I approach the door behind the bush. Though not as frightening as the old abandoned house where I had originally thought Rose was hiding, I am still wary and cautious. Frightened of what's behind the door, or frightened of being shut in behind it, I don't know the answer.

Just frightened. That's all.

I knock, at first lightly and with no conviction. Then, harder and with a take-no-prisoner thump.

I don't know whether to be surprised relieved, or a little of both when the door swings open to admit Rose's beautiful face. Her hair is combed and draped over one shoulder, she looks bathed and clean. Her face is smooth, and free of any emotion at all. She does not smile; she does not speak. She looks, for all intents and purposes, like she does not know me at all.

"Hello Rose, it's me Sonnet. Do you remember we spoke the other day? You invited me for tea?" I will my voice to not shake or quiver with the emotion behind my words.

Rose wrinkles her forehead. "Did I? Was it today? Oh dear. I am dreadfully sorry to have forgotten. Come in, come in." Her face wreathed in the most stunning smile I have ever seen on a person, she opens the door wider and beckons me in.

"Please excuse the mess. I've been busy, you see. I do like to keep busy. I find it relaxes the mind, don't you?" She gestures to the area inside, probably the parlor if I'm not mistaken. It is strewn about with paper. Paper everywhere, paper with drawings and paper with words and paper with nothing at all, but blank whiteness. They are piled willy-nilly here and there and everywhere.

"I don't like the words, you see." Rose sighs very loudly. "The words and the photos. He keeps them from me because he knows they upset me, but sometimes I find them. The doctors used to write things down, and I hated that, and I hated them. Words, words, words! Stupid letters, stupid pictures. I hate them all. They all have to burn." She glares at the offending piles and kicks one. The pages flutter to the floor like autumn leaves. Then she turns to me, and it's as though the last moment hasn't happened. Her face is cherubic again and she claps her hands together.

"But we must have our tea, sister! I will fix it. Is it four o'clock already? I don't know where today has gone...really I don't. But the civilized ladies take their tea at four o'clock every day. You stay here, and I will be ever so quick." She bounds out of the room like a little rabbit.

Emotionally exhausted already, I sink down into a nearby chair. Will I have the mental stamina, I wonder, to be able to deal with this on a daily basis? The mood swings and the memory lapses are intense and disturbing. I do not know the best way to go about this. Do I agree with everything she says? Do I gently correct her when she's wrong? It's nowhere near four o'clock, but that seems to be the least of our worries.

Rose enters the room again with a tray.

"I put lots and lots of sugar in your tea, sister, but no milk. Just the way I'm sure you like it. I'm never wrong about how people take their tea." Rose hands me a chipped teacup very gingerly. "It's very hot now, take care. We wouldn't want you burned, would we? Here, I'll blow on it for you." She leans down and puffs a cool breath on my tea and for a moment our hands are wrapped around the cup together before she lets go.

I raise the cup to my lips as she does with hers, but it is as I feared when my hands first grasped it, the cup is empty and the tea does not exist.

Chapter 27

I hold my imaginary tea gingerly, as though the fragile cup holds a steaming brew that could tip. I even find myself bringing it to my lips as Rose daintily sips hers across from me. I don't know what to say to her, this girl that is my sister. Fragile and wounded, yet fierce and alarming, she bewilders me to no end. It turns out, I don't have much opportunity to speak at all, because once she is finished with her pretend tea, she hugs her knees to her chest like a little girl and begins to talk. Her voice is melodious, sing-song like, in a higher range that is unlike my own raspy, deeper voice. She speaks lightly, tripping over the words carelessly, like a babbling brook.

"When I left the hospital there was so much to do. I needed to find you, needed to find Mother and Father. I knew you were all Lost, you see, just like me but you were always traveling without me. I was awake, did you know that?" Rose doesn't wait for me to answer. She is no longer looking at me, but seems lost in her meanderings. "I was awake most nights. I couldn't sleep. When the traveling got near, I would get the most terrible headaches. They were so bad I would cry and cry and then of course I couldn't sleep. Mother should have known that would be the night we were to travel, and she slept anyway. Without me! You all left without me. I just sat there, crying and alone until Old Babba came." Rose pauses. I want to speak to comfort her, and say how sorry I am, but my throat feels sewn shut. Rose continues, "There were plenty of Lost in the hospital and Old Babba knew things too, things she told me when I made her tell me. I figured things out eventually. But anyway, that doesn't matter now." She finally turns her liquid blue eyes on me and smiles brightly. "More tea?"

"No, thank you." My throat and lips are working again, yet this is all I say.

"Suit yourself. How is Father?"

"He's well," I choose my words carefully, "That is, well enough. He misses you so much, and Mother too. He is sad much of the time."

"Is he?" Rose shrugs. "He shouldn't be. He's alive, isn't he? I'm alive." She smiles almost mischievously. "That must have been quite a revelation for you, Sonnet. Seeing me the first time after all those years. Did you think you'd seen a ghost? You looked so white in that coffee shop when you saw me in that chair. I wanted to laugh when you tripped like that. You're a silly girl, a silly, silly girl. I wasn't sure you'd know me, but you did, didn't you? You knew it was your poor missing sister, come back to haunt you. It was easy to get into your room and crawl into bed with you. Did I hurt your arm? You're very easy to frighten, by the way."

"I wasn't frightened. I was confused. I'm still actually very confused, Rose."

"Of course you are. You've been confused this whole time. Maybe you're like me. The doctors used to tell me all the time how confused I was!" Rose laughs. It's high pitched and terrible sounding. I cringe. "Maybe you're just like me!" She stops laughing abruptly and leans forward. She is so close to me now. I will myself not to tremble when she raises her small hand and strokes my cheek. "Are you like me, sister? Are you mad too?"

"Stop it!" With a sudden movement, I jerk back from her touch and stand. "Stop playing with me. I came to take you back with me, to get you help. Come back and let us help you. Please, Rose?"

Her eyes narrow and she regards me with suspicion. "You're worse than Mother. I don't like you at all."

"You don't even remember Mother; you were only four years old."

"Don't I? I don't remember the songs she used to sing, the way she made soup, her hair, and hands? I don't remember, do I? The way she looked when I would cry, the way her arms made me feel suffocated and imprisoned, the way I knew she loved you more than she loved me?"

"That's not true. Mother was devoted to you."

"Devoted to her crazy little girl... I don't think so," these words are spat out forcefully. "She was scared of me. Even when I was small she was scared of me. She used to hide from me. Don't you remember?"

I falter. What do I remember? What's real and what are dreams?

"You should have seen her face that night." Rose puts her hands up to her mouth as though covering a smile. "She looked like you at the coffee shop, so shocked. I tried to talk to her, and tell her what she did to me by leaving me the way she did. I guess I didn't go about it the right way. She wouldn't listen. She never listened."

A terrible feeling begins to dawn on me, one so horrible that I push it from my mind as hard as I can. Yet, the words bubble up out of me in spite of myself. "What night, Rose? What are you saying? Mother is dead. She's been dead for years and years."

"Of course she has been, pet. She's quite, quite dead. I was there, so I should know."

"What do you mean, you were there?" I feel very cold and such a large tremor goes through me that my body shakes like a leaf.

Rose smiles again. "Didn't I tell you? I know how to travel on purpose. I can go wherever I like, whenever I like. Such a pity the rest of you haven't figured it out. Maybe you have to be like me. I'm very special. Very, very special."

Ordinarily such talk would fascinate me, haven't I wanted to know the meaning of the Lost? The cause and effect, the purpose, the goal, the ability? But I can only focus on one thing now and that is Mother.

"You were there when she died?" I keep my voice even though my body still shakes.

"She kept backing away from me." Rose scowls. "I only wanted to tell her things, that's all. That's all at first. But she was scared of me, I knew that look on her face well enough. Haven't I seen it often enough on others?

She was no better than some of those nurses at Bedlam. They wouldn't look in my eyes, like what I had was catching. Don't get too close to the Gray girl. You might catch her madness, they'd whisper. Mother was no better, and she made me so angry."

"So angry and then what?" I whisper.

"I pushed her," Rose replies in a matter of fact tone. "I pushed her. I suppose I shouldn't have. Now you'll want me to apologize, won't you?"

I want to curl up in a ball and find someplace inside myself where I can be alone, and not hear these things. I am torn between wanting to flee this house, and the desire to pick Rose up and shake her like a rag doll. I cannot find the courage to do either one. All I can do is hold my breath. I am getting adept suddenly at not breathing.

"Oh, don't be such a spoil sport!" Rose frowns at me. "You're upset with me now, and after all the lovely tea and talks we've had!"

"Yes, I'm upset. You just told me you murdered our mother."

"Oh, that! You're making a big deal out nothing! Stop judging me! I'm sick, you aren't allowed to judge me!" She picks up her tea cup and throws it at my head. I see it coming and duck and it shatters on the floor behind me. "I don't like you at all, Sonnet! You're a mean sister!" She makes a grab for my cup as well, but I slap it out of her hands and it too, shatters.

Rose makes a sound like she is screaming inside her head, but cannot let it escape through her clenched teeth. She stomps her feet like a child and her eyes well up with tears. Without another word, she whirls and marches back into the kitchen. I hear another piece of china shatter, and then another.

I am left standing there, surrounding by shards of glass that may as well be the pieces of my heart. I want to leave, I want to stay, I want to sob, I want to shout, I want to hurt her, and I want to love her. This wounded shell of a girl who has done these horrible things. What am I to do with her?

I find myself stooping to clean the glass. I know that I should leave, now, while Rose is occupied with throwing things in another room, but all I can think of at this moment is her bare feet and all this glass. I have never seen her wear shoes. I will pick up as much as I can and then I will leave. There is nothing more for me to stay for.

Where will I go? Down the street to a neighborhood not far enough away?

I could find Officer Walter Andrews. Will a three-hundred-year old murder interest him? Should my sister be locked up? Do I have the fortitude to make that happen?

The shattering of china seems to have stopped. There is silence from the kitchen now as I cup my hands and gently brush tiny shards of flowered ceramic into them. The miniscule remains slice my fingertips in a half dozen places, like the brambles and thorns of a blackberry bush, but I do not care. Soon my fingers have tiny lines of blood running down the way Rose's had when she chewed her nails. My ears are trained towards the room where Rose disappeared to, and I can hear the soft humming of a tune.

She is singing as though she hasn't a care in the wide world.

Then my ears detect another sound, it's the front door opening. From my spot, kneeling on the floor behind the settee I cannot see the person who has turned the knob, but I know it is not Rose because Rose has come back in the room. Smiling and looking angelic, she acts as though she has forgotten my presence entirely, and passes by me at her feet without a glance.

"Hello," I hear her say. And then tenderly, "I missed you so much."

"Hello, my love. I missed you even more," says Luke.

The sound of his voice is so gentle, and so familiar, the way he sounds when he's smiling. He is so full of betrayal, and it makes me feel nauseous. I stay frozen to the floor, on my knees, hands full of sharp, and bloodied slivers of china. I am at a loss for what to do, so I wait.

"I brought you some cake," Luke continues. "Doesn't it look good? Cake for dinner, you and me. Aren't we lucky?"

I hear what must be Rose, clapping her hands in delight. "I love cake! With tea?"

"Naturally. What did you amuse yourself with while I was gone? Besides tearing apart books?" I hear the teasing in his voice.

Rose sighs. "I told you not to leave them around. I went for a walk and I put on my new dress. Do you like it?"

"You look absolutely beautiful."

"Better than ever?"

"Better than ever. Come on, let's get some forks and have some supper."

Once again not breathing, I will my heart to stop thudding in my chest so loudly and stay rooted to my spot. If Luke does not turn his head far enough he may not notice me huddled on the floor, in a heap between the settee and an old chair.

And if he does? If he does, what will I say? Or should I skip the speech and slap him as hard as possible?

He does not turn his head. From behind them, I watch them as they walk into the kitchen. His arm around her tiny waist, her face turned up to his with a saintly smile. When they are out of my sight, I hear him chiding her for the broken dishes.

"You can't break things, my love," he says. "You'll hurt yourself. What made you so upset?"

I will myself not to panic.

I hear Rose sigh. "Nothing. It's the traveling is all, you know how that makes me. I get so confused. I took care of that girl. She's all taken care of, Luke. I did it all by myself like I said I would. Aren't you proud of me?"

"I'm always proud of you, you know that. You also know I hate it when you travel without me, even if you're only gone for a day. It worries me."

"I come back to you, Luke. I always come back to this dreadful city. I wouldn't leave you behind, never. Kiss me, please?" I hear her passionate sigh and then a whispered word, 'more,' and I feel sick.

I raise myself to standing as silently as possible and on feet that are more like wings, I leave that house forever.

Chapter 28

I replay my awful tête-à-tête with Rose again and again. Home again and alone as well, I sit on my bed hugging my pillow to my chest and feeling numb. I surprise myself by not crying, but the tears threaten to spill and my head pounds. My throat has that uncomfortable lump in it, but I do not cry. I think I am too confused as to what to cry over first, Rose's madness, the death of my mother, or Luke's betrayal. Should I categorize my sorrows alphabetically or numerically? The thought makes me choke back a bitter laugh.

I hear Israel come home, there is no mistaking the heavy tread of his boots. Dad is light on his feet and Dr Smythe has a soft stride as well. Israel practically marches.

I tell myself to run to him, but my body ignores my commands. I can't move from this bed.

His footfalls approach until our bedroom door opens and I manage a shaky smile to greet him.

"What a day." Israel yawns, tossing his coat onto the desk. "I thought twenty first century America was busy. You wouldn't believe some of the things I saw today."

"No? Wouldn't I?" I reply grimly. "I could say the same to you."

"Oh? Did you try to talk an old lady out of using leaches so often she's weak from loss of blood, too?" He grimaces. "Forget spiders, I'm definitely moving leaches into the number one spot of creepy things I don't like."

"No leaches, just imaginary tea parties with insane sisters."

"What?" He looks at me in concern. "What in the world is that supposed to mean?"

"Exactly what it sounds like. I found Rose here, here and now. She's," I pause. "She's really...how would we say it in modern terms? She's really messed up, Iz."

"Messed up how?" He sits beside me on the bed, causing it to sag and me to lean into him.

"In every way possible." I give a strangled laugh that is more like a sob. "She killed our mother. She knows how to control traveling and she went back in time." I feel as incredulous as I sound at the words coming out of my mouth. "And pushed our mother off that cliff. She's mad. I'm not diagnosing her myself, she spent I don't know how many years in Bedlam."

I feel, rather than see, Israel take a deep breath and I match my breathing to his. Our chests rise and fall together as we sit.

"How will you tell Noah?" Israel finally breaks the silence.

"I don't know. As gently as possible, I guess. How do you tell someone their daughter is back from the dead, killed your wife, and seems to want revenge on everyone else?"

"Revenge?"

"She's been toying with me. She was in my room that night I got the scratches on my arm. It must have been her who locked me in that house and left me there. I thought someone was trying to keep me from getting close to her, but it must have been her. Unless of course, it was Luke."
"Luke? Now what are you talking about?" Israel sounds as baffled as I feel.

"Oh, right. Forgot to mention that lovely part. After our little tea party and after she started throwing dishes at me, guess who walked in?"

"Is this where I say, Luke?" Now he sounds less baffled and more forbidding. "How long have they been...?"

226

"Together? And believe me, they are together in every sense of the word."
I laugh harshly. "Who knows? But I feel extremely stupid."

"He wasn't worth it, Sonnet."

"Worth what?"

"Worth your love."

"I didn't love Luke." I smile up at him in surprise. "Never did. I found him sweet, funny, and fun to be around. Maybe when I thought he cared about me it may have gone to my head a little, but no one was falling in love, Iz. You don't have to worry about a broken heart."

"You're sure?"

"I'm sure."

"Good," he practically growls. "Then I can stop waiting to do this." He tilts his head and kisses my lips, soft, sweet and slow. For a moment, everything slows to a wonderful perfect halt, and all is right with the world.

* * *

Later, I tell Dad about my time with Rose, and about Luke's betrayal of us. Though my mind still feels cloudy from confusion, and possibly from all the kissing Iz and I have been doing, I explain things as best I can. For a long while Dad is quiet as he sits across from me. His tall legs dangle in front of him and his long arms dangle to his side, like a dejected marionette. It is a while before he speaks and when he does, his voice sounds hollow.

"Your mother and I knew that Rose wasn't right. Prue knew, of course, but you were just too young. We hid her as best we could from people. but she was so violent even as a tiny thing, barely walking. Old Babba threatened to take her away from us. She had the 'Sight,' or at least claimed she did. Seeing into the future and all that. She warned us nothing good would come from Rose, that she would bring nothing but misery and death to us, but naturally we wouldn't listen. She was our child, our little girl, and we loved her. Sometimes she would seem almost normal, like a typical child, other times she'd lash out, or even worse, seem as though she was in a trance.

She was like your grandmother when she would get like that. You come from a special line of madness, Sonny. It's time you knew that." His voice is so wavering and apologetic. His hands still dangle uselessly by his side, and it is strange to not see them actively straightening his collar or fingering his whiskers. He seems broken, like someone has snapped his strings.

"Truth be told, we were all a little scared of her," Dad continues. "You were the only one who wasn't, and we had to shield her from you as much as possible. She got pleasure from hurting things, and we didn't know what she'd do to someone as trusting and loving as you were. Oh, we let you play with her of course, but we were always right there ready to scoop Rose up, or take you elsewhere if she started getting upset."

"She seems to think she can manipulate traveling," I interject. "Do you think that's possible? The whole reason we're here is because she led us here somehow. And if she really did kill Mother, she had to go back in time to do it."

"I don't know the answer to that. I know your mother always felt a traveling spell coming on. She would get headaches that lasted for days until she could hardly stand it anymore, and she knew it was coming. She didn't know how to manipulate things to get where she desired though. She didn't have time to learn," his voice broke a bit, "But she said her mother knew."

"The mad grandmother?" I ask, skeptically.

"Yes. She died in an asylum. She was mad as a hatter, but not dangerous. She lost her memories as an old woman, and with it the ability to travel somehow. She must have spent the last twenty years locked up. She was taken care of, and seemed content enough the last time your mother and I saw her. She didn't know Caroline anymore, didn't know me. We were strangers to her, and somehow it seemed kinder to leave her in one spot."

"Well, Rose seems to be dangerous," Israel interrupts. "And she seems out for revenge. I don't think it's safe to stay here, and we shouldn't bet on Prue being safe either."

"Are you talking about getting out of here? Getting out of London?" I ask. My hand is cold in his, and I'm so grateful for the warmth. I'm so grateful for him.

"I don't see any other alternative. We should be able to disappear. As far as I can tell, it's some kind of coincidence that she found us in America to begin with."

"She could have traveled far enough in time to get records and track us that way."

"Everything legal from that time is under the name Emily Winn, remember? And she doesn't know me or know you'd be with me."

"Wait. The night the police brought you home, Dad," I turn my attention back to him, "Did you tell them your name? Did they take you to the station before they brought you home?"

"I probably did." Dad begins to stroke his mustache in a worried fashion. "I was drunk, you know."

"Yes, we know." Indulgently I pat his hand. "Then that's how she found us. Police records of some sort. It's not that difficult to find someone with a computer and a name. So she traveled back to kill Mother, and then she came to us to scare and mess with me. But why'd she bring us here next?"

"1887 London." Israel shakes his head. "There has to be something special about the here and now."

"Besides the corsets?" I mutter, sitting up straighter as a whale bone is sticking into my rib. "Because that seems like revenge enough to me."

"Wait." Dad's fingers freeze to his mustache and his eyes widen. "1887? Is that the year now? I didn't think to ask. I knew the basic era of course, but 1887? December. Boxing Day?"

"Yes."

"Then this is a pivotal night in history."

"Is it?" I reply slowly, wondering what he's getting at. "What of it? I'm racking my brain and nothing from history is standing out."

Dad unfolds himself from the chair and it's as though his puppet limbs come to life. "She's out to hurt everyone who she thinks deserted her. She's had opportunity to hurt you, but hasn't taken it. What if she wants to hurt us by hurting the ones we love?"

"Dad, I still don't know what you're getting at. What about the date has you so upset?"

"It's Emme," he says, grimly. "This is the night that some legends say Jack the Ripper murdered his first girl. I think it could be Emme."

Chapter 29

If my hands were cold before, they are frozen solid now. Although my first instinct somehow was to pull away from Israel and run out in the night, he has held me fast. Now I've begun to shake as the weight of my dad's words sink into my flesh, my skin, and right through the marrow and bones of my very self. My heart feels as though it is in a vise.

"Just hold on," Israel whispers into my hair as he holds me tight. Maybe it's his rock hard arms that make me feel as though I'm in a vise, albeit a welcome one. "We'll figure this out."

"It's quite possible his first victim and most authorities believe she never existed because the body, if there was one, disappeared. She was never truly identified the way the other victims were. The press called her Fairy Fay." Dad's history lesson sounds like a professor, but his voice is shaky and full of sadness. "What a time to remember my trivia..." he trails off.

You look like a fairy princess. In a corset.

That's what the boys call me.

"Emme Fay," I whisper. This time I do pull myself out of Israel's grasp, but he reaches for me again, and holds me still a moment longer.

"Coats," he says. "It's snowing. We can't help her if we freeze to death on the streets looking for her."

I know he's right, but I hate the precious wasted seconds, the miniscule time it takes to find and then button my long coat. The costly moments it takes to wind a scarf around my hair and ears. I hate fact that there is no telephone, no way of communication, no instantaneous way of locating Emme, no warning for Bea. I hate what I already know we will find. Because the name is right, the timing is right, and the story is right. Who else, but one of the Lost would be hard to identify? Would only have a nickname? What kind of body just disappears besides the Lost? She doesn't belong here. It would be as if she never existed. She would be a legend.

The door slams behind us as we run.

* * *

I am beginning to hate winter. I don't want to be cold any longer. I want to wake up tomorrow in a tropical paradise, with Emme by my side. We can swim in the ocean and wear grass skirts. Grass skirts, inwardly I laugh at what Emme would say to that. They would go the way of my poor Garfield T-shirt.

My mind can't settle down. We run through the night, my long dress a bother that whips around my legs as I force them to move faster. Dad is leading because he has checked in with Bea only yesterday and knows the way. I have been too nervous to venture near this part of town since the first time, and now the guilt I feel for it eats away at me and invades my every thought.

"What other details do you know, Dad?" I shout to him as we run. The three of us and our six long legs eat up the ground beneath us.

"I can't think of anything else. No one even knows if Fairy Fay ever really existed, much less was murdered. The real Jack the Ripper murders begin in earnest soon." His voice is muffled by the time it floats back to me on the air. "I can't believe I didn't connect the time period earlier."

You're better at history than I.

Emme's words come back to haunt me. Why didn't I see this before? One of the most famous stories in history is going to begin with the death of Emme.

When we reach the door to Bea's home, our breath comes in ragged, gasping puffs. My lungs ache. Israel bangs on the locked door with excessive force and shouts Bea's name. It seems an eternity before Joe swings open the door. When he does, Iz shoves me inside and slams it shut behind me without a word. He and Dad leave me there with a confused Bea, and I know the reason.

They do not want me with them because they do not want me to find Emme's body.

I don't know what to say to Bea and for once I am incapable of lying. I sit a sleepy Joe up at the table with a pile of cookies in the hopes that the sugar will keep him occupied and awake. We cannot very well allow him to be the only one to sleep tonight. She knows something is wrong and her eyes are frightened, and her hands shake. I place my hands on her face at first, as I speak the words I don't want to say, and then I move them to her shoulders because her legs give out. We both sink down to the couch and I hold Bea. Besides Prue, Bea is the closest thing to a mother I have ever had, and we await the inevitable.

Unbidden, more choppy and incomplete words enter my mind.

Cheer up, ducky! The possibilities are endless!

You're so naïve, pet. What kind of boy wants a whore for a mum?

I always thought it'd be you and Israel, actually. I'm never wrong.

Yeah, well, I ran out of time is all.

It's not a palace but it'll do for now. I'll move up, Sonnet. You'll see.

I remember another conversation too. One that makes me tremble with anger.

There are bad people here. I met a bad man yesterday. He won't hurt me though, he told me so. He said I was a good girl. He might hurt you though."

"Why would he hurt me?"

"Because you are a bad girl! He wants to hurt the bad girls." I took care
of the girl, Luke. All by myself.

Rose knew about Jack. Rose even met Jack. And if Israel was right about
her need for revenge and wanting to hurt the ones I love, Rose sent Jack
straight to Emme.

I've heard people say that the waiting is the worst part. Worse than the
news that your loved one is dead, worse than the news that the cancer has
spread, or that someone didn't make it through the surgery. It's true, the
waiting on that couch with Bea was worse even than when Israel and Dad
came back with Emme's body. She is wrapped in Israel's long coat, the
bundle is small in Israel's arms, almost like he carries a child. He lays
Emme down on the floor by the fire as Bea covers her eyes and moans,
retreating further into the couch as if it could consume her wholly.

"Where's Joe?" Dad's voice sounds thick with emotion.

"Asleep at the table," I reply hollowly. He had fallen asleep only minutes
before, and I didn't have the heart to wake him, danger of traveling or
not.

"We couldn't just leave her body there. We'll have to find a place to bury
her tomorrow. We'll let Bea decide," Israel opens his arms and I move
into them. I inhale his familiar scent and want to disappear inside of him.
He can't hold me tight enough right now.

I swallow hard as I look at the wrapped body. "How bad is it?" I whisper.

"Not that bad," he answers, gently. "She's been stabbed through the
stomach, but nothing else. Not like the other girls will be."

"You're a doctor," I trip over my words, "Was it quick, Iz?"

"Yes, it was quick."

The words are like balm to my heart even though I know he would lie to protect me. I will still take comfort in spite of that knowledge, as I pull back the coat from Emme's face.

She looks like she is sleeping, angelic as always. I smooth her strawberry colored hair away from her face, and kiss her softly. The tears that fall from my eyes land on her cheek and they glisten there, like diamonds in the firelight. Almost like her very own tears if the dead could cry.

There is nothing to say, nothing to do until morning. Words are inadequate when grief is so deep, and for a long time the only sound is that of Bea's keening. After a while, even that stops and we all sleep.

* * *

It is late morning before any of us wake. Though my shoulders ache from my strange position curled up on Israel's lap all night, I stay where I am, in the warmth of those arms I love so much.

When Joe stumbles bleary eyed and yawning into the room, Dad springs into action and is immediately by his side. Explaining something about a walk, he bundles Joe up and they leave through the front door. I know it is to explain to the little boy what has happened. I stay where I am for a moment longer, but I know what I must do. There are three people I need to find, Inspector Walter Andrews, Luke Dawes, and my sister. I don't expect Inspector Andrews to believe anything I have to say, but I will try to make him understand that Emme's killing was a foreshadowing of more terrible things to come. As for Luke and Rose, I only know that I am angry, angry enough to force a confrontation. I will grieve later.

"I'm coming with you," Israel murmurs when I unwrap myself from his arms. His eyes are still closed, but he is fully awake. Energy courses through his body and nearly gives off sparks whenever I touch him.

"You won't like where I'm going," I answer.

"I never do, but I'm coming anyway."

"Get your coat then." As I say it, I realize just what I've said and an almost hysterical laugh nearly bursts out of me. He can't take his coat, as Emme's body is still wrapped inside it.

"Bea," Israel goes over to the couch, "Bea, I know you'll want some time alone with your daughter. I'm going to send a cab for Prue and she can help you with dressing Emme. She'll know what to do. Wait for her, all right?"

Bea nods and though I am reluctant to do so, we leave her. It is a sleeting chilly morning, a bad time to be without a coat, but it only motivates us to move faster. Israel gives everything in his pocket to a driver and sends him to collect Prue.

"I wouldn't want Bea to see all that blood on her dress," he explains softly. "Prue is better suited to take care of everything."

I nod wordlessly, and swallowing back the tears my body wants to spill, I tell him of my first meeting with Inspector Andrews.

"Do you think he'll listen? There's no way to explain how we know anything that makes any sense."

"I know," I agree. "But we have to try."

"Maybe a letter then. I don't want him locking you up in a loony bin."

"Ha ha. All right, a letter. Dad can write one, he's the historian. Maybe he can remember another victim's name or something more helpful."

"There are thousands of prostitutes in London, especially the Whitechapel district. I don't think we're going to change history, Sonnet. I don't think we can, as much as you want to."

"Speaking of being crazy, what do you know about Bedlam?" I change the subject. "You're a doctor, have you studied the history of one of the oldest hospitals in the world?"

236

"I know that the inmates don't like to be called crazy, and the proper name is Bethlem Royal Hospital," he deadpans.

"Sorry. How bad do you think Rose had it there?"

"Depends on the time period she was there, I guess. It's been around for a long, long time. If she was there during the thirteenth, fourteenth, or fifteenth centuries, it would have been horrendous. Not much better after, although at least they stopped manacling them to the walls or floors. In the early eighteen hundreds, just a few decades ago, they would let the patients out at night for dancing in the ballroom."

"That sounds bizarre and maybe a little scary. All those poor people dancing their cares away all night?" I think of Rose sipping her imaginary tea, and suddenly I can picture her dancing in her red dress, and bare feet in a dusty old ballroom with the other mad patients twirling and spinning. A crazy snapshot. Somehow the picture fits very well with what I know of my sister. "She said she danced there."

"Is that where we're going?" Israel asks.

"Bedlam? No. No, I want to talk to Rose. I want to know," I falter, "I want to know why. Why she hates me so. I also want to know how she does it, manipulates time, I mean. I want out of here," my last words are spoken viciously, and I realize suddenly how true it is. I do want out of London, this place of cold and death.

"I doubt she knows herself," he replies. "She must be capable of some kind of power, but I wonder if she knows how to harness it."

"Well, then maybe Luke will know. Obviously, he's Lost too and has been keeping all sorts of secrets." I can't help the bitterness that creeps into my voice.

Israel glances over at me. Something flickers across his face, whether it is jealousy or concern I don't know. Impulsively I step in front of him and kiss him, lifting my head to his. I have to stand on my toes in my boots.

He is warmth, light, hard curves and I am shadows, softness, and gray. He tastes of life and I taste of tears.

"Sonnet," he pulls away, "That night with Dawes? It's not that I didn't notice your dress. It's just that you always look that beautiful to me."

Standing there, kissing in the street with the sounds of horses' hooves coming too close for comfort, jogs us back to reality. We approach Rose's house quickly. Amazing how long it seemed to take to our fevered imaginations last night when we were racing against time to stop a madman who wouldn't be stopped. In the daylight it is a short walk to Dr. Smythe's house and only a few more blocks to Rose's.

"If Dawes knew about Jack and Emme, you do know I'm going to kill him," are Israel's last words before I lift my hand to the knob on Rose's door.

"I know," I whisper, and the door opens before I can turn the handle.

"Gray." Luke's face is ashen when he sees me. He reaches out his arm to close the door again? To embrace me? I hardly know. In either case, I slap his hand away and push the door further open.

"I want to see Rose," I say flatly.

It's apparent he didn't realize I knew about him and Rose, his face becomes even paler. She really had forgotten I was there, crouched besides the broken tea things, when her lover got home. Must have slipped her fragile mind to tell him about her little tea party with Sonnet.

"She isn't here, she's gone. I don't know where. Come in." Luke nods stiffly to Israel, who is so tightly wound right now I am afraid he will spring into some sort of violent action at any point. I can feel his hand in mine, and it feels as though it seethes and throbs with a barely controlled strength.

238

We enter the house, and it is as I remember it. The same books are torn apart, photographs strewn about. I push a pile to the floor and sit on the chair where it had been. No fire burns in the fireplace, and it is cold in the house. Colder here somehow than it had been outside.

"Why don't you start at the beginning?" Israel's voice is like an animal growling.

"Whose? Mine? Rose's?"

"The one that will explain to me why you're helping a criminally insane murderer."

"She's sick." Luke throws up his hands and his words as though that simple explanation will cover over the offenses.

"No one is debating that. What's your plea if she has the insanity one going for her?"

"I'm not insane, but love makes you do crazy things. Look at her," Luke nods at me, "Wouldn't you do anything for her?"

"I wouldn't ask him to," I answer him myself. "Rose is using you."

Luke shrugs. "I know."

"And that's enough for you?"

He looks at me, tipping his head to the side as he considers the question.

"Yes," he replies.

"Then you might be worse than she is," Israel says. "Did you know about Jack?"

Luke strokes his hair back from his forehead. "Not until this morning, I swear it. Rose imagines all sorts of people she thinks she's talked to. She told me about meeting someone bad, but I confess I didn't pay much attention to it. This morning she told me she sent him to Emme. It took me a while to connect the dots. When I did, it was too late. I did go out to see if I could find you or Emme, but you weren't home."

"We were taking care of Emme's body," I answer coldly.

"I'm sorry, Gray. Truly I am. I didn't know how far she'd take this thing, this revenge. She's obsessive about it and she isn't going to stop. I'm the one who let you out of that house after she locked you in. I realized then that she had every intention of letting you die in there. When she told me about your mother, I didn't know whether or not she was telling the truth. I guess I chose to believe she wasn't. When we caught up with you, she used me to get close to you. I thought it was harmless enough, or that maybe your Dad deserved it for abandoning her as a baby, or Emme deserved punishment for taking Rose's place as your sister in a way. I didn't expect to start caring about you."

"Oh, what a lovely sentiment." I am sarcastic. "You didn't care enough, did you?"

"No." His voice is flat, exhausted. "I'll always take care of her, I'll always do what she wants. I love her."

"How does she do it? How does she choose where to travel?" I am feeling sick to my stomach, and don't want to hear any more about his fixated love and commitment for Rose.

"I don't know. Believe me. If I could do it the way she can, I'd have had us living in Utopia by now. Or someplace where I could get her some help. But I'm just like the rest of you and the Lost. I've traveled maybe twenty times my whole life, never knowing ahead of time, never seeing it coming. I fit in anywhere now. I left my family to be with her. I lied about the artist mother and the absent father, I guess that's obvious now. I have both a father and a mother, and a couple of sisters. I left them all behind for Rose. I'll never see them again unless she takes me back.

Somehow, she figured something out in the hospital as far as bringing the traveling on and how to steer its course, it's how she got out. She seemed so helpless, so childlike and innocent. I told her I'd always take care of her, and we've been together ever since." His true voice begins to seep out, now that he isn't pretending to be someone he isn't. Heavily Australian more than anything else, though there's a guttural element that makes me think Russian.

"Were you there when my mother...when my mother died?" I asked, swallowing hard. I need to know how badly I will always hate him.

"No. She had just come back from there when we met. Please believe me."

"But you knew why she picked America, why she wanted to get close to me and Dad."

"I knew, and I helped track you, but I never thought she'd kill you off one by one. The night we traveled here I was out on your porch like I said, but she was with me too. By then I wanted it all to stop, but she's the one with the power. Sometimes I think she's not as disturbed as she seems. Sometimes I think she has it all figured out, and she's playing the rest of us. In any case, one thing she hasn't figured out is how to stop ending up here. She can go anywhere, any time, but she'll always bounce right back here to London. At least it's familiar to her, like home in a way." Luke looks tired, like he could sink down to the floor and fall asleep.

"And you don't know where she is now?" Israel asks.

Luke shakes his head. "I'm worried she's traveling again. I have some medication for her that helps her stay more even. She won't let me give it to her regularly, but sometimes I can hide it in her cake. With it, she could pass for normal, at least for a little while."

"Well, you and your cake can stay here, but I'm going to find her." I am out of patience. "And I think we'd better find Dad and Prue too."

"Go. I'll keep her away for as long as I can, you have my word, but, Gray," the warm eyes I used to lose myself in narrow as they gaze into mine, "Hurry. Get out of here. Disappear. Vanish."

I hold his gaze for a minute more and then I nod. "We will, but first," my gaze and my voice falter for a moment, "first, she has to understand what she's done. She has to be put somewhere where she can't hurt anyone, Luke. You understand that?"

In a flash, I realize I've gone too far. What a fool I am. He already told me he would do anything for Rose, anything. His loyalties are not in question. He won't be a party to anything that may hurt her. I understand this incredibly quickly, but I am not as quick as Luke. In one fluid movement he has reached the front door and turns the lock. When he turns again, this time to face us he has pulled a pistol.

"You aren't taking her back there." Luke snarls. "You don't know what it's like. You don't know what she's been put through. I saw it. I know."

"You can't just let her roam through time, killing people!" I should be feeling fearful, but instead I'm angry. "She's collected us! Like a bloody stamp collection! She's brought us all here and she's going to pick us off, one by one. And then what? What will she move onto next? Your family maybe? Your mother and father? Your sisters? You can't stop her and you can't make her love you. She's twisted. She isn't capable of love."

"She is capable and she does love me," Luke hisses. "You'll never understand what we've been through. She saved me, and now I'm going to save her. I can redeem her and we can be together, you'll see."

"I thought the same thing, but it isn't going to work. She's past redemption. You have to let her go. She has to be stopped." I intentionally lower and soften my voice as if I'm talking to a child, as if I'm talking to Rose herself.

"Not if it means going back there." The pistol is steady in his hands. "I won't go back either."

I feel Israel stiffen beside me. "That's where you met her then?"

"Oh, I didn't mention that?" Luke smiles. "Inmates together. Quite romantic really. You could write a book about our story, of course no one would ever believe it. But don't be nervous, Gray, I'm not mad. Not at all."

"Then what," I clear my throat, "What were you doing in a mental hospital?"

Luke waves the pistol in a frivolous manner that makes me wince at the thought of accidental gunfire pointed my direction. "Oh they put all sorts in there when they run out of room in the prisons, you know. Just label them criminally insane and off they go. Off I went to Bedlam. Chop, chop!" Unbelievably, he grins at me then and I feel slightly sick. "Actually, it was a little better there than in the House of Detention. Ever been there, Gray? Near Clerkenwell Green? No? Underground? Interesting place if you're the historical type. Haunted, you know."

"You said Rose saved you?" All I can think to do is keep him talking. Anything to keep him from shooting.

"She's my sanity, I suppose," Luke muses thoughtfully. "Ironic, isn't it? She keeps me rational. Keeps me from doing crazy things. I want to be normal when I'm near her, want to take care of her..." he trails off.

"You're hardly being rational at the moment." Israel's tone is still filled with barely controlled fury.

"Oh, that's where you're wrong. I'm being exceedingly rational. If I was my old self, my pre-Rose self, I would have shot you by now just for the fun of it. Instead I'm being kind enough to toy with you for a while. I've changed, you see. I'm a changed man. That's what love can do for you."

Chapter 30

"So what happens now then, Dawes?" Israel demands. His arm is steady around my waist as we stare at Luke and his pistol. "Are you going to shoot us?"

"I haven't made up my mind," Luke responds, coldly. "You, definitely. Her, I'm still deciding."

I am done trying to appeal to his sympathies, and so I make no reply. I simply stare at him, my blood coursing through my veins for what is hopefully not the last time. I hear something then, a sort of rustle from the kitchen, from behind and off to the side of Luke, and something tells me not to react, not to turn my gaze towards it. I desperately want to avert my eyes and see if I am hearing things, but I steadfastly do not react. Therefore, I am almost as shocked as Luke when a small bundle of something comes nearly flying out of the kitchen and collides with him. The pistol is knocked free and skitters across the floor. It's the first thing I make a dash for, and it is surprisingly heavy in my hands. Heavy and amazingly cold considering it was grasped in Luke's hands only seconds before.

Israel has torn off the bundle in moments and has Luke pinned up against the doorway. The bundle, it seems, is Lu. I embrace her so hard, I think I feel her ribs crack.

"Thank God," I murmur in Chinese. "What are you doing here?"

"He came sneaking around the house last night." Lu gestures towards Luke. "Asking for you, acting strange. I'd seen him before, hanging around, slinking around. He didn't know I could understand English well enough so he was muttering to himself, all about death and revenge. I followed him back here to see where he came from. When I heard about your friend I knew in my gut he had something to do with it, so I came over real quick – especially since I didn't know where you were and if you were safe. Saw you through the window and when the door was locked, I came in through the kitchen window."

"You're wonderful Lu." I smile fondly.

"I know."

"Iz?" I reach for Israel's shoulder. I see Luke's furious eyes staring at me, but I don't look away. "Iz, we have to go."

"Not before he's taken care of," Israel replies grimly, and savagely punches the wall near Luke's face. Luke doesn't flinch.

"There isn't anything we can do to him. The police won't be able to make heads nor tails of our story, and I doubt pulling a gun on someone in your own house is breaking very many laws, not in this day and age. He'd just say we were breaking in. Let him go. He won't follow us. He only cares about his precious Rose. Come on, we'll find a bedroom to lock him in or a closet." Fitting, I think, remembering my days locked in the abandoned house.

We find a closet quickly enough and a chair that can be wedged under the knob, effectively keeping him contained. Israel shoves him in with force while I keep the pistol trained on Luke.

"You're nothing, Dawes," Iz says.

Luke spits in his face. The door is slammed, the chair is wedged, and the pistol is pocketed in my skirts. God forbid I need it in the future.

* * *

The next day passes with no events to mark it. It is only the day that we mourn Emme and that grieving is the very essence of all we do. Dad has come up with enough money to pay for burial, whether through honest work or honest thievery we'll never know and I don't care. Normally, the people here would wait at least a few days to make sure the deceased really is dead and not in a coma, but we don't have the luxury of observing that tradition. We all know Emme isn't coming back.

Prue had arrived at Bea's when we were with Luke and had gotten Emme's body ready. We laid her on the bed in her good pink dress. Joe has taken the news of her death like most small children do, he alternates between confusion and a clear understanding with a fair amount of normal activity in between. Bea is stoic and silent, while Dad's eyes are red rimmed and puffy enough for the both of them. He seems to have stopped drinking these past couple of days, but I fear he is only saving it up for a real fall off the wagon eventually. Even Prue seems to have aged, if such a thing is possible for someone as old as the hills already. We all seem older and wiser in ways that we wish we weren't. I have not seen Luke or Rose at all, and I do not do them the misplaced courtesy of wasting thoughts on them. My thoughts are full of Emme.

A letter to Inspector Andrews has been written and rewritten several times. Nothing we can say makes any sense. Emme's death has caused little to no stir in a community where violence is the norm. It will take several more to grip the populace with fear, several more before they will be on their guard and lock their doors at night. No one knows what is coming, and no one will believe us when we warn them. The letter will most likely lie on some inspector's secretary's desk somewhere, gathering dust, never heeded, and never taken seriously. If it's read at all.

The day of Emme's burial it snows. Big, fluffy flakes of white that drift lazily to the ground and transform it from gray and brown puddles to picturesque accumulations of sparkling sugar. I think of the frosting on the shoe shaped cookie, and it seems appropriate somehow. Emme would like frosting on the world the day we say goodbye to her.

The curtains, both at Bea's and at Dr. Smythe's have been drawn the clocks stopped, and the mirrors covered with black crepe. Emme's body has been carried out feet first, as custom dictates, so that her lonesome spirit will not look back and beckon anyone left in the house to follow her in death.

Lu has helped Bea and I with mourning clothing and the black dress is too short. My boots stick out from the bottom, but it's the best we can do with short notice and little money. I find it apt that my fashion will be as disastrous as ever. If Emme's spirit is there, it will laugh at me and the spectacle I make in my veil, and yards and yards of ebony fabric.

The cemetery is silent and still, even more so by the soft blanket of snow falling from the sky. It turns our black clothing white and settles on my veil. In the middle of the dreadful preacher's dreadful soliloquy, Joe turns his face up to the heavens and sticks out his tongue to catch the snowflakes. The mood is transformed from something dark and dreadful to something sweet and magical. Everyone, except for the preacher, titters behind their hands and then laughs out loud. Dad with his chuckle I haven't heard in ages, Bea's soft giggle, Prue's snort, Israel's soft laughter by my side, and my own. I fling my veil back like a triumphant bride who is eager for her husband's kiss, and turn my face to the sky, letting the flakes fall on my eyelashes, cheeks, and lips. Death will not have the victory, not today, not yet. We will remember Emme as she was, full of life and joy, the closest thing to a sister I have ever had, or will ever have.

Wherever Rose Gray is, she will not be redeemed. Not by me. Not by Luke, I fear. We will leave this place and vanish. There will be no records that we were ever here, that we ever existed, that we ever loved, lived or died. We will not be remembered, but we will never be forgotten either.

We will travel, and we will live, and we will love. Someday when I am old and full of years I will tell my children the story of their mother and father and their legacy.

"Once upon a time," I will say, "Hundreds and hundreds of years ago, I was born..."

The end.

Acknowledgements

Thanks to my family, from the parents to the in-laws to the sisters and brothers, nieces and nephews. You always believe in everything I do...except for the detective agency.

Thanks to my sweet kids, Cora, Anna and Gianni. I love the chaos you surround me with.

Thanks to my other kids: Peter, Eddie, Marie, Calvin, Nate, Vic, and Konah, just because you taught me so much about myself and about teenagers. I hope I got some of it right.

Thanks to my fabulous Teen Forum, all two of them: Lauren and Joe. I love you guys and if you didn't live a billion miles apart I would have to play match maker with you.

Thanks to my Slave Editors: Kelly, JJ, Heather and Heather, Mandy, and Michelle. Any mistakes are definitely theirs. Haha! I totally owe you; put it on my tab.

Thanks to Genesis for the most wonderful cover art ever. I love my artsy friend. You come in ever so handy.

Most of all thanks to my husband who loved me first in overalls.

About the author

Melyssa Williams is a mom, sister, daughter, wife, friend, ballet teacher, ex-contemporary dancer, writer, and blogger, who resides in Southern Oregon. She was homeschooled back in the day when it was slightly odd and eccentric, which came in handy when she decided to be a writer. She drinks coffee too often and reads fiction at inopportune times. She has parented inner city teens and wants to sky dive, but that's the extent of her excitement. Other than that, she finds baking bread and sipping wine to be the most thrilling parts of life.

She can be reached at: http://melyssawilliams.wix.com/melyssa-williams

CPSIA information can be obtained
at www.ICGtesting.com
Printed in the USA
FSHW01n0145040718
49978FS